RUSTED HEARTS

S. I. ALMANZA

ISBN-13: 9798848974522

This is a work of fiction. Names, characters, places, and incidents are either the author's imagination or used fictitiously. Any resemblance to actual persons, living or dead, businesses, companies, events, or locales is entirely coincidental.

Trigger Warning — This book's content is for a mature audience and will discuss multiple forms of trauma, including intergenerational trauma, abuse, and violence.

Contents

The Transaction

There is no hunting like the hunting of man, and those that have hunted armed men long enough and liked it, never care for anything else thereafter.

—*Ernest Hemingway*

The deafening racket of the police and ambulance sirens. The chaos, the pandemonium. The panicked hubbub of a hundred revelers and partygoers all seemed to have no effect on the man who had caused it all. He sat casually on the bonnet of the red BMW and lit a cigarette, inhaling deeply, savoring the moment. Even as the police got out of their vehicles and (directed by the accusatory pointing fingers of the revelers) made a beeline towards him, weapons drawn, commanding him to show them his hands, he was unaffected. He took another pull on the cigarette, smiled, blew smoke into the mild night air, and calmly placed his hands upon his head.

***

The man sitting across the table was an enigma. Hard-bodied and lean. Somewhere between muscular and wiry, not particularly tall or short, with hands, forearms, and upper arms slightly larger and disproportionate to the rest of his body. It was almost as if some Frankensteinesque, mad scientist had attached a bodybuilder's arms onto a swimmer's torso.

Yet it was obvious that this wasn't the physique of an obsessive gym rat or even a professional athlete. Nor was it the physique of a man who injected steroids into his buttocks and stared narcissistically into a mirror whilst slowly lifting a weight up and down.

No.

This physique was too asymmetrical. The quality of the muscle was too mature and dense. Deep, defined, and refined over decades. Deep striations like steel cables and vascularity like a road map. Even the bones seemed to have expanded and hardened over time. This was a physique that had been molded unintentionally as a by-product of whatever physical activity this man had engaged in throughout his life.

He had used his arms a lot more than his chest, legs, or back. Therefore, his arms were bigger. It was that simple.

A blacksmith, perhaps? A lumberjack? Or maybe a Viking berserker from the previous millennia, who had spent hours, every day of his life, swinging a battle-axe and hopped into a time machine here to the twenty-first century? It would certainly explain why more than half of each of his arms were covered in scar tissues of various shapes and sizes.

His ethnic origin could have been anyone's guess, as could his age. He could have been an old-looking thirty; or a young-looking fifty. It was impossible to tell. Square-jawed with sharp-edged cheekbones, hollow cheeks, and a two-week, jet-black, thick, rough; growth of facial hair and a full head of equally black hair, slightly unkempt but healthy and just long enough to fall over his eyes.

He was dressed in black boots, black cargo trousers, a full-sleeved black t-shirt rolled up past his elbows, and a dark, bottle-green, leather hooded body warmer.

And his face. What a face it was. Constructed with a series of contradictions. Handsome but ugly. Somnolent yet tense. Young but old. Caucasian features but tanned and weather-beaten with an old scar across the bridge of his nose, trailing downwards and diagonally across his face, stopping just underneath his right cheekbone.

He also sported fresh marks and injuries. A deep gash above his right eyebrow, which had, an hour earlier, been glued shut by a medic, a tiny trickle of blood that was slowly escaping from his left nostril into his mustache, and a slight crimson swelling under his left eye.

Then there were the eyes.

These were by far the most unsettling features on this man. Ancient. Like they had seen a thousand lives. There was no way a pair of eyes could tell such a long and complex story if they had only lived forty, fifty, or even a hundred years. No. This was an old soul, peering through a pair of globular organs- so grey, they were almost colorless. Transitioning between empty and predatory, depending on what they focused on. Unable to conceal the evidence of centuries of arcane knowledge deeply embedded within them.

The man sitting opposite the enigmatic stranger had observed and analyzed all this information within a few seconds. He was Detective Chief Superintendent Carson. A highly decorated and extremely competent police veteran of twenty years. Early into middle age but at the pinnacle of a long and successful career with the Metropolitan Police. He was a tall but thin man, and with his neatly combed, light brown hair and clean-cut, smart appearance, he looked as if he could be the CEO of a large company or perhaps a smooth-talking lawyer.

Of the countless thieves, robbers, murderers, rapists, and every other kind of unsavory character Carson had physically wrestled with, arrested, interrogated, and conversed with over the years, the stranger sitting opposite him was by far the most intimidating and intriguing of the lot, though he had yet to utter a syllable or move a muscle. The mere ambiance he emanated was terrifying. Like a black hole, devouring everything around it into oblivion... and then there was the arrest report which only added to the air of apprehension in the room...

One dead nightclub owner; stabbed once in the jugular and three times in the chest with an illegal switchblade. And an entire security team of five men. Four in the hospital with crippling but non-life-threatening injuries, and one on life support with a dozen broken bones, including a smashed skull. Savagely beaten, hanging on to what would very likely be his final moments, by a thread.

All in the same night. All in the same location. All within the space of ten minutes. And all perpetrated by this mysterious man who was now sitting opposite the detective, hands cuffed in front of him, resting on the steel table.

Yet he had remained at the scene of the crimes for the ten or fifteen minutes it had taken for the police to arrive even though he had ample opportunity to escape, leaning against the bonnet of a car parked in the street outside of the nightclub, calmly smoking a cigarette. He had offered no resistance to the arresting officers, said nothing as he was read his rights, and was fully compliant with every instruction given to him. And now here he was, sitting in the interrogation room facing the detective, with no signs of fear, apprehension, or anger on his face.

It was an unremarkable police interrogation room with a table in the middle, three chairs and a single door, and a large two-way mirror on one side. Two CCTV cameras were fixed on opposite corners, and the room was brightly lit with two LED ceiling lights. A digital camcorder was perched on a tripod next to the table, facing the new arrival.

Carson took a deep but subtle breath. With his moderately deep voice and seasoned professional tone, he broke the loud unbearable silence.

"You've requested to speak to me specifically, and only me, after refusing to speak to any other officer; and waiving your right to legal counsel. Is that correct?"

"Yes."

His voice was low, gravelly. Carson relaxed ever so slightly. With his extensive experience, he could always tell how an interview would go by the first few exchanges. The man had not hesitated to answer the question, however simple it had been, not offered any belligerence or aggression, and answered verbally and efficiently using a single word, as opposed to shrugging or nodding or giving a vague reply. Not the worst start. The detective continued, "OK. We have found nothing on your person, no wallet, no keys, no weapons, no ID. No phone. Not even lint. Nothing at all. Also, fingerprints don't match up to anything we have on any of our systems. Would you like to tell me your name?"

"You may call me Azra."

"Is that your real name?"

"Reality is subjective. You may call me Azra. I have also been known as 'Alistair' and 'Roan.'"

He spoke calmly. Confidently. A British accent with a tinge of something foreign Carson could not quite put his finger on, and with the sophistication, authority, and finality of a college lecturer whose word was law in the classroom. Carson continued, "Do you have a surname?"

"I don't need one."

Carson paused for a moment. The non-compliance was starting to creep in. But at least the man was engaging with him. Add to this the fact that there was no pressure on Carson to extract a confession or any information from the man, as his actions were all caught clearly on CCTV and —observed by dozens of witnesses. They had him dead to rights.

There was no court in the world that wouldn't convict him with this much proof. Carson had no obligation to be here. There was nothing the man could offer him as it was an open and shut case. This was no "You help me. I help you" situation. The detective was in total control. It was curiosity, more than anything else, that was driving Carson to probe this man as much as he could. Still confident, he resumed, "OK. Azra-no-surname, you asked for me by name. Why?"

"I want to talk to you."

"So, talk. How did you know my name?"

"Oh, I know a lot more than that. Believe me."

"Oh really? Such as?"

The man replied with a dry laugh, breaking his intense eye contact for the first time and turning his face away slightly; as if enjoying some private joke. As he turned, Carson, for the first time, noticed a small tattoo of a coiled snake on the right side of his neck. Who was this man? An assassin working for some secret guild? Was that tattoo their brand?

"All in good time, Detective…" The man resumed with an unmistakable air of menace.

Carson stared for a few seconds. He would not play games with this man or exert more effort than he felt like. He was, after all, not obligated to be here. Masking his curiosity and annoyance with a confident and controlled front, he continued, "So, you seem to think you know a lot about me, but you haven't told me anything about yourself yet."

The man nodded disinterestedly. Agreeing.

"You want to tell me why you murdered the owner of that nightclub?" continued Carson.

"Humankind cannot gain anything without first giving something in return. To obtain something of equal value must be lost."

"What's that?"

"Alchemy's first law of equivalent exchange…" He flashed a wry smile. Completely confident, relaxed.

Carson couldn't help but feel, despite himself, like a young student being hypnotized by a professor. Gathering himself for a few moments, the superintendent narrowed his eyes and studied the man.

"What are you, buddy? Some kind of spook? MI6? CIA? Mossad? Or maybe an Al Qaeda or ISIS sleeper cell?" he said.

"How do you figure?"

"Well, for starters, as I've already mentioned, you're a ghost; fingerprints, facial recognition, nothing. We can't find you anywhere on any of our very sophisticated databases. And then there's the fact that you've murdered a man with precision wounding in exactly the right areas of the body, assassination-style, using a US Special Forces issue switchblade which I'm assuming belonged to you.

"And then there's the small issue of you singlehandedly and unarmed, sending the handiest, battle-hardened group of bouncers in this city, to the hospital, including beating one of them— the head doorman; a giant, and the handiest of the bunch— into a coma and quite possibly to death. The smallest of those doormen being six-one and a hundred and twelve kilos of martial arts-trained muscle. Not to mention you've barely taken a dent yourself, considering. Then you hung around the scene enjoying a smoke, though you had ample opportunity to escape.

"I think your target was the nightclub boss. It was supposed to be quick and quiet, but you messed up and were caught by security, who were obviously shocked at what had transpired and must have jumped on you before you had the chance to put your hands up, be compliant, etcetera, etcetera.

"Dog-piled and punched and kicked by five big men, you, of course, had to fight back to avoid being seriously hurt or possibly even killed. So, you did. Now the fight had spilled out into visible territory in full view of a hundred people and half a dozen cameras. So, at this point, you must have thought it was no point running, so after you incapacitated the security team, you walked over to the head doorman, who was already on the floor, bleeding and immobile next to his comrades, and stamped on his head twice with those heavy-duty boots you're wearing. You then went outside and smoked a cigarette, waiting for police to arrive.

"And now you're sitting here, facing life in prison, hours after a murder, possibly a double murder, and a massive brawl, but looking like you're relaxing on a park bench on a sunny day. We've checked you for intoxication; you're clean. It makes me wonder if the reason you're so relaxed is because you do this kind of thing for a living, and you're expecting whatever government agency you work for to burst through that door any minute and rescue you. Or, if you're some fanatic terrorist, you want to be imprisoned and become a martyr. You're not some random run-of-the-mill street thug or gang member. And this wasn't a random heat-of-the-moment murder. You planned this. That much is obvious."

The man stared intently at Carson for a few moments, with a gaze that could have burned through Iron. Then he smiled, clapping slowly and sarcastically.

"I'm impressed. Nice deduction, Detective Carson. I guess your reputation is well-earned."

Carson stared flatly. He didn't reply. Nor did he react to the empty compliment. The man continued, "But you're wrong, unfortunately. I have never worked for any of those organisations. Though I daresay, I have crossed paths and had dealings with them in the past. I'm no 'spook' or terrorist either. Not that any spook or terrorist would be capable of doing what I've done tonight anyway unless you believe Hollywood. Not to mention that If I were a spook and that nightclub boss was my target, wouldn't I be a little more low-key? Put a bomb in his car? Shoot him with a sniper rifle from a mile away? Why would I get so up close and personal and risk getting caught?

"And no, I'm not expecting someone from the "government," or anyone else for that matter, to come and save me. I'm no religious fanatic, either. Nevertheless, I'm still not going to prison." He spoke matter-of-factly, with no doubt in his voice, as if reading from an encyclopedia.

"How do you figure?" inquired Carson.

"Oh, don't worry. You'll know by the time we've finished this conversation."

"And what if I told you I've had enough of your bullshit; and that this conversation is over?"

"Do you consider yourself a good man, Detective?"

Carson had had enough. He slid his chair back and began to get up to leave. It was almost 2 AM. He had wasted a lot of time with this freak, but if he left now, he would still find his teenage son Jeff awake and playing XBOX. They would munch on snacks, laugh, joke, and play games for an hour or so and then call it a night. He would then slide into bed next to his wife of seventeen years, Kirsty, who would already be asleep, forget about this whole thing, and drift off to sleep himself. Bliss.

He was now standing, still facing the man, "Enjoy your life in prison," he said, flashing a smug smile, as he switched off the camcorder and turned to walk towards the door.

"Do you consider yourself a good detective?" the man repeated. No change of tone in his voice. No sign of urgency.

Carson continued to walk towards the door.

"How about a father? Do you consider yourself a good father?"

Carson shook his head dismissively, laughing dryly. He had now reached the door; his hand clasped around the handle.

"I mean, you're definitely an exceptional detective, your record speaks for itself...but you still weren't good enough to find your baby daughter... were you...?"

The superintendent froze in his tracks. The door was open at a forty-five-degree angle with his hand still holding the handle. He stayed in that position for a few seconds. Then he closed the door and turned, facing the man, feet planted to the spot. He glared at Azra, fury, anger and confusion, fear, and anxiety all coursing through him like a poisonous cocktail. A hundred thoughts ran through his head. How could the freak know about this? It wasn't possible. Nobody, not even his wife...Who the hell is this guy...how did he...

"Therrre we go," the man said. A satisfied look on his scarred, weather-beaten face. He was clearly gleeful that he had touched a nerve and made no attempt to disguise it.

"We're going to have some fun now, aren't we, Detective?"

Carson stood rooted to the spot. Jaw clenched. Eyes wide. He finally found some words. "What…the hell… did you just say to me??" He formed each word slowly and carefully, his voice the quietest it had been since he had entered the room but laced with pure venom.

The man's face split into a grin, moving his scar upwards a few centimeters.

"I said, you are a useless father and a spineless pathetic excuse of a man who couldn't do a thing to rescue his helpless, innocent baby daughter… but you are a good detective." His grin devolved into a smirk. He cracked his neck side to side mockingly, as if warming up for a fight, and waited for the detective to respond.

Swearing and cursing, Carson still did not move from where he stood. He had now lost his composure. Gone was the smooth, professional police chief who was in control. In his place was an angry man, losing control and lusting for blood. He took out his mobile phone, his hand shaking with fury, and swiped across the screen, punched a couple of buttons, and held it to his ear.

"Yes, of course, it's me! Listen, LISTEN! Switch everything off, get out of there and tell everyone to go get a smoke or a cup of coffee. YES! Don't let anyone back in that room or in here until I call you again. OK? Please hurry up and do it. NOW!

Anyone has a problem with this; I swear to God, I will have their badge and they'll be flipping burgers in McDonald's tomorrow. Do not test me on this."

"It's nice to have so much power. Isn't it, Detective?" the man remarked, still smiling, dumping yet more fuel on the fire. "But where was all that power when Harriet disappeared? It *was* Harriet, wasn't it? Your daughter's name? Oh! Look at me" — The man slapped his forehead in mock self-admonishment — "talking about her in the past tense, how insensitive of me. She might still be alive, mightn't she? She would be…about what? Twenty-five now? Ha! You know as well as I do, Detective, that is ancient in terms of street life. Probably a dried-up old hag now working in an illegal brothel in Thailand somewhere. Harriet. What an awful name for a baby girl. Sounds like an old schoolteacher or the old biddy next door…"

Carson slid the phone back into his trouser pocket, unfastened the top button of his shirt, took off his tie, wrapped it around his left wrist, and unbuttoned and rolled up his sleeves. Furious, he walked towards the table, took the spare chair resting next to the one he had been sitting on, and carried it to the corner of the room where one of the CCTV cameras was fixed to the wall. He then climbed onto the chair, reached up, and disconnected the camera. Jumping back down, he carried the chair to the opposite corner of the room; and did the same with the other camera.

He walked to the table slowly, deliberately, and with both hands, jerked it towards himself a meter or so. There was a loud screeching sound as the table moved away from the man and towards Carson, knocking over Carson's chair.

The detective walked around the table, eyes still piercing, slightly more controlled than he had been a minute earlier, but his chest was slowly moving up and down as he inhaled deeply.

He was now standing extremely close to the man with no obstacles between them. So close that their toes were touching. The man sat there, no change in his demeanor, no apprehension on his face, cuffed hands now resting on his lap, grey eyes looking up at the detective.

Carson was almost exploding with rage. Who the hell did this scumbag think he was? He needed to be brought down a couple of pegs. He needed to be taught a lesson. And a lesson was best learned in pain. In blood. A lesson in manners. And respect.

He had been willing to walk away. But the freak had taken it too far. He had no idea whom he was playing games with. The chief hadn't gotten to where he was today by rolling over and playing nicely. He could be ruthless when he had to be. This cretinous, arrogant piece of filth would learn that the hard way in a few seconds.

The man had already been involved in a large brawl a couple of hours ago, had a few minor cuts and bruises, and one relatively deep one above his eye. Nobody would pay attention to a few more new ones. Carson would be careful not to leave too many marks. Besides, nobody was going to look too deeply into the plight of a savage murderer who had stabbed a man to death and stamped on another man's head twice. Nor would they look too deeply into the most highly decorated and respected chief this department had ever produced. He had power. Influence. Leverage. Much worse had been swept under the rug. This was nothing. It was time to inflict some retribution. Nobody talked about his daughter. Nobody. Ever. Nobody knew about his daughter. He was going to get to the bottom of this…

The man continued to stare up at Carson. Arrogant. Assured. Fearless. As if he were sitting safely behind bullet-proof glass instead of an extremely angry man who wanted to tear him to pieces and had every advantage over him.

"Come on, Detective, are you going to stare at me lovingly all night?" he mocked. "Or are we going to get on with this?" The detective couldn't help but feel a sudden rush of admiration for the man's complete and utter fearlessness.

Carson had trained as an amateur boxer in his youth, and though, even by his own admission, he had been nothing spectacular, even seasoned professionals agreed that his right uppercut was a thing of beauty. It was like a sledgehammer attached to a well-oiled, highly powered, coiled spring. Fast, explosive, and powerful. Devastating. And he loved to throw it. It had been a while since he had, but he still took care of himself physically and occasionally hit the bag and pads.

He set his feet and body into a boxing stance, left foot forward, right foot back, squatted down further than usual to account for his opponent sitting down.

The man grinned and closed his eyes as if in anticipation of extreme pleasure.

"Let's see how funny you feel after this," Carson remarked menacingly.

He twisted his hip, leg, and upper body and, in one fluid motion, fired the most lethal weapon in his repertoire.

It was a cracking punch and, with the slightly added bulk of middle age, possibly the hardest he had ever thrown. It was a beautiful connection. His fist landed squarely under the man's chin with a sickening thwack. His head snapped back as if hit by a rifle bullet. A tooth flew into the air and clattered across the floor somewhere. He fell back with the chair and slammed into the hard floor, the momentum rolling him on his side.

Carson was sure he had knocked him out cold. That punch could have staggered a horse. For a horrifying split second, he even thought he had possibly killed him… until the man began to laugh, manically. It was a disturbing laugh. An ugly thing. Deep, guttural, demonic even. Gravelly as his speaking voice.

Sitting up, he carried on laughing and shuffled back a couple of meters on his buttocks so that he could lean against the wall.

"Now that's the Eric Carson I came to see! Show me more!"

Infuriated, Carson grabbed the fallen chair and slammed it back into its original, upright position. He then grabbed his victim with both hands by the collar, lifting him off the ground and dropping him aggressively back into his chair. Wasting no time, Carson grabbed the back of the man's head and slammed it forwards four times in rapid succession, cursing with each slam into the edge of the steel table. He then stood back, breathing hard, chest heaving, admiring his handiwork.

The gash above the man's right eyebrow, which had been glued shut a few hours earlier, had re-opened. Blood poured down into his eye, dripping into his short, rough beard. There was blood on the table.

Blood on the floor… but he was still defiant. Still confident, unaffected even. He spoke, his voice as dark and rough as ever, but his tone was conversational, polite. Even hesitant. Almost like a father who was attempting to divulge an uncomfortable truth to his young son whilst trying to spare his feelings.

"Detective, I can appreciate your enthusiasm, but you must understand, I've had my testicles burned with a blowtorch, courtesy of Mossad, been water-boarded and electrocuted by the CIA, and on one occasion, thrown into a pit of African Fire Ants by a South African warlord. Lots more fun experiences, of course, which I don't want to bore you with, but my point is, this little love-tapping session won't get us anywhere. You're just tiring yourself out and making a bloody mess!"

Still intoxicated with hate and rage, Carson tried to think rational thoughts. Who was this… this thing? It wasn't a man. It wasn't human. It couldn't be. It was like a red-hot piece of steel in a blacksmith's forge. Beating it didn't break it. It just changed its shape.

Carson's hand was still throbbing from the initial punch. It had felt like punching a marble statue. He worried his hand might be broken, the pain blunted by adrenaline. He had dealt with plenty of tough, defiant, and bullish criminals in his time. But this man was something else. He wasn't putting on a front or projecting a fake image of machismo. He was genuinely enjoying this. Carson could see it in his eyes. He could feel it.

Hiding his apprehension, Carson continued to project a fake image of machismo. He bent forward so he was face to face with the man, stared him straight in the eye, and spoke in a low, calm voice and an icy tone. "Are you ready to give me some answers, you son of a—?"

Standing so close to the killer, rage, and adrenaline beginning to wear off, Carson felt the mysterious energy again. It emanated from the man in electrical waves. It was petrifying. It made him want to curl up on the floor in a fetal position and cry profusely. Even now, in custody in a police station, hands cuffed, bleeding, and battered, Carson felt this man was still as dangerous as an animal in the wild.

And he was right.

Before Carson could finish his sentence, the prisoner threw his head forward like a whip, faster than a cobra, connecting his forehead with Carson's mouth with a savage head butt. The chief was knocked backwards off his feet.

The man grinned; mouth full of claret. "'Lex Talionis.' An eye for an eye, Detective. Equivalent exchange. Remember?"

Carson landed on the floor, seated on his buttocks. He stayed in that position for a few seconds, collecting himself, wiping and spitting the blood from his split lip, breathing hard, and glaring at his assailant.

"Come on now, Detective, enough of this silliness. Take a moment, then get up and sit down. I am ready to tell you everything."

Carson, without uttering a word, like a child ordered to clean his room, picked himself up heavily and reluctantly, dragged the table back into position, and plopped himself back down in his chair. His breathing was much calmer. The red mist was wearing off. He sat patiently, waiting to learn what revelations would spill forth from the enigma in front of him.

"Now, let us..." The man paused. Blood was still seeping from his newly re-opened wound, much of it pouring into his right eye and in his mouth. It must have been vexatious and obscuring his vision.

"Detective, before we begin, would you kindly fetch me a glass of water and a towel, perhaps?" he asked casually, gesturing towards his face. "You look like you could do with a few minutes to freshen up, yourself."

Carson, feeling slightly defeated and exasperated, gave no reply; but rose from his chair and left the room for the first time.

***

He returned a few moments later, carrying half a dozen paper towels and a plaster in one hand and a Styrofoam cup filled with water in the other. He had rinsed his face and hair, and his mouth was no longer bloody.

He handed the cup and towels to the man.

"Thank you kindly," he said, sounding genuinely grateful.

Hands still cuffed together, he wiped his face and mouth thoroughly with three towels. He then spat blood into two more, and drained the entire contents of the cup, throwing his head back, gurgling, spat it all back out into the cup. He then dried, and patted himself off with the remaining towel, crumpled them all together, and placed them and the cup to the side of the table. He tore open the packet containing the plaster and placed it over his open wound. It was all very fluid and precise. He hadn't spilled or drank a drop of the water, and Carson was, or perhaps wasn't at this point, surprised he hadn't asked for more, so he could drink some.

The man patted the plaster over his eyebrow gingerly, making sure it was securely in place. They both knew the wound needed medical attention, but the plaster would suffice for now. He leant back in his chair, inhaled deeply, exhaled, and began. "Detective, does the name Fernando Estevo mean anything to you?"

"No."

"How about Oliver White?"

"Yes. The head doorman; probably on his deathbed right now."

"Ok. We'll get to him later... Fernando Estevo is, well, was, the nightclub owner I...purged earlier tonight."

Carson gave a slight nod.

"Mr Estevo was, unfortunately, despite appearances, not just a simple nightclub owner. He was, in fact, the ringleader of one of the largest international human-trafficking organizations in this country. He was also, amongst many other things, I'm sure, a murderer, a rapist, a child molester, drug dealer, extortionist, thief, and thug. The nightclub was simply his legal front. He—"

"I couldn't give a shit about all that. Tell me about my daughter! What you think you know. And how you know it," Carson interrupted, his temper beginning to rise again.

"I will get to that, but please don't interrupt me again, or I promise you, you will be sorry." He didn't raise his voice or change his calm demeanor. But the words cut right through Carson, giving him goosebumps. He took a breath and gathered himself, absently fingering his cut lip.

"Thank you. Now, where was I? Oh yes, Fernando Estevo. Do you know what I despise more than anything, Detective? Those who are placed on this Earth and, right from their very first moments, are

28

blessed with every single advantage and opportunity in life yet squander it all and become lower than scum. Especially when the motivation for this behavior is merely power, greed, lust and narcissism. Not for a greater good. Or for survival or necessity. Not for an ideology, a country or community, or love, or for a belief out of a misplaced sense of righteousness. You know, 'The road to hell is paved with good intentions,' and so forth. But purely for base, self-serving, animalistic pleasure.

"I mean, one can understand, if not excuse, when a person born into poverty, squalor, and/or abuse develops into a deficient human being and makes morally bankrupt decisions. But to be born with ample health, wealth, love, food, warmth, education, and shelter yet still become an ingrate and choose to destroy and poison hundreds and thousands of lives merely for one's own lust and greed? This is true evil. True darkness. The greatest tragedy—"

Bit rich coming from a savage killer, thought Carson, resisting the urge to verbalize it.

"This was Estevo. His father was a first-generation immigrant from Brazil. A lawyer. His mother, a full-blooded native here. A schoolteacher. Wealthy, good, loving parents. A happy marriage which provided a happy childhood. His parents enrolled him into the best private schools, college, and university money could buy. From a young age, Estevo showed a particular aptitude for mathematics, chemistry, and biology. His proud and hopeful parents wanted him to become a surgeon. But young Fernando had other plans…

"Whilst halfway through his third year of a degree in medicine, Estevo, out of the blue, dropped out. Quit. Just like that. His parents were mortified. What was he thinking? His path was so clear. He was doing brilliantly. He had all the talent and ability and was so close to his goal.

"What they didn't know was that throughout his years at university, though he was never left wanting for finances as his parents supported his education and living fully, Estevo had been working part-time as a nightclub bouncer. Through his moonlighting, over the years, he had built up a vast number of associates and contacts within the criminal underworld.

"Ruthless, intelligent, charismatic, and Machiavellian, and heavily into aggressive martial arts and illegal competitions, Estevo carved a bloody path through the hierarchy of the criminal underworld. Decimating anyone and everyone who stood in his way. Including murdering his own younger brother, his only sibling, who was supposed to be the 'black sheep' of the family. Ha. If only.

"After selling his soul and proving his worth to some particularly powerful entities at the very top of the pyramid, he became, so to speak, king of the jungle. He settled into his new position comfortably and gave himself a new name. An alter-ego for the law-abiding nightclub owner Fernando Estevo. A name that would strike fear into his allies and rivals alike. The Surgeon."

Carson's interest peaked slightly. This moniker was familiar to him.

"The Surgeon. An appropriate name for the precision and cunning and violence with which he operated… and a homage perhaps to his poor parents' broken dreams, and perhaps, somewhere deep down in the recesses of his blackened heart, his own.

"I asked you moments ago, Detective, if you were familiar with Fernando Estevo, and judging by your reaction just now, and from what I know about him, you are familiar with his alias but were not aware of his true identity and birth name."

Carson nodded. "We know all about The Surgeon. Agencies all over have been hunting him for years. His name constantly cropped up. But nobody knew who he was, where exactly he operated from, or even what he looked like. We began to doubt he was even real and thought maybe it was a group of people and not an individual. We just had an inkling he, or they, operated domestically. But that's all."

The man nodded back, agreeing. "Yes, he was very careful. Surgical, you might say" He chuckled to himself. "After he had annihilated all his opposition, which was anybody who could identify him, he operated purely from the shadows. Never did his own dirty work, never showed his face in dealings. Lead a double life. Fernando Estevo, the high profile, highly recognizable, charismatic nightclub owner on one side. And The Surgeon, a mysterious, demon-like, faceless, and enigmatic figure, pulling the strings in the underworld on the other.

"He was cautious. Very cautious indeed. Never even made a mistake. But you throw filth and feces and corruption into the Universe. It throws it right back. You upset the balance, the harmony, and it recalibrates. Bucks you off. Destroys you, no matter how many identities you hide behind and how much you fortify your castle. There is no escape. Your body becomes food for the worms, and your soul receives its appropriate recompense..."

Carson, despite himself, had been listening intently. He knew the man was telling the truth. Small pieces of the puzzle were beginning to come together now. But he was conflicted with a variety of emotions. The curiosity to learn more, the anger and frustration of a man who was accustomed to being in control and calling the shots but being at the mercy of this mysterious drifter, and the anxiety and confusion of what secrets would be uncovered about his daughter...

The man continued, "So we move on now, to Oliver White... who, by the way, has just passed on."

Carson stared. "What? Passed on? You mean died?"

The man nodded slowly.

"How the hell could you possibly know that?"

"You can make a few phone calls to confirm if you would like?"

Carson shook his head, tired, fed up.

The man resumed, "Ok, let us proceed, shall we? First of all, you mentioned earlier. You are familiar with Oliver White?"

"Yes."

"How?"

"He's definitely in our records. Very well known around these parts. We've picked him up for a variety of charges in the past. He's been convicted and gone to prison a few times. But this was all a decade or two ago. Recently, though he's definitely been involved in things, we've never been able to prove anything, and so he's not been jailed or convicted of any crimes for the past ten years or so."

The man nodded casually, his grey eyes fixed in a thousand-yard stare, looking right through Carson.

"Oliver White. This man was the polar opposite of Fernando Estevo. Born into an inner-city housing estate right here in this city. A violent, alcoholic, and soon-to-be-absent father and a drug-addicted mother. From the moment he could walk and talk, he had been a 'problem child.' He exhibited all the childhood signs of psychopathy—bedwetting, pyromania, and cruelty to animals.

"As he grew into adolescence, it was clear that he had become a volatile, violent, aggressive, and nasty individual. By the age of fourteen, he was already well over six feet tall and over two hundred pounds of pure muscle. Classmates and teachers alike were terrified of him.

"Fascinated by violence and itching with the need for aggressive conquest, he started his own fight club with his fellow students. But these were not minor playground scuffles. These were incidences of pure savagery. Held after school and at night, in alleyways and car parks, and backyards, many of these fights were almost to the death.

"Growing bored of fists and legs, White even introduced blunt weapons into these fights. Hammers, chains, baseball bats, knuckledusters, and more. Of course, it was a very niche market, and only the most reckless and aggressive of his classmates would even consider entering into these competitions and fighting each other, winning prizes which often consisted of nothing but bragging rights and horrific injuries. News spread, and other boys from other schools joined in the savagery. The club grew to gigantic proportions... with franchises springing up here and there in towns and cities far away... but nobody would ever want to fight White. One or two had tried and failed miserably, discouraging the rest.

"So White introduced a new rule just for himself. An equalizer. He would allow two opponents to fight him simultaneously armed with weapons, whilst he, himself, would be alone and unarmed.

"The two boys tried their best and even managed to break a couple of White's bones, but before long, White got the better of them. Crippling one of the boys and beating the other one to death.

"White was charged and locked up as a juvenile for involuntary manslaughter, spending two years in a juvenile detention facility. He was released just after his seventeenth birthday, and he knew that only one thing was certain. His life of crime and violence… had just begun.

"An ex-con with no formal qualifications who hadn't even finished school but armed with a legendary reputation, White found unlicensed, under-the-table work as a debt collector, bouncer, and minder.

"Over the years, his legend grew, and it wasn't long before he was picked up, not in person, of course, by The Surgeon. The Surgeon hired White as his number one enforcer. Punishment, threats, debt-collection, torture and interrogation, assassination. All these departments for The Surgeon were handled by White. He was the Biblical Benaiah to The Surgeon's

King David. The Pedro El Negro to The Surgeon's Santa Claus. A mad dog unleashed by its owner upon those whom he wanted ravaged and torn to pieces. And he was compensated very handsomely for it. More than he could ever have acquired finishing school and leading an honest life as a doctor, or an engineer, or an electrician.

"As the years passed by, White became weary of being hassled by the authorities. Constantly in and out of courtrooms and sometimes even prison, he decided to take up legitimate employment, as a front, as the fully badged and licensed, suited and booted, head of security at the nightclub owned by Fernando Estevo. Unbeknownst to him, right up until his very last breath, that the boss he was running security for at the club was the very same boss he was killing, raping, and torturing for in the criminal underworld...

"But, as I said before, the Earth recalibrates itself. Cleanses, detoxifies, purges. And in this case, all it took for the Earth to wipe the kingpin's big bad invincible enforcer from existence was a couple of stamps to the head, from one, of a size ten, pair of boots on these feet..."

Carson yawned and glanced at his watch, 2:45 AM. He had listened intently throughout. He was genuinely intrigued. But he was also tired, cranky, confused, and hungry. Hungry in the traditional sense, but even hungrier for information and answers about his daughter. And information about how any of this was connected to him. Or her. And lastly, of course, who, in God's name, this human-like creature was.

His temper was beginning to rise again. His patience was running out. He would give the man one final chance - one chance to begin speaking about the things Carson wanted to know. If the next words from his mouth were not relevant, the chief would get nasty. Very nasty. This freak had seen nothing yet. Carson would make what happened earlier look like a picnic.

"Bored, Detective?" the man inquired.

"No. Just tired," Carson replied truthfully.

"Well then, grab yourself a cup of coffee if you like. Because we have, at last, arrived at the precipice of this twisted tale. You. Detective Chief Superintendent Eric Carson. You. And your daughter Harriet…"

Finally, thought Carson. Throughout the man's monologue, Carson had sat, leaning back in his chair, arms crossed in front of him. He now sat up, leaned forward, resting his elbows on the table, and waited.

"Detective, before we start, would you tell me everything you remember about what happened on the eve of your daughter's disappearance?"

Carson hesitated. It wasn't a fond memory, and he very rarely revisited it.

"Why?"

"It doesn't matter. Equivalent exchange. Give, and you shall receive."

Carson inhaled deeply.

"It was twenty years ago, a few months before I joined the police. I was twenty-two at the time. Harriet was six. I hadn't met my current wife yet, and my son hadn't yet been born-another life. Harriet's mother wasn't around, and I was a single father. It was springtime. A Friday afternoon.

"I was working as a self-employed painter and decorator at the time, so I could be flexible and start and finish work as I pleased, around Harriet's schedule. Quite often, if a job was unfinished or needed more work done for that day by the time I left to collect her from school, I would return with her after picking her up and keep her with me whilst I finished the job.

"As it was a Friday, I decided to finish early and not return. I would collect her from school, and we would drive straight home. After picking her up in my work van, we drove to the shop to buy a few things for the house, looking forward to a weekend of cartoons, games, and playing in the park. Just me and my girl..." Carson paused, hesitating.

"Go on..."

"She... she was tired that day. As was I. It... it was Friday. We'd both had a long week."

He paused again. He could feel the change in his own demeanor. He no longer felt like the powerful, confident, and controlled chief of police. Or the intimidating interrogator gripped by bloodlust. He felt timid. Vulnerable. Full of pain and regret. He swallowed and forced himself to continue.

"She'd fallen asleep by the time we'd arrived at the shop. She looked so comfortable. Peaceful. I… I didn't want to disturb her. It wasn't my fault. It could've happened to anyone. I… I left her in the van. Sleeping. Remembered to lock it and everything. I only needed a few minutes in the shop. But when I came back… the window on her side was smashed… and she was gone."

The man stared at Carson, his expression blank, unreadable.

"Then what?" he asked.

"What d'you mean then what??" Carson snapped. "That's it! I never saw her again! I went crazy, of course, running up and down the street, screaming her name, went into all the nearby shops, asking if anyone had seen her. Called the police. They launched an investigation, of course, and a nationwide manhunt, but there was nothing. No leads, no evidence, nothing to go on. Absolutely nothing. No witnesses and it happened outside the line of sight of any CCTV. Eventually, the investigation was called off…"

The man raised his eyebrows as if to say, "Really? That's what happened?"

This enraged Carson.

"Why the hell are you looking at me like that?"

"Are you sure that's what happened? Think harder! What really happened that day?"

That was it. Carson exploded. He leapt up, knocking his chair over.

"WHAT THE HELL IS WRONG WITH YOU, YOU GODDAMNED PSYCHO?"

The man also leapt up. Hands still cuffed together, and, like greased lightning, he lunged forward and grabbed the detective's wrists, holding on tightly.

Carson began to shake violently. He felt an electrical current surging through his body. He stood there, stuck in the man's vice-like grip, shaking and shuddering. He felt his eyes roll to the back of his head, and foam bubbled out of the corner of his mouth as though he were having a seizure or being electrocuted.

The room spun at a hundred miles per hour. Carson didn't know what was happening. He felt like he was dying. And then, it all went dark… and the terrible memories came flooding back like a dam had been broken.

***

It was the turn of the millennium. The year 2000. Twenty years ago. Friday. Eric Carson had just collected his daughter from school and was driving his work van towards the city exit. Heading out of town. About to complete his final job. The job that would change his life forever. The job that would set him up for life and make all his dreams and ambitions come true…

It all started around a year ago, 1999. Eric had just entered his twenties and had nothing. Very basic qualifications from schooling he had barely completed, a dead-end job painting houses and rooms now and then, and a crummy little apartment in a crummy part of town. No prospects, no family, no future. Few friends… and a five-year-old daughter he hadn't planned on having, the result of a drunken back-alley fumble. The mother of his child had dumped the baby with him soon after she was born and disappeared forever, leaving Eric to pick up all the pieces and raise the baby on his own. He could barely take care of himself. Let alone a needy, fragile baby too.

After five years of struggle and hardship, jumping from job to job and girlfriend to girlfriend to help look after his daughter whilst he worked and stole to survive, Eric had decided enough was enough. He started his own sub-par painting and decorating business so he could at least have a stable, if not sufficient, form of income whilst he figured out what he would do with his life… along with his business, he had also formulated a plan…

For as long as he could remember, Eric had always known that he was special. He was ambitious, charismatic, and more intelligent and good-looking than anybody he had ever met. There must be a reason he had these qualities. He knew he was destined for great things. He was sure of it. He could feel it in his very bones. It was just that he had been dealt a bad hand in life and was going through a bad patch. But the phoenix always rose from the ashes… and Eric knew he would rise again, no matter what it took. He had always been ruthless when it came to the pursuit of his own goals. It was all about him. Nothing else mattered. Nobody had ever achieved greatness worrying about other people.

His plan was a little strange. Actually, it was downright crazy. He was almost certain it wouldn't work. But desperate times called for desperate measures. He had to do something. If it didn't work, he would have lost nothing. But if, by some miracle, it did? Everything he had ever wanted and deserved would be laid out to him on a plate.

A friend of Eric's was heavily into the occult. The study of demonology, black magic, devil worship. That sort of thing. He had told Eric stories about those who had "given themselves completely" to darkness and now had wealth and power beyond belief. Of course, Eric, who had no belief in religion, the paranormal, or supernatural, had scoffed at this, asking his friend why he hadn't tried it himself if he was so convinced it was all true. His friend replied that he was too scared and that it was a line he wouldn't cross.

Pathetic.

That was the difference between Eric and other people. He was willing to go all the way and cross lines that others wouldn't dare to.

So, he borrowed one of his friend's books and prepared to follow the instructions which would lead him to greatness. Silly as it seemed, what did he have to lose? If it didn't work, he would be in exactly the same position as he was now, only now he could mock people who believed in this crap because he had attempted it himself and seen its futility. But if by some miracle it worked? Nothing to lose. Everything to gain.

Eric left his daughter in the care of one of his friends. According to the book, he needed to be alone in his apartment for three nights and days. No distractions or disturbances. He followed every instruction to the letter. First, he moved all furniture and appliances out of the room, so it was completely bare. Then, he disconnected his landline. Next, he switched all the lights off, shut all the curtains, and lit a candle.

He then stripped down completely nude and sat cross-legged in the middle of the lounge.

After this, he took a razor and made a small incision in his forearm, bleeding into a cup. Once the cup was suitably full, he dipped his finger into it and then drew a circle around where he sat. He then added the appropriate shapes and symbols to the inside of the circle and began to chant.

The first night passed, then the day. Nothing.

Night and day number two passed. Still nothing. At this point, after barely having moved a muscle in over forty-eight hours, aching and feeling like he was dying, and sitting in his own urine and excrement, Eric began to lose hope... until...

It made contact on the third night. A dark, mysterious entity. All Eric could make out was a black shadow. A silhouette. Vaguely reminiscent of the shape of a man. It appeared out of nowhere outside the blood circle. At first, its appearance petrified Eric. But after a few moments, he managed to pull himself together, reminding himself who he was, what he was about, and why he was doing this.

The shadow spoke. It told him everything. From what Eric was to do from that very moment to what would happen after he did it, to exactly what he would receive and how and when he would receive it.

He was to complete six tasks. Each task would be more difficult and testing than the last. He would only find out information about the next task once he had completed the previous one. No more rituals were necessary. The entity would come to him. Eric was ecstatic.

The first task was easy. Too easy. A walk in the park. All Eric had to do was to say something hurtful to someone close to him without offering any form of apology or explanation.

Eric was at home, watching cartoons and eating dinner with his daughter.

"Harriet."

"What, Daddy?" asked the little girl. Eyes wide and innocent, gazing at her father.

"You're ugly and very smelly."

She was visibly hurt, upset, and rather confused, but she'd be ok. She was barely six years old. She would forget about it in a few minutes and go back to eating her spaghetti alphabets and watching cartoons.

That night the entity revisited Eric whilst he slept. He was awoken suddenly by a pressing sensation on his chest and realized he was struck with sleep paralysis, unable to move, with the familiar shadowy silhouette standing above him. It acknowledged that his first task was complete and informed him of the second. It would continue to do this after the successful completion of each task.

The second task was even easier for Eric. Too good to be true. All he had to do was destroy and "disrespect" a holy book. He visited a library the very next day and walked into the Religious Books section. He selected a book and, making sure he was out of sight, tore the book to pieces, taking some of the torn pages home with him. Upon arriving home, he threw some of the torn pages into the toilet, flushed them away, and stored the rest as toilet paper for future use.

The third task was still relatively easy too. He was instructed to desecrate a specific grave- in the local cemetery and urinate on it.

The fourth task was slightly more challenging and exciting than the first three. He had to set fire to an unoccupied place of worship.

The fifth task was messy.

He was to butcher a domestic animal that belonged to somebody. Eric chose the cat next door, which, unfortunately, his daughter had grown rather attached to. But it was Ok. She would get over it.

After making sure its owners weren't home, and luring the dumb creature into his own garden, and then stabbing the furry little creature to death with a kitchen knife, he buried it in the woods where his daughter or its owners would never find it and assume it had simply run away and got lost.

One task away from success and greatness, Eric slept that night, content and with a smile on his face. He woke up the next morning, ready to complete his mission and fulfill his destiny...

***

It was the turn of the millennium. The year 2000. Twenty years ago. Friday. Eric Carson had just collected his daughter from school and was driving his work van towards the city exit, heading out of town. About to complete his final job. The job that would change his life forever. The job that would set him up for life and make all his dreams and ambitions come to fruition…

Harriet was asleep next to him in the front passenger seat, still in her school uniform. The little girl was tired from a long day at school but still insisted on going straight to the park before going home. They had barely driven for five minutes in slow-moving traffic when she had fallen asleep, head leaning against the window, her light-brown, shoulder-length hair loose and covering most of her rosy, flushed cheeks.

Eric drove over a deep pothole, the van bouncing and jerking, and Harriet woke up, rubbing her eyes and yawning.

"Daddy, where are we?" she asked groggily.

"Going to the park, remember?"

"This isn't the way to the park! I've never been here before."

"I know, but we're going to a new park, a better one, much more fun things to do there."

She frowned. She was only six, but she was already very perceptive and intelligent for a child her age. She was also very garrulous.

"Then why didn't you say that before?" she asked suspiciously.

"Because I wanted to surprise you, of course!"

She craned her delicate neck, looking around the interior of the van and behind the seats.

"Ok. But Daddy, where's your jacket? It's quite cold outside today."

"It's not cold."

"Of course, it is! It's still springtime. It's not even summer yet! You're so silly, Daddy! You're a grown-up, you should know that! Here, there's a blanket behind your seat. You can wear that when we get out. Did you bring the frisbee? What about the—"

"Harriet, would you SHUT UP!"

She jumped. Startled. Then shrunk down in her seat. Upset. Dejected. "You don't need to shout at me, Dad. I just don't want you to be cold and catch the sniffles. That's all. We both don't have a mummy, so I need to be like TWO mummies, so I can look after both of us."

"I'll be fine," Eric replied coldly.

After another fifteen minutes of driving, following the Sat Nav, Eric pulled into what looked like a large, abandoned industrial complex, with large buildings and factories littered around everywhere. He parked the van outside one of the desolate buildings and switched off the engine.

"Daddy, why are we stopping here? Is this the new park? Eww. It's so ugly and boring! The other one's much better. Can we go back there, Dad? Pleeeease?"

"No. Be quiet."

Harriet huffed and crossed her arms, scowling. "You're being really mean today, Dad. AND you called me 'ugly' and 'smelly' the other day!"

A minute or two later, a black Range Rover with tinted windows pulled into the complex, rolling to a stop, adjacent and a few meters away from Eric's van. The Sun was beginning to dip, and the earlier spring sunshine had disappeared, giving way to grey clouds, darkening the day.

Two men emerged out of the vehicle. There were possibly more inside.

"Daddy, who are those men?"

"They're just Daddy's friends. They've come to play with us."

The first man was around medium height. Medium build. Dressed all in black. Black shoes, trousers, shirt, and blazer. Even black sunglasses. He looked to be around his late forties and had mousy brown hair, which had all but disappeared on top but was still rather thick around the sides and back.

The second was younger. A giant. Almost six and a half feet tall. He had hands like dinner plates, shoulders like a bull's, and a neck thicker than most men's legs. His hair was cut very short and formed a dark-brown stubble over his large head. He was dressed in exactly the same attire as the first man, including the sunglasses.

Eric was sure he recognized him. They had gone to school together. The giant had been a couple of years above him and was always getting into trouble and suspended for fighting. He had, apparently, even started his own fight club and ended up killing another boy from another school and getting locked up for it. White. That was it. Something... White. Was it Harry? Mallory? Whatever. It didn't matter.

Eric got out of the van with his daughter in tow, holding his hand. The first man approached, but the giant stayed by the Rover, hands placed one above the other, over his lower abdomen, head moving side to side slowly, like a secret service agent, scanning the area.

"Good evening Mr Carson," The first man greeted Eric. His words were measured. He sounded posh. Sophisticated. Like an aristocrat.

"Hi," said Eric flatly.

"I trust we're ready to proceed with the transaction?"

"Of course."

The man gestured to the giant. The giant removed his sunglasses and walked over slowly, approaching Eric and his daughter. He stopped two paces in front of them, looking down curiously at the little girl holding her father's hand. She was looking him straight in the eye. Unblinking, fearless.

"Ain't you scared, little girl?" His voice was low, booming, like what a gorilla might sound like if it could speak.

"No," she said. Smiling. Unfazed.

"Why not?"

"Because you're Daddy's friend. He told me. And if you're mean to me, he will beat you up. Really, he will. I don't care if you're a huuuge giant. My Daddy will still beat you. He's the strongest, bravest, funniest dad in the whole wide world! Even stronger than Spiderman! I don't even have a mummy, and I don't even need one because I've got him!"

The giant chuckled menacingly, then stooped down, hand reaching out, to take the little girl. Harriet squealed, her confidence evaporating in an instant, running around to the back of her father, still holding his hand tight.

"Daddy, help! He's trying to take me! Is he a stranger? I thought he was your friend?"

The two men looked at Eric with expressions that said, "Deal with it, or we will."

Eric turned and picked up his daughter. Trying his utmost best to avoid eye contact, he tried to calm her down.

"Harriet. It's Ok. Go with him. He's Daddy's friend. He's going to take you on a fun ride."

He handed her over to the giant as she kicked and screamed. Confused. Frightened. Sobbing. Tears poured down the flushed, tender skin of her little face.

"Daddy, no! What are you doing? Pleeeease! There's no rides here! Where are you taking me, you big ugly monster? Put me down, NOW! My dad's going to beat you up! Daddy, help!! Heelppp!"

Holding the thrashing, screaming girl in one hand, the giant took a syringe out of his pocket with the other, inserting the needle into her neck. Her movement stopped almost immediately. She stopped kicking. Stopped screaming. And lay limp and motionless in the giant's massive arms.

The giant carried her to the Range Rover and placed her in the back, closing the door. He then put his sunglasses back on and resumed his position, standing by the vehicle, hands placed in front of him, head moving side to side slowly.

"What are you going to do with her?" Eric asked the older man.

"Does it matter Mr Carson? Are you concerned?"

"I heard something about some up-and-coming new guy in the streets. 'The Surgeon' or something? Specializes in child trafficking and other things? Is that who you're taking her to?"

The man chuckled. Amused.

"No, Mr Carson. I assure you, though she will initially be taken to The Surgeon, there are entities much higher up the food chain than the likes of him. Entities who require pure blood to continue functioning. Your sacrifice will be very well received. Very much appreciated. It will serve a very important purpose. Larger than us all."

Eric wasn't quite sure how he felt. He noticed a very slight pang of guilt creeping up on him. Very slight. He dismissed it easily. He was above such emotions now. Guilt, honesty, love, fear, remorse, pity, empathy. These were all emotions for the weak. Emotions which were conditioned into people from a young age to keep the population docile and easily controlled.

But the elite? The ones at the top pulling the strings and orchestrating the world? The ones that really mattered? You wouldn't find these people exhibiting those pathetic emotions. There was no good or evil. Just power. Survival of the fittest. There were those who were too weak and unwilling to go the distance. And there were those that weren't. Eric knew he was the latter. And that was all that mattered.

Besides, the mother was the one who had abandoned her. It was usually the father who did a runner. But Eric had taken her in. Looked after her. Fed her. Raised her. Done everything. And what had he gotten for it? A rubbish, insignificant and pointless life with barely enough money to survive. A constant miserable struggle. A pitiful existence.

Ha! Look at me, thought Eric. Getting all defensive and trying to justify myself. Who gives a damn? There is no good and evil, remember?

And with that, Eric completely dismissed the thought of his daughter from his mind.

The man was studying Eric curiously.

"Chief of police, eh? Interesting choice. Most people just want to be celebrities. You know, singers, actors, athletes. That sort of thing. But chief of police? Interesting indeed."

"President or prime minister wasn't available."

"HAHA, brilliant! Brilliant!" The man chortled, appreciating the humor.

Eric hadn't been joking.

"So, what happens now?" he asked.

"Now? Well, we go our separate ways, and you prepare for a life of success, prestige, honor, wealth, and power. Your handler, the one who visits you at night, will be in touch very shortly."

They shook hands and walked back to their respective vehicles. Eric stopped.

"Wait!" he called out.

"Yes?"

"One last thing."

"Go on."

"I was told about some memory thing."

"Memory thing?"

"Yeah, something about my memory of this whole thing being wiped out and replaced with a new one or something? So, it, you know... doesn't ever come back to bother me in the future or in my dreams?"

"Ah, yes. Well, in a few moments, you will experience a blackout. Upon awakening, you will find yourself in another location, going about your daily business, shopping in a local supermarket. To your mind, it will be as though your daughter is outside, having just been collected from school, sleeping in your parked vehicle. You will leave the shop and find your vehicle with a smashed window and your daughter absent. You will panic and grieve for a very brief time. A heart as rusted as yours? It really won't take long for you to forget her and enjoy your new life. She will become a very distant memory before long.

"The memory erasure will start from the moment you first performed the ritual and made contact with your handler and end in a few moments after we have exchanged our very last words. Everything in between, completely erased."

Eric breathed a sigh of relief. Satisfied.

The man smirked and offered a salute and a wink. "Live long and prosper, young Eric."

Then it all went dark...

***

It was now 3:30 AM.

Detective Superintendent Carson was lying flat on his back in the interrogation room. Hyperventilating. Gasping for air. Sobbing uncontrollably.

The man stood, looming above him. He had somehow broken out of the handcuffs, which were lying on the floor a few yards away. He looked larger and more menacing than before. Grey eyes, piercing as ever. An energetic, satisfied look etched across his scarred face.

"Eric," he said, referring to the detective by his first name for the first time. "That's right. Eric. No more of this Detective Superintendent rubbish. That is not you. Not the real you. It is but a facade. An illusion. Eric is the real you. Eric, the poor, young, sniveling, cowardly, weak, evil, pathetic excuse of a man, who sold his baby daughter for two short decades of a bit of power and wealth." The man's face was now etched with complete and utter disgust and contempt as he looked down at the floor, at the pathetic wreck in front of him.

"No, p…please," Carson pleaded, still suffocating, bawling like a baby, barely forming his words. "I'm…I'm sorry! I'm so soorrrrry!"

"SHUT UP!" The man bellowed. "Don't you dare! You are not sorry for your actions! What you are sorry for is that your fairground ride has finally reached its end!" he spat.

For the first time, there seemed to be a hint of sadness in the man's eyes when he spoke.

"Aaah, young Harriet," he sighed. "Beautiful, pure, loving, innocent, intelligent, brave, angelic, selfless little Harriet. How fiercely she loved you, Eric. How completely she trusted you. And how dark and painful and terrifying was her recompense for this?

"But no matter, no matter, for she is now, surely in lush, beautiful gardens under which clear rivers flow. Picking and eating fruits from trees no mortal eye has ever seen. The moment her pure, tiny little heart stopped beating and her soul left her delicate, pierced, and bloody body, she forgot everything in an instant. All the events that transpired in her short lifetime on this ugly, insignificant, cruel battleground. On this floating little ball of dirt in outer space. This thresher. All gone in an instant. She remembers neither the cruel mother who so quickly abandoned her nor the callous, cowardly father who delivered her to her horrific, premature demise.

"She is protected and guarded by angels with many wings. Angels of love and mercy who provide for all her needs. With billions and trillions of other children just like her, taken too soon, running and laughing, eating, drinking, and playing as they please. Just like the parks, she so loved to visit with her father. In the final park she will ever visit. A vast expanse. Endlessly and unimaginably better than the park you so cruelly told her you would take her to, deceiving and delivering her to a lonely and painful death.

"And love you say? The love she is provided with is unfathomable even to the purest of hearts. She is shrouded with an eternal love and comfort, far beyond even the powerful, unconditional love she gave to you. The fierce love. The pure, selfless love of a pure and innocent child. The love which you so recklessly rejected and defiled with your filthy, rusted heart.

"And so, she shall bask in its warm embrace for all eternity. No fear, no pain, no grief, no regret. No sorrow. Ever again."

Carson was still sobbing uncontrollably. He tried to move, but he couldn't. His body wouldn't co-operate.

The man continued. "And as for you, my narcissistic, sub-human friend. I would advise you to cease your sobbing. You'll need to save your tears. For you shall surely run out of them where you're going.

You shall now meet the entities you denied. The day you believed would never arrive. It is here, my friend. Your ugly pungent soul will attempt to fight it. Attempt to stay in this wretched body. But it shall be dragged out. Oh yes, it shall. Ripped out and torn like wet wool on a skewer. There is no escape. You will taste what your own hands have sowed. The rotten fruits of your rotten labour."

The man lifted his right foot and brought it crashing down on Carson's windpipe. Crushing it. Destroying it. Carson coughed and spluttered, gasping for air, spitting out blood over his face. He had moments left.

The man gazed calmly. "In my nine hundred years, of all the assignments I have completed. All the tyrants, the oppressors, the evildoers. This has been, by far, the most satisfying."

Carson continued to splutter. Blood spurting from his mouth. His breaths were short and sharp, life rapidly escaping him. He somehow managed to gather the ability to speak a few words. His final words.

"A…a…are…y…you...the…the…Devil?"

The man laughed incredulously.

"Goodness, no! I am but a lowly errand boy. A taxman. A debt collector, if you will. The proper forces on the other side shall make themselves known to you very, very shortly, young Eric. Not long at all now. My job is done. I must take my leave."

And with that, he was gone.

***

It was almost 5 AM. The chief had still not made contact. Surely, he couldn't still be questioning the man, could he? What were they even talking about in there? It was a slam-dunk case. The suspect was caught red-handed.

The chief had warned them that if anyone disturbed them, he would have their badge. And he would do it too. Carson didn't mess around. But they had called his phone three times now. And there had been no answer. Something was wrong.

The officer decided he would check on them, but he would do it via the observation room so that Carson wouldn't see him and flip out.

He opened the door and walked in. He looked through the two-way mirror, and his blood ran cold.

The chief lay lifeless on the ground, flat on his back, the chairs scattered across the room, the table flipped on its side. Blood was pouring out of his mouth, and his chest was not moving. His eyes stared upwards, glassy, empty. Dead.

Broken handcuffs lay a few feet beside his body. The suspect was nowhere to be seen…

Martyr

I am the Sword of Peace
I am the Sword of Justice
I am the Sword of God
I am the Wolf that walks alone

Chapter 1: Fat Boy

Zander gazed in awe.

It was a surreal view. The man sat atop his shiny, beautifully maintained Harley Davidson Fat Boy motorcycle against the backdrop of the bleak, ruined landscape. A small amount of dust on the sides of the tank and tyres were the only sign of travel. He was leather-clad from shoulders to toes, black shades covering his eyes.

The low rumbling of the idling motorcycle's (quite possibly the last of its kind on Earth) engine was the only sound spoiling the serene silence of the ravaged and dead land, which stretched as far as the eye could see.

The man reached behind him to his right, into the saddle bag attached to the Fat Boy, and pulled out a sawn-off pump-action shotgun, the black, brown, and grey of the archaic instrument of death (this too, quite possibly the last of its kind) blending in perfectly with the collective hue of the land and sky. He raised the weapon and pointed it one-handed at Zander, who stood twenty yards in front of him.

Individual perspectives are a funny thing. Funny in that they are so similar yet so different whilst being oblivious and unsympathetic towards each other.

Zander could imagine that from the Fat Boy Rider's perspective, there must have been something wrong with him. There he was, a young man, alone in the Badlands, gun pointed at him, yet he had not raised his hands in surrender or armed himself. Nor had he tried to run or even so much as startled or flinched.

From Zander's perspective, there was plenty wrong with the man sitting atop his motorcycle, pointing a shotgun at him.

In his early twenties, Zander was still young. He was wearing scruffy, dirty brown cargo pants, scuffed, dirty brown boots, a slate-grey, military-style windbreaker jacket with many pockets, and a black and grey shemagh scarf wrapped loosely around his neck, most of it resting on his chest, underneath a bandana and pair of goggles. A huge sword lay strapped to his back. His longish hair and shortish beard were prematurely greying, and he was rail thin. Handsome, in a gaunt, pinched sort of way.

But people would always say that it was his eyes that stood out the most. An impossibly bright emerald green, a stark contrast to the rest of his appearance and attire. Piercing, intelligent, wise, old, young, happy, and playful with a hint of sadness, all at the same time.

He stared at the huge leather-clad man.

The man was not much older than himself, if at all, and the first human being he had seen in the last one hundred miles or so, on a vehicle he had only read about and seen pictures of, pointing a weapon he had never seen straight at him.

The man looked eerily similar, almost identical to a man on a battered old poster he had seen on a scavenger hunt as a child, right down to the shades, the motorcycle, and even the hairstyle. They used to make these things called 'Movies' long ago in the old world. Actors acted out fantastical stories, which would then somehow be visually recorded and transferred to devices, both tiny and large, for people to watch and be entertained. He had been fascinated by that poster as a child. The actor in the image looked seductively magnetic and awe-inspiring. Cool, calm and intimidating. Dressed all in black leather, wearing black shades sitting on a motorcycle, a stylish warrior.

Zander remembered someone telling him that this actor and this movie had been one of the most famous ones. The movie was called Exterminator Judgment Day or something or other. The actor had a long, complicated name Zander could no longer recall. And he had been a big guy. Back in the days when people had enough time, food, and energy to spend hours in places specifically designed to provide them with heavy plates of iron and machines to lift up and down, not for work or slave labour or anything like that, but completely voluntary, for no reason other than to look bigger and get stronger. In fact, people would pay to use these places. And this guy was even bigger than that Exterminator guy. But who the hell was he?

Fat Boy Rider, gun still raised in the same position, spoke.

"I need your clothes, your boots, and your motorcycle."

Zander glanced to his right. Kaz, his horse, had died a few dozen miles back. Since then, his only transport and travel companion had been an ancient but reliable, eleven-speed rugged mountain bike with huge tyres, which he had carried, strapped to his back as backup transport whilst he had ridden Kaz. The bike now lay against the log he had been sitting on moments ago, resting, before he had heard and spotted the roaring Fat Boy in the distance and gotten up.

"I have no motorcycle. It's a bicycle," he said.

Fat Boy Rider's expression was unreadable through the dark shades, his lips a thin straight line. He didn't move.

"I said, I need your clothes, your boots, and your motorcycle."

Zander, still unabashed and confident but confused, thought for a second. *Why would a man riding such a rare and beautiful beast such as that want my rusty old bike? He can't ride both at the same time, and if it's one or the other, surely, he's not going to leave his and take mine?* That would be like swapping a healthy young stallion for a lame old donkey. Even worse. Perhaps he was almost out of fuel?

"You can't have my clothes. I need them. Same for my boots. If by 'motorcycle' you mean my bicycle, you can't have that either. Same reason. But if you want some food or water, I have plenty, and I don't mind sharing…" He added, "None of you will have true faith until you love for your brother, what you love for yourself."

Fat Boy Rider now began to hold the gun with both hands instead of one, firming his grip, showing Zander he meant business. "Last chance, douchebag."

Zander stared. His thoughts were somewhere between Do what you have to do. And what in God's grey Earth have you been smoking?

He muttered a supplication under his breath, "Sufficient for me is the Lord, and he is the best disposer of affairs," and if there was any sense of even a minuscule amount of fear remaining in him, it evaporated.

Fat Boy Rider remained in this position for a few more seconds and then suddenly guffawed uncontrollably, pointing the gun away from Zander and throwing his head back as he roared with fits of laughter, "Goddamn boy! You a damn fool, you s'posed ta say, 'You forgot to say please' Donchu know nothin'?"

Zander continued to stare. Baffled.

Fat Boy Rider immediately ceased his laughter and redirected the gun back to Zander, removing his sunglasses, exposing a pair of widely stretched, unfocused eyes with nothing in them but pure, unreasonable insanity. He bellowed at the top of his voice, spit flying out of the corners of his mouth in an insane rage, "I SAID YOU S'POSED TA SAY, 'YOU FORGOT TO SAY PLEASE!' YOU RETARDED OR SUMMIN' BOY?! SAY IT NOW, OR I SWEAR TO CHRIST I'LL FILL YA GODDAMN RETARD FACE FULLA BUCKSHOT! SAY IT!"

"You forgot to say please," said Zander, flatly with no hint of fear or urgency in his voice.

Fat Boy Rider's rage disappeared in an instant, and he began chuckling again, "There ya go, that weren't so goddamn hard now, was it, boy? Can't do the next part, though, now, can we? Ain't got us no cigar, or pool cue and all that crap have we, douchebag? Ain't no nothin' out here but rocks, stumps, and rocks now, is there, boy?"

Zander was unsure whether to nod or shake his head. He settled for the shake.

"So, what's your name, douchebag?" asked Fat Boy Rider.

"Zander."

Fat Boy Rider nodded slowly and thoughtfully as though he had received a satisfactory and complex answer to an extremely important question.

"And you are?" asked Zander amicably.

There was a deafening blast as Fat Boy Rider fired the shotgun into the air. His face turned beet-red, returning to rage mode. He yelled at the top of his voice, "DONTCHU THROW ME NO QUESTIONS, BOY! WHO YOU! HUH? YOU THE POE LEESE? YOU FIVE-OH? YOU INTRAGATING ME, BOYY? DONTCHU EVER! EVER! ASK ME NO QUESTIONS RETARD. I ASK THE QUESTIONS, DOUCHEBAG!"

"Okay, sorry," said Zander, still composed. And though unshaken, he projected submissiveness and worked towards appeasement. He would have to play this maniac's game for a little while just to stay alive and complete his journey. And his task. Possibly the most important assignment in history. The last mission he would ever complete.

Fat Boy Rider's rage again dissipated as quickly as it had erupted, and he dismounted the bike, wheeling it over to Zander and letting it rest on its kickstand. Still holding the shotgun in one hand, but in a much more relaxed manner now, dangling it by his side, he asked, "You said you had food and water, douchebag. What food you got? I need me some protein, boy, feed these here biceps, man, whatcha got? Whatcha got?"

"You like lizard? Roast lizard?"

"Hell yeah, boy!"

"Caught two yesterday, ate one, was saving one for breakfast just now, but I have plenty of other things to eat, so you can have it, brother."

Fat Boy Rider's eyes widened. "Choo just call me?"

Zander hesitated. "Brother..."

Fat Boy Rider stared. It was impossible to predict how this man would react from one minute to the next. More like one second to the next. He was the kind of man who would shoot you in the face on a whim and then offer you a drink a moment later. And then shoot you again. But now, his face split into a grin, and he slapped Zander on the back, hard, with a monstrous hand that felt like a bag full of concrete. "You aight, kid, you aight."

Zander walked a few paces to his hiking pack and took out the roasted lizard wrapped in a light-brown cloth, handing it to Fat Boy Rider. He took out a bag of dates and a full water skin for himself.

They sat close, opposite each other on the scorched, barren Earth and ate together. Fat Boy Rider, cross-legged with the shotgun in his lap, and Zander in an Asian squat. Close up. Zander realised that Fat Boy Rider was even more gargantuan than he had initially thought, at least six and a half feet tall, with a neck that was thicker than Zander's legs, a lantern jaw but a fresh-faced, healthy quality about his skin, no roughness or wear and tear, like a high-school jock. It didn't make sense to Zander for a human being living life in this harsh new age to lack signs of aging, scars, wear and tear.

Fat Boy Rider demolished the roast lizard, which was the size of a small tabby cat, in three bites. As he sat there, chewing and grinding the tough meat with his perfect white teeth, he ruminated and frowned thoughtfully at his new companion.

"Ya know Zee, you'da fort after they dropped all them nooks back then, at least summa these lizards woulda got massive from the raydation or summin', wouldn't ya? Like in the movie Godzilla?"

"There are rats the size of dogs where I grew up."

Fatboy Rider's face lit up. "That's awesome, cuz! Like Stuart Little on steroids, boyy!"

Zander nodded with an agreeing smile as he chewed on his dates, even though he had no idea what the man was talking about. Although curious about this stranger's story was, he refrained from asking questions. Firstly, because he had been warned in no uncertain terms not to, and secondly, because he had a feeling that this was the kind of man who enjoyed the sound of his own voice and would reveal everything about himself, right down to the colour of his underwear, without any prompting.

Zander was right.

Fat Boy Rider finished chewing and swallowed hard, forcing the last of the dry, tough meat down his throat. He gestured to the water skin next to Zander, who handed it to him. After draining most of its contents within a few seconds, he threw it back to Zander, burped loudly, wiped his mouth with the back of his hand, and said, "So whatchoo doin' out here all by yourself, Zee? Wait, screw that, man, Imma tell you what's up, and you gonna listen, yeah you are, Zee, and you know why? Cos I'm givin' you the honour of bein' my first follower. Yeah, that's right, Zee. You gon' be my lieutenant, my right-hand man, my number two, Zee! You know, like 'I'm Michael Jackson, you Tito.' I'm Scarface, and you Manny, I'm the president and you the vice president, ya dig that, Zee?"

Zander spat out a date seed, nodded, and smiled, widening his eyes in feigned excitement.

"Now you see, after the world done went crazy Zee, and they dropped all em nukes? Only two types people survived. The special and the lucky. You one dem lucky ones, Zee. But me? I'm special. See, my great grandaddy was the top military scientist in what they called back then thee Yoo Knighted States of Merica. Now when it all went down, him and his family and friends, they had one thee golden tickets, ya know? Like Willy Wone-ka's chocolate factory? So, they was down underground, in some place they used to call Yoorope, safe, protected in thee beautifullest underground mansions you ever seen Zee. Oh yeah! They had everything, Zee: best food, water, drinks, medicine, vehicles, toys, books, comics, DVDs, even swimming pools, gyms, and jacuzzis bro, and enough of it to go for a hundred years, man! So—" He suddenly paused, frozen, staring at Zander, eyes empty as if he were a machine whose owner had decided to switch him off for being too loud.

Zander narrowed his eyes. For God's sake, what now?

Fat Boy Rider switched back on, his face looking as though he'd suddenly experienced an epiphany.

"Hold on, hold on, hold on," he said. "First, I needs to know if you tough enough, Zee."

"Tough enough for what?" Asked Zander.

"Well, if you goan be my number two, ain't no good havin' no fag fairy as my backup now, is it, Zee? And no fence, man, but you ain't exactly no Rambo-lookin' fella now, is ya? Lookin' like if it gets to be a lil' windy, it would blow your skinny ass away."

Zander held his gaze but said nothing.

Without warning and incredibly swiftly considering his size, Fat Boy Rider lifted the shotgun out of his lap and smashed the barrel, hard, into Zander's face.

The blow missed Zander's nose but struck him in the mouth, knocking him backwards off his feet from the squatting position. Zander lay on his back for a second, staring at the dark, murky sky, conscious but bleeding from the mouth. He bolted back up and spat a tooth at Fat Boy Rider, grinning. "For such a big guy, you sure do hit like a little girl, don't you?"

Fat Boy Rider roared with mirthful laughter, dropping the shotgun back into his lap and clapped aggressively. "Goddamn Zee, you tougher than you look, killa! Say no more, man! You be my number two, it's all good, it's all good! So where was I, Zee?

"Oh yeah, so my great granddaddy and his family went on kicking back, chillin', livin' it up down there, ya know, for years and years, and then somewhere down the line, I popped out. An' I had it all, Zee, growin' up down there with education, toys, movies, video games, music, gym, learned how to read, write, drive and ride, swim, felt like I was livin' just how folks was livin' in the old world ya know? Never even saw this hellhole up here 'til I was about fifteen.

"Anyway, 'bout a year ago, news starts comin' bout the same time I start havin' these dreams. News about some big don in the East, s'posed to be some kind of Messiah, Anti-Christ, profit, God or whatever. Different stories and 'pinions, from different people, ya know? People sayin' he raisin' up the dead, controllin' the weather, raisin' an army to take over the world or some sheet. You believe that, Zee? Anyways me, I start havin' these dreams, man, real dreams like I'm awake, seein' that I'm killin' this douchebag an' takin' his place, ya know? An I kept havin' these dreams, man, every night. So one day I got to thinkin', and you know what I realised, Zee? This douchebag ain't no Messiah or Anti-Christ or whatever. This dude's nothin' but a poser. A pretender, a faker. I'm the real Anti-Christ, Zee, ya dig? So, it's my job, wait, it's my… what's that word? Oh yeah! My destiny to waste this dude and take his place, and you'll be right there with me, Zee, right there when I bust open his face with buckshot. You my right-hand man! We goan rule this whole joint, playa!"

Zander stared poker-faced, masking his disbelief and forcing his lips to curl into an approving smile. Fat Boy Rider's eyes were wide. Manic. The delusions of grandeur spilling out of them like water escaping from a broken dam. He bolted upright to his feet, again with a swiftness that was baffling for such a behemoth, and exclaimed excitedly, "Come own, Zee! Let's get it ownnn!"

Look on the bright side, Zander thought, at least you get a free ride to where you're going.

Chapter 2: Eastbound

"In the name of God and all praise is for God. How perfect He is, the One Who has placed this (transport) at our service, and we ourselves would not have been capable of that, and to our Lord is our final destiny."

Zander whispered the prayer under his breath just as the Fat Boy's engine roared to life.

Zander swung his leg over and sat snugly behind Fat Boy Rider, choosing to hold the sissy bars behind him for support instead of holding the rider himself.

"Hey!" Zander shouted over the machine-gun engine.

"What?" Fat Boy Rider replied.

"What do I call you?" Zander braced himself for an elbow or a backhand to the face.

"Bossman!"

"Bossman?"

"Bossman. Gotta problem with that, Zee? Huh? Ain't I the man? Ain't I the Boss??" "Boss" came out, "Baaos."

"No problem. Bossman." He hesitated, then said, "One more thing."

"Dammit, Zee, choo think this is? Question ta-am?"

"We're going to need more than your shotgun and my sword to get to where we're going. There are bandits, robbers, hundreds of them… and God knows what else."

Bossman half-turned and grinned, opened one of the saddlebags so Zander could see what was inside. The bag was filled with a dozen or so metal, ball-like objects with something attached to the tops Zander had never seen before.

"What are those?"

"What's wrong witchu, man, dontchu know nothin'?"

Zander stared blankly.

Bossman rolled his eyes. "They called grenades, dummy."

"What do they do?"

"Watch 'n learn, Zee."

Bossman pulled one of the grenades out of the bag, removed the pin with a click, and hurled it in front. The grenade flew a good thirty metres in a high, wide arc and landed in a shallow ditch. A few seconds of silence, and then… the ditch exploded with a deafening boom causing Zander to flinch. Dirt, shrubs, stones, and other debris rained down and Zander thought he saw a lizard's tail amongst it.

"Nice," he nodded approvingly.

"Got these too, baby," said Bossman, opening another saddlebag. This one held an M16 Assault Rifle with four or five extra magazines and a Glock 9mm with a similar amount of extra ammunition. Zander recognised those. Bossman had certainly come prepared for his delusional crusade. Physically at least, if not mentally or tactically... or in any other department for that matter.

Bossman took a large, tough-looking matte-black crash helmet out of seemingly nowhere, slipped it over his head, kicked the bike into gear, and twisted the throttle, shooting the bike forward like a rocket, the G-force making Zander feel like his head might fly off his shoulders.

***

They had been riding for about half an hour. It was almost noon, and the shy sun had decided to make an appearance through the dull, dirty-looking sky. The winter, which had been brought on by humanity's grandest act of stupidity and barbarism, had lasted over twenty years, but the climate seemed to be warming steadily over the last few decades. Zander thought that had it not been for the wind chill from the speeding bike, it would have been warm enough for some sweat to begin moistening his underarms beneath his scarf, coat, and shirt.

Bossman handled the bike expertly. Occasionally slowing only slightly to weave in and out of burnt-out vehicles, debris, and potholes, and then resuming his aggressive but steady 90 or 100 mph. He seemed to be one with the bike, just as Zander had been with Kaz.

The vehicle was an extension of himself. That kind of flow and harmony only came with years of practice and experience.

After a few mini heart attacks, Zander began to enjoy the ride. He could feel the warmth of the sun beating down on his face, despite it being wrapped by a bandana and a worn pair of goggles. The deep, low, steady rumbling of the engine, the sun, the wind, the bike's speed, and the landscape flashing by was lulling Zander into a Zen-like state. He felt like he could sit there forever, and yet he was only a passive passenger. Bossman must have been enjoying it even more.

Zander still couldn't believe he was sitting there on the back of this lunatic's motorcycle, whipping through the air at almost 100 mph. He could have rejected Bossman's invitation. Sure, the man was a violent (likely homicidal) and unpredictable nutcase, not to mention roughly the same size and weight of a Silverback, but had it come down to it, Zander was fully confident that he would have been able to separate the man's head from his body, with one swing of his sword… or maybe two swings, Zander thought as he stared at the back of the man's thick neck.

So why hadn't he? Zander couldn't explain it. Except that he felt as though an invisible hand had been guiding him in the right direction over the past few years. A protective and caring hand that sometimes seemed as though its arm was draped around his shoulders, assuring him that he was making the right choices and would be ok no matter what.

Zander was alerted back to the present moment as he felt the bike slowing down significantly. They must have been travelling on what they used to call "motorways" or "freeways" in the old world. As Bossman halved his blistering speed, Zander saw battered, illegible signs overhead which must have meant they were entering a city soon. A couple of hundred yards ahead, most of the entire width of the road was jammed with the burnt-out shells of vehicles, as far as the eye could see, with only the smallest of gaps through which the bike just might have been able to squeeze.

Bossman had now brought the bike to an abrupt and complete halt, still twenty yards from the sprawling wreckage. He clicked off the engine with a turn of the key and, with a flick of his heel, engaged the kickstand, jumping off the bike (almost knocking Zander off in the process). He threw his helmet on the ground with force and released a tirade of curse words.

"Relax, brother. I think we can make it." Zander assured him.

Bossman turned to Zander, who had now also dismounted the bike, the wild, unreasonable fury back in his eyes. "CHOO SAY FOOL??!!"

"We'll make it," Zander repeated. "God willing."

Bossman continued to stare at Zander as though he was struggling to decide whether to punch him, shoot him, or humour him.

"Look," said Zander, gesturing towards the wreckage. "There are small spaces we can get through, and if there are any blockages, I'm sure we can move them between the both of us. Hell, look at you; you could probably move most of it on your own."

Zander did not find out whether his words had made any significant impact on Bossman because Bossman had, all of a sudden, raised the shotgun and was aiming at something in the distance, towards the wreckage, barking, "FREEZE! HANDS ON YOUR HEAD, FOOL!"

Zander turned and saw a man standing just behind one of the first wrecked vehicles, holding what looked like an ancient bolt action rifle, trained on the pair of them.

"STOP RIGHT THERE! YOU NEED TO TURN AROUND AND GO BACK THE WAY YOU CAME!" He spoke fluent English with a hint of a Spanish accent.

"YOU NEED TO DROP THAT DAMN PEASHOOTER OLD MAN, 'FORE I BLOW THAT STUPID SPIC HEAD TO PIECES FOOL!" replied Bossman, inching forward and pumping the shotgun to punctuate his point.

"WAIT!" yelled Zander, placing himself between the line of fire of the two men. He looked Bossman in the eye and said, "Just wait a second, Boss, let me talk to him. Please. He might be able to help us. There's no need for this."

Bossman swore and snarled. "Out the way, Zee, or I'll blow yo stupid damn head off 'fore I do his."

"Listen! We're almost out of food and water. We've still got a long way to go. You mentioned we're low on fuel, too, right? How much extra are you carrying in that can? At this rate, we won't even make it to France. We need supplies. Let me talk to him. Please."

Bossman stared at Zander as though he wanted to cut his heart out and eat it, and, for a moment, Zander thought he would pull the trigger and make good on his threat. But then, huge chest heaving from rage, he jerked his head, gesturing Zander to go ahead, shotgun still trained on the man.

"Thank you," said Zander, relieved.

"Whatever, douchebag."

Zander raised his hands and approached the man slowly.

"Sir! We mean you no harm."

"Say all men with a gun pointed at them." The man paused, then said, "What brings you to these parts?"

"We're headed far East. We have work there."

Something changed in the man's face. Suspicion, perhaps, mixed with a touch of curiosity. "East? Now, what work could you possibly have there? Nothing but trouble up there in those parts. War. Terror. Evil. Something big brewing up there, things no sensible man should want any part of."

Zander was now only slightly more than an arm's length away from the man who still had his rifle raised. Close up, he saw the man was in his early sixties at least, with a lean, weathered face and dark, wise, kind but forceful eyes, as though he would make a good friend but also a formidable enemy if necessary. He was probably a father. Probably a grandfather.

"Sir, please," said Zander. "All we need is directions to the closest place to replenish our supplies. Food, water, and fuel. That's all we need, and we'll be on our way. I give you my word. Can you help us?"

The man said nothing for a long few seconds. Zander could see the cogs turning behind his perceptive eyes. He glanced at Bossman with suspicion, dislike, and caution, then at Zander with something like respect and acceptance, as if struggling to decide which man was in charge and would have the final say about how this interaction would end. He must have decided it was Zander because he slowly lowered his rifle.

"Sorry, my friend. Can't be too careful these days."

"No problem at all, sir, completely understandable," replied Zander, holding out his hand. "I'm Zander. You are?"

"Osvaldo." He shook Zander's hand with a strong, working man's grip and flashed an amicable smile.

Bossman finally relaxed and moved towards them steadily, shotgun now held in one hand by his side, barrel facing the ground.

"There's only one place in this city where you can still get the things you need," said Osvaldo. "But it's going to cost you. A lot. Probably everything you have but the clothes on your back, in which case you'll probably have to carry on, on foot, so there would be no point in purchasing fuel. My advice? Trade in the bike and a few weapons. That will get you at least a week's supply of food and water. Keep the bike? And the fuel alone will cost you everything else with nothing left over for food or water."

Zander chewed on this for a few moments. Bossman, now standing next to him, suddenly fired the shotgun in the air and spoke.

"So where dis place, old man?"

Osvaldo fixed Bossman with a disapproving glare; they might have been father and disobedient son.

Zander hastily filled the silence.

"I apologise for my friend; he's very tired. Could you please tell us how to get there?"

Osvaldo tore his gaze away from Bossman and turned, pointing behind him, beyond the wreckage. "You want to go about three miles north until you get to what used to be the Cathedral. You'll recognise it because they have placed ten broken statues in a row as a landmark. When you get to this, turn right and keep going for another mile; make sure you are going very slowly at this point. Keep going until you hear gunshots and bullets hitting the ground next to your feet. When this happens, you need to stop immediately and do as you're told." He gestured to Bossman without looking at him. "And you might want to teach your friend here some manners. He'll get himself killed out here before long."

Bossman sneered. "Thanks, old man."

And with that, he lifted the shotgun to Osvaldo's face.

And pulled the trigger.

Osvaldo's head exploded, fragments of his flesh, blood, and bone flying in every direction. A second ago, he had been a living, breathing human being, communicating, offering advice, companionship, emotions, and ideas. He had been thinking, acting, affecting the environment around him. Now, dead before he hit the ground, he was a lifeless mess of organic matter, lying on the ground doing, offering, affecting, and communicating nothing. He no longer even had a name. That was the great miracle of death.

Zander's ears were ringing, temporarily deaf from the gun firing so close to his head. He was filled with dismay and shock and utterly stunned, lost for words, thoughts, or actions. After a few moments, he gathered his bearings and yelled, "WHAT THE HELL HAVE YOU DONE?"

"Aah, quit yo jawing Zee, or you be next, fool!"

"HE WAS A GOOD MAN! HE WAS HELPING US! I GAVE HIM MY WORD, YOU LUNATIC!"

Bossman pointed the gun in Zander's face now and pumped it loaded. "I SAID, QUIT YO DAMN JAWING FOOL. YOU DON'T TELL ME! I TELL YOU! YOU GOT THAT, ZEE?"

Zander felt his arms twitching. His left hand wanted to backhand the shotgun's barrel away from his face, whilst his right hand would simultaneously reach up and unsheathe his sword from behind his back, hack horizontally and cut through this murderer's thick neck and separate his head, all in less than a second, before Bossman's brain would even register what had happened.

But he didn't.

Zander again felt the proverbial, comforting arm around his shoulders, willing him to be patient, to relax, and carry on for a while. Everything would be ok; this was supposed to happen. Lean back. Relax, and flow with the current.

Zander walked towards the bike and rummaged through his backpack, taking out a rolled-up mat. He walked towards the edge of the road and spread the mat on the ground. He removed his shoes and stood ramrod straight on the rug, like a soldier on parade.

"The hell you doin', Zee?"

"Dhuhr."

"The hell?"

"Midday prayer."

"The hell you prayin' to, dumbass? Ain't nothin' worth praying to here but me, fool!"

Zander ignored him. Still standing to attention, his hands were now placed one above the other, on his abdomen, eyes trained on the mat in front of him, seeing nothing but the area his forehead would touch in a moment when he prostrated, lips moving in silent prayer.

"HEY! SPASTIC! I'm talkin' to you, Zee!" said Bossman raising the gun, with one hand, to Zander's head.

Zander was unperturbed, as though he were praying alone in a silent temple. Not even his gaze flickered. He bowed forward, from one-eighty to ninety degrees, palms now on his knees, back and legs still utterly straight, stood up straight again, then down into prostration.

"I'M WARNING YOU, ZEE!" He held the gun to the back of Zander's head as he lay, still in prostration, face on the ground.

"I ain't playin'! Five… four… three… two… one…"

He pulled the trigger.

The gun made a disappointing click.

"Sheeit! Mann, you one lucky sumbeetch!"

In his peripheral vision, Zander saw Bossman plod back to his bike, reach into one of the saddlebags, draw out a pack of Marlboro Reds, take one out, and light it. Smoke curled into the warm afternoon air. When he was done, Zander was still praying, now sitting on his knees, hands resting on them.

Bossman flicked the finished cigarette at Zander. It landed less than a yard beside him, the orange tip glowing for a few seconds before resigning and lying there, cold and lifeless like a lonely forgotten corpse on the edge of a battlefield.

Chapter 3: Zander

The Harley Davidson Fat Boy had lasted a lot longer than Zander had anticipated. He sat pillion, wind and dust blowing through his hair and battering his bandana and goggles, no longer enjoying the ride as they steadily approached the Turkey-Syria border.

Over a week ago now, Osvaldo's information had been accurate, and Zander had felt a pang of sadness and regret as they had spotted the ten broken statues in the distance, remembering the way the man's head had exploded before he'd even had a chance to defend himself. Murdered by this insane psychopath with delusions of grandeur.

Upon reaching the refuelling area, stopped by the guards as Osvaldo had warned, Bossman had opened fire with the M16 and thrown grenades instead of surrendering his weapons. Zander could only look on and contain his barely restrained anger, the invisible metaphorical arm, again around his shoulders, holding him back from intervening, assuring him that this was all part of the plan.

The ensuing violence and mayhem had supplied them with enough fuel, weapons, food, water, and medical supplies to last them two weeks, more than enough to see them to their destination and decimate a small army on the way. It had also cost them.

Bossman had taken shrapnel in his left shoulder, and Zander's left hand had eaten a bullet from an AK47, and his conscience had taken a hefty beating as he had allowed, though not participated in, the slaughter conducted by this unsophisticated accidental artist of death, his insane travelling companion.

The rest of the week had gone by without any major incident. They had experienced a few close calls with the occasional wasteland bandits, but the average band of robbers with their melee weapons were no match for the arsenal possessed by the two travellers. Bossman made short work of them on the odd occasion whereupon merely flexing their firepower hadn't been enough.

As he sat there now, on the back of the motorcycle, wind and dust blowing against his almost entirely covered face, fast approaching the unmanned and unsecured border, Zander felt a strong sense of foreboding and apprehension about what he was soon to face. It was close now. Too close. This was happening, and as the sun dipped on the horizon, Zander doubted he would ever see it again.

The feeling grew stronger, and Zander recognised it. It was a faded remnant of an extreme and traumatic episode he had experienced regularly in his childhood.

***

Sara embraced her boy as he sat atop her lap, screaming and crying in an all-encompassing terror.

"SSh, it's ok, baby, you're ok." She tried to soothe, stroking his hair.

Zander continued to bawl and scream. It wasn't the cry of a child throwing a tantrum or cowering under the bed covers, afraid of a thunderstorm. This cry was tearing out from the core of his very soul. His eyes were wide open in horror, but he wasn't awake. Not asleep either. Trapped in some sort of dreadful limbo.

His mother would ask him, when he grew a little older, old enough to articulate experiences, what he used to feel in those dreadful moments. And Zander would tell her that the word to describe it had not yet been invented and probably never would be. It was as if the absolute extremities of fear, terror, panic, hopelessness, and anxiety were all transformed into solid objects, melted and mixed in a huge vat, scooped up with a jug, and thrown over him violently over and over again until the vat was finally empty.

These night terrors would occur once or twice a week and last around ten minutes each time until it abated, and Zander would go back to sleep most mornings without any memory of the episode the night before.

But this wasn't the only monster Zander had faced. As he grew from childhood to adolescence, the *night terrors disappeared and were replaced by vivid nightmares. At least once a week. The dream was always the same. He would be standing alone in the ruins of some large ancient structure, like the remnants of a Roman colosseum. The air would be uncomfortably warm and humid, and he would feel it in every atom of his being, more real than the real world. It would always be moments before twilight, the Sun about to set from a brilliantly bright day, casting a golden glow over everything.*

A terrible feeling would begin to brew in the pit of his stomach, a sense of intense foreboding as if he were about to face something unimaginable and otherworldly. Then, as if a switch had been flipped somewhere, the ruins would suddenly be full of people. Hundreds, possibly even thousands of people, shouting, cheering, and jeering as if watching a gladiatorial contest or a public execution.

Then the pain would hit him like a tsunami.

It was pure, physical agony as if every inch of his skin were ablaze, and a thousand tiny knives were forcing their way out of every part of his body. He would collapse on the ground and writhe around in agony, and at that moment, he would truly believe that this pain would never end. After an immeasurable amount of time, he would finally wake up in his bed, shaking and sweating profusely, sometimes in tears.

"Why is this happening to me?" a nineteen-year-old Zander asked his mother.

"We've spoken about this. You know why," said Sara.

"I've had enough. I don't want this anymore. What have I done to deserve this? Hm? I pray, I fast, I stay away from sin, I try my utmost best to be a good person. I could easily be like one of them. Some of them are out there killing, looting, raping, and pillaging, yet they're living happier lives than me?"

Sara stared at her son, her eyes betraying pain and sympathy, but mainly steel. She set down the leather jacket she had been sewing for Zander, the sleeve had torn off during today's scavenger hunt, and clasped his hands, looking him straight in the eye.

"Stop it. I taught you better than that," she said sternly. She had not yet hit fourty but looked twenty years older, battered by the radiation from the nuclear fallout, the harsh living, the stress. What was left of her hair was grey and wispy, face marred with premature wrinkles and a makeshift eyepatch over one eye. Yet her strength and dignity somehow erased all this and made her beautiful. And she was still very physically strong, her casual grip unintentionally hurting Zander's hands.

Zander tore free from her grip, stood up, and bellowed, "TAUGHT ME WHAT?"

Sara stared at her son, unabashed. Patient, as if waiting for him to say what he wanted to say, knowing it must be expelled from his system, like pus from an infected wound.

"TAUGHT ME WHAT? To just accept the fact that I was born for no other reason than to suffer? That I was created just to be tormented and battered? To struggle and strive to be 'Good' and get nothing for it? While others go around committing every sin under the sun and still sleep better at night than I do?!" His voice was full of anguish, frustration, and sadness, and he struggled to hold back the tears and keep his voice steady as he ranted.

"Sit down, Zan," said Sara tenderly.

"No. I've had enough."

"Sit down. Please."

Zander's chest heaved. He stood there for a moment, then wiped his eyes and sat down.

Sara looked at her son, dark circles under his eyes. Nineteen years old in the face but twice that in the eyes. He'd had no adolescence. He'd gone straight from childhood to adulthood, as had many of the children born in these dark times.

She leaned forward and brushed a wisp of hair from his face, clasped his hands again, this time more gently.

"Listen to me, Zan. You are a diamond sculpture."

"What are you talking about?"

"Diamond, Zan. Like diamond, you're one of the toughest, most valuable, and beautiful materials that God created on this Earth."

Zander said nothing.

"And do you know how diamonds are formed?" continued Sara.

Zander shrugged.

"Under extreme heat and pressure over billions of years. You can't become what God has destined you to become overnight. It doesn't work like that. It takes time, extreme pain, prolonged suffering. The stronger the soldier, the harder the battle he is sent to fight in. You're on fire right now. Your pain and suffering are just the impurities and the weaknesses being burned away from you. Like a crucible. Like a sculptor creating a statue. God is the sculptor, and you are the statue, and he is hammering and chiselling away your rough edges to mould you into his final beautiful product. The more beautiful the sculpture is, the longer the process of hammering and chiselling."

Zander stayed quiet, breathing deeply, drinking his mother's words.

"The meat we ate earlier. Would you have eaten it raw? Or half-cooked? Of course not. So, it had to be cooked, slowly roasted, until it was done and ready and it became fit for our purpose. Like that meat, you too are being cooked and seared until you too are fit

for your purpose. So, my son, don't give in before the sculpture is finished or the meat is cooked. We are never afflicted with more than we can bear."

Zander gave a slight nod. His mother's words always had a calming effect on him, and even now, at nineteen, he always felt like an insolent spoiled child if he argued with her because he couldn't argue against her logic or wisdom, he could only complain that it wasn't fair.

"Basically, you need to man up, buddy." Came a gruff voice behind Zander.

Zander turned in his chair to see a lean, muscular man leaning against the door frame, arms crossed, grinning mischievously, a strand of ash-grey hair hanging over his face.

"You're going to regret those words when we spar later," said Zander, with no sign of his earlier vulnerability now, just machismo and confidence.

"Oooh, tough guy," said the man, mock-shaking his knees then winking at Zander before slinking back out of the room.

Smiling faintly, Zander turned back to his mother.

She smiled and said, "Take it easy on him; he's getting old, and you know he's the only sibling I have left."

Zander looked at his mother with disbelief. "Me? Take it easy on him?"

***

THWACK! The wooden stick hit Zander's upper back as he tried to concentrate on what he was reading in the book, propped open and upright on the shelf in front of him. He sat on the hard concrete floor, cross-legged with his back straight and his hands on his head with his elbows as far back as they could go.

"Straighten up, princess; it's only been twenty-five minutes!" Yelled Uncle Mourad.

Zander ignored him. He knew his back was straight; the strike and the remark were only meant to distract him. He continued to read, eyes darting left and right across the page.

THWACK! This time in the ribs. The first one hadn't hurt. This one did, but Zander still stayed in position.

"DID THAT HURT LITTLE BOY? Boo hoo, shall I call mummy in here?"

THWACK!

When this training first began at age six, he would have to remain in this position, without lowering his arms, bringing his elbows forward, or bending his back even the slightest amount, for at least five minutes. Now, thirteen years later, after small incremental increases over the years, it would last at least sixty.

This was a boring book. Some soul-destroying novel about a loner called Steve, watching birds in the park. Uncle Mourad wouldn't ask what the character's name was. That was kindergarten level. Too easy at this juncture. So, this Steve is sitting on a bench blah blah blah, munching on an egg and cress sandwich which tasted good as he hadn't eaten since breakfast blah, blah, blah, wearing a blue windbreaker coat— remember that. He might ask about that—

"BLAH, BLAH, BLAH, RED, YELLOW, GREEN, BLUE, PINK, SILLY SAUSAGE, ONE, TWO, THREE, FOUR, FIVE, ONCE I CAUGHT A FISH ALIVE!"

THWACK!

Lower back this time. That hurt more than the first one but less than the second. Zander's shoulders began to ache slightly from holding his hands on his head.

"STOP SMILING AND START READING, FOOL! I'M EXPECTING NO PENALTY MINUTES AT ALL TODAY!"

THWACK!

Zander continued to read. Steve continued to sit and watch birds and talk about the weather and his incredibly boring past.

Uncle Mourad bent forward, his mouth centimetres away from Zander's earhole, "HURRY UP, RETARD, ASK ME TO TURN THE PAGE ALREADY!"

Zander, expecting this, did not flinch. Continued reading. He gave the nod. The only form of communication permitted, other than answering questions, during this exercise.

Uncle Mourad would place a random book on the shelf in front of Zander. Zander would have to read four or five pages of this book whilst in the stress position and with Uncle Mourad turning the pages for him. During the reading, his uncle would hit him hard with the wooden stick if his posture slackened... or at random. He would also shout loudly and aggressively in Zander's ears, make noises and disparaging remarks and generally try his best to distract Zander and prevent him from absorbing what he was reading.

"FINALLY! THE IDIOT FINISHES THREE PAGES! THERE IS YET HOPE IN THE WORLD!"

This is getting slightly more interesting, Zander thought, although his upper back was starting to ache. Steve was witnessing a murder taking place, and the murderers didn't know he was there. What weapons were the murderers using? That will very likely be one of the questions.... It was a—

"LITTLE DONKEY, LITTLE DONKEY, ON THE M25! GOT RUN OVER BY A ROVER, BUT HE STILL SURVIVED! CONCENTRATE, MAGGOT!!"

Once Zander had read the four or five pages, Uncle Mourad would swipe the book, put it aside, with

Zander still in the stress position, and bark twenty questions at Zander about the content of those pages.

"Name two of the characters."

"What was John doing at the park?"

"When was Alexander born?"

"What colour was the car Linda was driving?"

"Which Hadith was narrated?"

"What animal was in the cage?"

"Which supplication was recited?"

"What year did the battle take place?"

Upon answering all twenty questions, Uncle Mourad would place another book in front of Zander, and the same process would begin again. This would go on until the sixty minutes were up.

If more than five questions were answered wrong during the quiz at the end of each read, a one-minute penalty time would be added to the sixty minutes.

"This will condition you to think and speak and conduct memory recollection under pressure," Uncle Mourad had finally explained to a twelve-year-old Zander. "You're going to face huge challenges, impossible situations that will scramble your thoughts and make you want to soil your pants. You need to be calm and have clarity of thought under pressure and in danger. You need to be present enough in these situations to take the right action, the appropriate response, remember and recite the right supplications and verses, pray with concentration and focus with a

sword blade at your throat or a loaded gun to your head."

Back and shoulders on fire, Zander finally lowered his hands from his head, stretching and grimacing, massaging and rolling his shoulders.

"Sixty-five minutes," said Uncle Mourad, and Zander heard the ever so slight undertone of pride and happiness beneath his uncle's stoic, matter-of-fact tone. "That's your best so far."

Zander, now standing, rolled his shoulders in circles and massaged his neck.

"Not good enough," he said. "I should be down to sixty-one or two by now."

"You'll get there, don't worry."

Zander didn't reply to this, then said, "When can I get some more firearms training?"

"I don't know. You know how rare those things are these days. Like gold dust. Anyone who happens to procure one on a hunt isn't going to waste it by handing it over to us to train with. There will be limited ammunition, and it will be put in the armoury to be used in our defence. These days, a man with a few guns can rule an entire country. They're like the nukes of the old world. Anyway, you know the basics, aiming, loading, safety, trigger discipline. Plus, all the books we have. That'll have to be enough."

Zander nodded, taking a sip of water from his canteen, and stared at the bare wall, zoning out.

In a flash and seemingly out of nowhere, a scarred, solid forearm knotted with dense muscle wrapped itself around Zander's throat from behind.

"So, you going to make me regret what I said earlier now, tough guy? Let's see what you got!"

***

The Harley Davidson Fat Boy, thirsty, dusty, and exhausted, sputtered and finally died.

Zander dismounted first, not wanting to be knocked off by Bossman.

Bossman jumped off the bike, letting it crash to the ground on its side.

"GODAMMNIT!" He stamped on the Bike viciously, cursing and yelling.

"It's ok; we'll just travel on foot. It's not far now. We should get there in a few days." said Zander, now bone tired. The travelling and events of the past couple of weeks were finally catching up to him. They ate and slept sparingly. They would sleep in shifts, a couple of hours at a time, while the other kept watch for bandits and animals, both mutant and regular. Two days ago, Zander had impaled a three-pincered scorpion the size of a cat.

Even Bossman was beginning to show signs of wear and tear. He seemed to have aged ten years in the past week, lost a little weight (though still huge), and his face was tanned and rather desiccated. Zander marvelled at the fact that Bossman was still standing, especially considering the amount of energy the maniac expended on a minute-by-minute basis. Insanity and delusion were, it seemed, very efficient driver. The man was convinced he was the Antichrist after all.

Bossman had cauterised the shrapnel wound in his shoulder using gunpowder from a bullet and a matchstick, claiming it had worked for a character named Rambo in one of his favourite movies. He had howled in agony then guffawed maniacally when his theory seemed to pan out, and he saw that his arm hadn't blown off. He had then advised Zander to do the same for his hand. Zander had followed suit but without the gunpowder. Instead, he had simply heated a knife and pressed it against the wound.

Bossman had then chugged half a bottle of Oramorph, throwing Zander a single bottle and keeping half a dozen for himself. Bossman had been drinking it like water ever since.

But overdosing on the liquid morphine seemed to have no major side effects on Bossman… or perhaps they just melded with his already chaotic personality and were difficult to differentiate.

"No way, man, I ain't leavin' her!"

"B, listen, we're out of fuel, and we've still got a fair distance—"

"SHUT THE HELL UP! I AIN'T LEAVIN' HER! I'LL WALK HER UNTIL WE FIND MORE GAS!"

Zander sighed. The day was warm, the warmest in a long time, and rather arid. Or maybe it was just this area of the world as it had always been warmer here, even in the old world. He was curious to see how long Bossman would last, wheeling the three hundred-plus kilo bike in this climate and terrain, especially after the stresses of the past week and the shrapnel buried in his shoulder.

Back straight, with perfect form and technique, Bossman deadlifted the bike off the ground, kicked out the kickstand, removed his helmet, and collapsed on the ground, resting on his back. He lit a cigarette. "But first, we goan chill."

Zander didn't complain. He took out a date, only five left now, ate it, spat out the seed, and removed his rucksack. He pulled out a canteen of water and drank deeply from it.

Bossman was still staring at the sky, smoke curling out of his mouth and trailing into the air above him. He looked like a human-shaped industrial factory, polluting the air.

Zander pulled out the prayer mat from his rucksack, spread it on the ground a dozen or so yards from Bossman and the bike, and began to pray.

The air grew warmer with only the slight occasional gust of wind, blowing dust and dirt around. The landscape was barren and empty, a few dead trees scattered about sparsely, with no buildings or landmarks as far as the eye could see, just sand, rocks, and rubble.

A few hills in the near distance made Zander a little nervous as there could be anybody, or anything, concealed behind them.

The midday prayer was one of the longest of the five, especially when Zander decided to take his time, praying slowly, deeply, blocking out everything, as if his creator were right in front of him. Fifteen minutes in, he was only halfway through and in the zone when he heard Bossman snoring and saw him in his peripheral, flat on his back, arms splayed out, lit cigarette still smouldering in his hand. But it was an abstract hearing, an abstract vision, disconnected from reality as if it were in another dimension that didn't affect this one. He also heard the roaring engines of a dozen vehicles appearing over one of the hills and bearing down on them.

And Bossman, waking up with a start, shouting and cursing, and opening fire.

Chapter 4: Guerrera

Jordan Guerrera was a hedonist and a pragmatist. If a pursuit was pleasurable, it was worth pursuing, and if it ensured his survival and an easier life, even better. Morality didn't enter the equation.

He was also ruthless and efficient, shrewd and calculating. A master tactician and a charismatic, Machiavellian manipulator, and at the ripe age of fifty-eight, he still ruled his men with an iron fist.

Quite literally.

He had lost his hand in a skirmish a few years ago and had it replaced with a perfectly crafted surrogate one made of iron. It was a beautiful piece of engineering that allowed him to push a button on the palm with his other hand, causing it to curl into a fist. Push it again, and the fist would re-open into an open palm, fingers splayed. He had been seen on many an occasion beating men to death with this fist for insubordination, disrespect, or just garden-variety incompetence.

In the old world, Guerrera could have been a lawyer. Or a politician, an army general, a police sergeant, a drug kingpin, a businessman, or a salesman. In this new dog-eat-dog world, with most of those professions virtually non-existent, it only made sense for him to be the alpha dog. The ruler. The shot caller. The man at the top of the food chain. And he had been, for a while… until the emergence of the real alpha. The apex predator. The man they called The Messiah.

But was he the Messiah? Or was he the Antichrist? A prophet? A God? *The* God? An impostor? A con man? A magician?

It didn't matter.

What did matter was that he existed and harnessed more power than anybody on the face of the Earth. He was ending year-long droughts and causing it to rain again, bringing the dead Earth back to life. He brought dead people back to life. He conjured Paradise and Hell in front of their very eyes and threw people into either one. What could one possibly gain from opposing such a man? The opposition was weak and dwindling by the day and would soon be gone completely. Pockets of them remained, hiding like rats, waiting for some kind of miracle that would never come. How does one defeat someone who controls the rain? And brings the dead back to life?

That was the pragmatist in Guerrera.

Then there was the hedonist in him, and his new master ticked both boxes. After swearing fealty to his new lord, Guerrera was awarded the world and everything in it. His already large harem of women was multiplied tenfold. He was given his salubrious living accommodation, the best food, personal vehicles, and an impressive personal armoury of the most hi-tech weaponry preserved from the old world.

He never wanted for anything so long as he served his master.

Guerrera's loyalty and service had paid off in a big way most recently. He had been entrusted and honoured with the task of capturing the man, the boy really, from the prophecies made by the soothsayer and bringing him back to his master to make an example of all those who dared attempt to stand against his power. Nobody other than Guerrera could be entrusted with a task as monumental as this. Nobody.

The rewards would be immense. Guerrera fantasised about the powers he would be endowed with after this.

But what more could he possibly gain? He already had it all and had become jaded a long time ago. After a while, all carnal and material pleasures were the same. He had tasted every type of woman. The vehicles could only be so nice, so fast. The food could only be so delicious, and the weaponry was already sufficient to defend himself and destroy an entire army. What else was there?

The pragmatist.

Hedonism had its limits and, after a certain amount of time, became pointless and empty. But pragmatism was forever. Doing this would cement Guerrera's position with his master, and it was better to stand with the Devil than in his path. That was enough. To merely be alive and comfortable in this new world when so many others weren't.

***

"So, what do you think, Esteban? Is it him?"

"I think so…. what do you think?"

"Hard to be sure at this distance, but… young… is he though? Hair goin' grey! Green eyes, slight build, noble face… can't really tell the colour of his eyes from here, but the rest of it sure fits."

Esteban nodded slowly in agreement.

"Shall we call Guerrera?" said the other man.

Esteban, lying prone just behind the peak of the hill, binoculars still fixed to his eyes, nodded slowly without looking at the other man.

"But what if it ain't him?" said the other man. "We best be sure. I don't wanna get beat to death by that goddamn metal fist of his. Crazy bastard."

"It doesn't matter. We're never going to know from this distance anyway. We have to approach them regardless. There's no other way."

"You sure, man?"

"Yes, now shut up, put on a fresh pair of panties, and make the call, Nathan."

Nathan, hand trembling, picked up his radio and made the call.

***

As they approached in convoy, Guerrera in the armoured truck in front, followed by three jeeps and four motorcycles on each wing, Guerrera studied his target intently through his binoculars. They were less than fifty metres away now, the noise of the eight vehicles aggressive and loud, yet the boy still hadn't broken from his prayer, his back to them at a slight angle, standing straight, facing East. This had to be him.

The other one, also just a boy, albeit a huge one, had jumped up as soon as they'd gotten to around a hundred metres from them. This one seemed to be the complete antithesis of the boy. Whilst the boy appeared lithe and graceful, this one looked like a lumbering oaf. Whilst one looked calm and serene, the other appeared insane with bloodlust and rage. The cheetah and the rhinoceros; an unlikely duo.

Guerrera's men had asked him whether they should just dispose of the oaf, place a bullet between his eyes with a sniper rifle from afar, as they had no use for him, and he may offer resistance given the chance. But Guerrera had said no. There was always a potential use for someone, especially a genetic freak like this. People were a resource.

***

Bossman stood behind his bike, picked up an M16, screaming, "SAY HELLO TO MY LIL FRIEND!" and opened fire.

The gun, on full automatic, fired rapidly into the first truck, the windshield must have been bullet-proofed as small cracks appeared, but it did not shatter. Bossman emptied the entire magazine, squatted low behind the bike, frantically pulled the crash helmet over his head, grabbed a Kevlar vest from the loot, strapped it on, and reloaded the final magazine into the M16.

The convoy had now stopped about thirty yards away, around thirty men exited their vehicles, taking up firing positions behind them.

As Bossman took aim again, he turned his head to look at Zander. "WHAT THE HELL YOU DOIN' YOU DUMBASS DUNE COON? YOU GONNA GET IN ON THIS OR WHAT?"

A hail of return fire came back at him from an assortment of firearms. Uzis, M16s, handguns, MP5s. Of the hundreds of bullets whizzing towards Bossman, many hit the ground around him, many others slammed into the bike, whilst three found their target. One hit the front of his helmet where his forehead would have been, cracking the dense Kevlar but not penetrating his skin, the second grazed his right arm, and the third buried itself in his shoulder, in the same spot the shrapnel still sat embedded from the week before.

Bossman was knocked off his feet, flat on his back again.

The convoy had now stopped in a single row.

***

Guerrera, standing under cover of the open door of the armoured truck, nodded at Esteban, who was to his right, standing in the same fashion by his Jeep.

Esteban spoke.

"HEY, KID! IF YOU'RE STILL BREATHING, LISTEN! WE DON'T WANT TO HURT YOU. YOU FIRED FIRST, SO WE FIRED BACK. ALL WE WANT IS THAT FOOL OVER THERE PRAYING. DROP YOUR WEAPONS, WALK OVER TO HIM, PICK HIM UP AND BRING HIM TO US, BIG MAN. YOU WILL BE REWARDED BEYOND YOUR WILDEST DREAMS. WE CAN PROMISE YOU THAT!"

Still lying on the ground at a slight angle, only the kid's massive legs were visible, poking out from behind the rear wheel, almost parallel to the Harley.

Guerrera and his men watched. Waiting. Was he dead?

Then a heavy-booted foot twitched. Then the leg. The kid rose slowly, first the cracked helmet appearing from behind the bike, followed by his tree-trunk neck and the rest of him. Standing straight, facing them, he was no longer holding the M16 but had his hands clenched into fists, held down by his side.

"He's holding something in his hands," muttered Guerrera nonchalantly.

"DROP WHAT YOU'RE HOLDING!" yelled Esteban; he sounded like a SWAT team commander.

"Whatever happens with this kid, do not hit the boy. He must be taken alive," Guerrera warned his men.

At this distance, Guerrera, squinting in the sunlight, could just about make out a broad grin on the kid's face, under the open visor and behind the mouthguard of the crash helmet, with a few small, thin objects protruding from his mouth, held between his teeth.

"GET BACK!" he roared to his men.

With incredible speed, and before any of Guerrera's men had registered his command, the kid spat the pins out, screamed, "GET SOME! BITCHES!" and hurled the grenades, three in each hand, at the centre of the convoy.

When they all landed almost simultaneously and roughly on target, there was a panic as the nearly three dozen armed men attempted to scramble away, some of them firing a few shots at the kid in the process.

A few seconds, then six large booms, in rapid succession.

Bodies, vehicles, glass, pebbles, dirt, and debris flew in every direction.

Carnage.

Then there was silence.

***

Bossman sat on the ground with his back against the Harley, laughing maniacally, "WOOO, YEAHH! Din't expect that one, did ya now, chiefs?" His laughter rang in the stillness. "YOU DON'T MESS WITH THE BAOS BRUH, NO SIRREE, NO YOU DON'T FAGGOTS!"

He coughed and spluttered whilst ranting and guffawing. Bossman had caught another four bullets. One in his left arm, a few inches below the shrapnel, and the other bullet, two in his vest, and another one in his crash helmet, which was now ruined and falling apart.

Still sitting and chuckling, he dragged the helmet off his head with his right hand, with an exhausted groan, and threw it on the ground. His left arm now useless; Bossman took out a cigarette with his blood-soaked right hand, screwed it into his mouth, lit it, then pulled out a Glock 19, cocked it using his left armpit, and sat back, spent, blowing smoke into the air. He pointed the Glock at Zander.

"YO, ZEE! YOU COOL OVER THERE, HUH DOUCHEBAG? YOU CHILL? I'M FIXIN TO AIM

THIS AT YO DUMB GREY HEAD, CRACKA, AND BLOW YO GODDAMN BRAINS OUT ALL OVER THAT MAT. GOT A FULL MAG THIS TIME, I WON'T MISS. YOU GOT ABOUT TWO SECONDS TO LIVE, YOU STUPID SILLY SON OF A—"

Fierce gunfire erupted, showering the Harley and all the large boxes, containers, and bags full of supplies strapped all over it. It was much more ferocious and enduring this time.

Plain business.

And when it finally ceased, the bike, now a wrecked mess, lay on the ground, on top of Bossman's legs, who lay on his back, Glock still in his motionless hand on the ground, cigarette still lit and hanging limply in his mouth.

***

Guerrera and his, now down to twenty, men approached cautiously, locked and loaded, weapons trained mostly at the apparently dead, giant man-bike hybrid, but a few pointed at Zander. One of them flinched and almost pulled the trigger as Zander suddenly bowed in prayer.

Watching Zander, there was no doubt at all now in Guerrera's mind that this was indeed the boy.

They reached the huge kid, still flat on his back, spread-eagled, legs crushed underneath the bike. He still held the Glock in one hand, the red cherry of the cigarette still burning, almost falling out of his slightly open mouth, a stream of blood escaping it, eyes shut. The Kevlar vest was shredded, and there was blood all over it, his arms, neck, and face. It was impossible to tell where it was all coming from.

The smell of cordite, copper, and smoke hung thickly in the air. Guerrera now stood directly over the kid, accompanied by his men, gazing down at him.

"Kid's a loon," muttered one of Guerrera's men.

"Damn, man, look at the size of him," said another.

The kid's eyes suddenly flew open, his lips pursed over the cigarette, securing it in his mouth. His right hand weakly attempted to bring up the Glock to Guerrera's face.

Guerrera, who had anticipated this, quickly stamped on the kid's wrist. The Glock fired at nothing, trapped beneath Guerrera's foot.

"Aaargh!" the kid cried, still sucking on the cigarette and blowing smoke up at Guerrera.

Holding a Glock of his own, Guerrera gazed down at the kid, looking into his eyes. The eyes that were still overflowing with that irrational rage and uncontainable fury. With a mixture of disappointment, sympathy, and contempt, Guerrera said, "Look at you. You've still got fight in you. Even now." He paused, then continued, "You took out ten of my men, do you know that? Had you joined us, you could have accomplished great things."

"Shut yo hole, you silly old faggot!" The kid attempted to yell but was no longer able to raise his voice. He spat out the cigarette, then attempted to spit blood up at Guerrera. It landed back on his face.

The men laughed.

Guerrera said nothing.

He sighed and pointed the Glock at the kid's forehead... but the kid wasn't done yet. He jerked his head forward violently and yelled, "GET BENT, YOU MOTHER—"

The single shot cut short his final words like a premature exclamation mark. He lay staring up at the sky, eyes open, the hole in his forehead oozing crimson over his forehead, the ground underneath his head slowly darkening.

Chapter 5: The Take

"Is he still praying? Goddamn fruitcake, I'm tellin' ya."

"After the show *this* fruitcake just put on," Guerrera's man kicked Bossman's lifeless body, "I think we've earned some easy game."

Guerrera reminded Esteban, "Remember, no matter what happens, he needs to be alive and well enough to stand and talk. You kill him? And you might as well take that gun, put it in your mouth, and blow your own brains out."

Esteban nodded, and handgun raised in front of him, slowly began to advance towards the boy, who was still kneeling in prayer, seemingly unperturbed. Two more of Guerrera's men flanked Esteban, one holding an AK47, the other holding a heavy set of manacles.

The boy was now sitting on his knees, palms flat on his thighs, head angled slightly downwards, eyes directed at his knees, lips moving in silent recitation. As the trio reached him, Esteban took position in front of him, just beyond the mat, gun pointed at the boy's head as if for an execution. The man with the manacles stood directly behind him, eyeing the great sword strapped to the boy's back, and the man holding the AK placed himself to Zander's right. Guerrera and the rest of his men stood thirty yards away, at an angle, affording them a side-view of the scene. They stood, breaths abated, watching intently. But for the faint whistling of the warm desert breeze, there was utter silence.

***

"Come on, kid, that's enough. Hold your hands behind your back, and you won't get hurt," said Esteban evenly.

Zander stayed in the same position, palms on thighs, eyes still on his knees, lips still moving. The breeze blew a strand of grey hair serenely about his face. The index finger of his right hand suddenly raised and pointed forward for a second before falling back down to his thigh like a meerkat.

"HEY!" Esteban raised his gravelly voice now, more assertive. More commanding like the SWAT team commander from earlier. "I said quit that shit! And put your hands behind your back!"

What happened next happened very quickly.

Failing to get a reaction from Zander, Esteban gestured to Manacle man to restrain Zander and attach the manacles to his wrists.

As the gesture was made from Esteban to Manacle man, Zander turned his head right, whispering to his right shoulder, then did the same to the left.

Just as Manacle man began to bend down to secure Zander's wrists, Zander sprang up faster than a jack-in-the-box, still facing Esteban. He met Manacle man halfway, the back of his head smashing brutally into the man's face. Before Manacle man had even hit the ground, Zander, now standing, reached behind him and unsheathed his sword and, in one fluid motion, swung it at Esteban's neck, decapitating him instantly. His head thudded on the ground and rolled like a rudely discarded bowling ball; the rest of his body still upright, still had the gun pointed at Zander for a good second before crumpling into a heap.

The sword carried on in its left-to-right trajectory; after cutting through Esteban's neck like melted butter and it didn't stop there. Using the momentum from the initial swing, Zander swung it further until it batted away AK man's AK47 like a Baseball player going for the home run. AK man could only stare in shock as the blade was drawn back and ran right through his chest, with a good eight inches poking out between his shoulder blades.

Zander pulled the blade out with a sickening squelch, and AK man dropped to his knees, bleeding profusely from the mouth and chest, eyes wide with horror and confusion. He attempted to say something but merely gurgled. Then fell flat on his face.

The moment from which Esteban had gestured Manacle man to the moment when AK man had been impaled had lasted no longer than two seconds in total.

***

Guerrera and his men stood rooted to the spot. Awestruck. They were still attempting to register the events that had just transpired before their very eyes. One second, the boy had been on his knees, serene, utterly relaxed. Then, in the time between two blinks of the eye, there was a decapitated head on the ground and three bodies, and the boy, who now walked towards Gary who had the manacles, and was still semi-conscious, brought his sword down through his chest with a savage thrust, the blade going all the way through and into the ground beneath him. He stayed in this position, hands still gripping the sword hilt, and turned his head towards Guerrera and his men, fixing them with an icy glare.

Although unsettled, Guerrera did not show it. A veteran of hundreds of battles and skirmishes, he had never seen a man move so swiftly and fluidly. Much less a scrawny kid.

Of the remainder of his crew, now down to seventeen, a few stood frozen, others looked uncertain, and some holstered their guns, then dropped the holsters on the ground, drawing machetes, knives, hatchets, cattle-prods, and an assortment of other melee weapons. One carried a taser gun; another had a fisherman's net. They all looked at Guerrera, awaiting instruction.

"Remember. Alive and well enough to stand," Guerrera reminded them sternly.

"Caint we just shoot him in the laig or summat baoss?" drawled one of his men.

"No. Too risky. Might miss, might hit an artery. Leave your guns here. Keep the taser."

Guerrera sent them all on ahead, barring three, who stayed with him.

As they advanced towards the boy, he calmly turned his gaze away from them and pulled the blade out of Gary's diaphragm.

He slowly walked towards the gang of men, face serene, eyes gazing into the distance dreamily. When there were less than twenty yards between them, he suddenly thrust the sword into the ground, the first six inches of the blade disappeared, the hilt still reached his chin. He then thrust his left hand out in front of him, palm facing forward like a cop stopping traffic, and yelled, "WAIT!"

The men stopped abruptly in their tracks, exchanging confused and uneasy glances. The looks on their faces were a mixture of what is he up to? And why are we following his instruction?

***

Whether they had stopped in fear or merely due to disarmed confusion, it didn't matter. Satisfied, Zander casually took off his coat and his scarf, placed them calmy on the ground revealing a pair of lean, scarred, vascular arms poking out of a loose-fitting brown T-shirt. He placed his hands on top of each other resting on the hilt and closed his eyes. He began speaking quietly, too quiet to be heard by the men in front of him.

"Oh Lord, protect me from my front, behind me, from my right and my left, and from above me, and I seek refuge in your Magnificence from being taken unaware from beneath me."

Zander could see, in his mind's eye, Guerrera's men continuing to exchange nervous glances, until Zander suddenly raised his voice, shouting like a church preacher, his eyes still shut. He felt the men startling and turning their heads back in his direction.

"INDEED! THOSE WHO WERE BEFORE THEM ALSO DEVISED PLANS! SO, THE WRATH OF GOD STRUCK AT THE FOUNDATIONS OF THEIR BUILDINGS, AND THEN THE ROOF FELL ON THEM FROM ABOVE THEM…" Zander's eyes sprang open.

Judging by the looks on the faces of Guerrera's men, the look in Zander's eyes must have been terrifying. He felt the energy. The pure, righteous fury coursing through his veins and escaping from his eyes, and as he delivered his final words, they were spoken much more quietly. Pensive. Gentle, even.

"...And the Divine punishment came to them from whence they never perceived."

The fourteen men stood rooted to the spot. They looked as if their blood was running cold and as if a strong chill rushed through them. It was almost as if each man could see the other was experiencing the same feeling as they exchanged uneasy glances. Then, as if desperate to expel the ice from their veins and warm their bodies, they broke out of their stupor, roared, and charged forward.

The first three, who had reached Zander ahead of the others in a semi-circle formation, were disposed of in under four seconds.

Zander snatched his sword out of the ground and decapitated the man to his right. Before this man's head hit the ground, Zander delivered a powerful front kick to the lower abdomen and groin area of the second man who was directly in front of him, raising his hatchet whilst elbowing the third man who was attacking to Zander's left, in the centre of his throat.

As the Hatchet man doubled over in pain from the kick, Zander drove the sword through the base of his neck. Throat-struck man, coughing and spluttering, swung his machete at Zander's head. Zander ducked, feeling the blade caress the edge of his hair, then pulled his sword out of Hatchet-man and drove it through Throat-struck man's chest and pulled it back out.

Zander suddenly felt a jolt of sharp pain seize his entire body, forcing him to drop his sword and fall back on his buttocks.

"HE'S DOWN! GET HIM!" came a cry from in front of him.

Urgently trying to make sense of what was happening, Zander looked down at his stomach, from where he could feel a sharp pain like a needle prick. He saw two wires protruding from his shirt, followed them with his eyes, and saw they were connected to one of the men holding what looked like a yellow toy gun pointed at him.

Zander yanked the wires out of his stomach as another half-dozen men rushed him. He had just enough time to reacquire his sword as more machetes, clubs, hatchets, knives and a couple of cattle prods came at him from every direction.

A net rained down on him, which he managed to avoid with a forward roll on the ground. The fact that most of the men seemed to be aiming for his sword more than his actual body made things even easier.

Then, as the remaining eight men scrambled forward to join their comrades, he began to swing his sword all around him. Zander felt like a dexterous conductor of an orchestra of death, a savage symphony, as he hacked and slashed in every direction; limbs, heads, and blood flew left and right. He felt totally calm. At peace. His body and sword moved as one, like two highly trained synchronised dancers in a flow state. *Mushin*. His mind was empty, and he felt like he could do this forever.

But a crackling sound rudely interrupted his harmony, followed by a white-hot jolt of pain shooting through his lower back down to his buttocks, causing Zander to cry out and drop his sword. He fell to his knees, tried to get back up, but felt it hit him again in his arm. This time, he fell flat on his face and attempted to get up again. The crackling jolt hit him yet again. And again. And again.

Then darkness took him.

Chapter 6: *Barakah*

Zander awoke with a headache, throbbing pain, and soreness over most of his body. It took him a second or two to gather his bearings and register his final memories and his current situation.

He tried to move but found he couldn't. He felt a trickle of blood running down his forehead and cuts stinging on his lips. He was in a moving vehicle, and his hands were chained together, feet chained to the floor. He must be sitting in the back of a van.

He was startled when he realised he wasn't alone and looked to his left to see two men. One was sitting by his side a metre to his left, and the other was a little further down opposite him, near the rear doors looking out the windows as dusk fell.

The man sitting next to him was slim and blond, with a conflicted look on his face, looking at the floor as if contemplating some important future decision. He had either not noticed or cared that Zander had awoken.

The man by the rear doors turned his head to look at Zander. He looked rather older than the first man. Possibly in his late fifties or early sixties. His hair was iron-grey like Zander's own but slightly shorter, and a thick stubble of the same hue covered his cheeks and chin.

Whoever or whatever this man was, he was clearly a survivor. A saying Zander had once read during his reading exercises came to mind, fear an old man in a profession where men die young.

Deep scars and lines marred his once-possibly-handsome, lean features, and Zander felt a pang of sadness as he was reminded of Uncle Mourad. It was difficult to differentiate between the scars and lines. His eyes were also grey and had a shrewd intelligence and deep steel to them. There was no change in those eyes as he gave Zander a very faint, slightly cocky smile and said, "Good morning, sleeping beauty."

Zander said nothing.

"You must be thirsty," said the man.

Zander didn't reply.

The man picked up a canteen off the floor, and Zander realised something was wrong with him.

One of the man's hands wasn't real.

The fingers were frozen in place, and the entire hand was smooth, solid, silver, and glinted in the light from the single tubular lightbulb running across the van's ceiling.

The man followed Zander's gaze and, holding out the canteen to Zander with his real hand, said, "Oh, misspent youth."

Despite his thirst, Zander did not accept the canteen. He wondered what was going on. These men weren't your average wasteland bandits. They had decimated Bossman and his bike and had not seemed interested in any kind of loot. They had asked Bossman to hand Zander over to them before they had killed him and then done their very best to capture Zander alive, despite incurring heavy losses in doing so. They weren't interested in spoils, nor were they mindless indiscriminate murderers. They had even offered Bossman a chance of amnesty if he cooperated in capturing Zander.

He contemplated for a second. Surely, he, his family, and his people couldn't be the only ones with knowledge and access to the prophecies. There must be others that knew. Why else would these men have captured him? What was he without the prophecies? Nothing. Just another faceless survivor in this dark new world. Nobody anybody would hold any interest in capturing or killing unless he stood in the way of loot or conquest. Which begged the question, if he were being targeted for elimination due to his prophesied role, why hadn't they killed him?

And, so, the main question was, what did they want with him? He couldn't afford to be side-tracked from his mission. Not after all he had been through up until this point. Not when he was so close.

**

Guerrera studied the boy.

Zander.

He had finally awoken after being knocked out by almost half a dozen hits with the cattle prod. After the clash with the other kid, this kid had taken out almost the entire remainder of his crew. But the other kid had used guns and explosives. This kid had slaughtered fourteen men with nothing but a sword. He sat there now, battered and bleeding, helpless. But he still appeared calm and serene, asking no questions and offering no pleas. Although the kid was small and slight, there seemed to be an inextinguishable fire in his eyes and a sinewy harshness about him. Almost as if he had never known true comfort or rest and probably never would.

Guerrera knew this look. It was a look shared by many of his men and, he dared say, even himself. Those men were the hardest workers and the most determined soldiers. No matter how much comfort and pleasure they sought and acquired, it never quite filled them, and they always reverted to find some purpose to toil and suffer for.

Zander spoke at last. "Who are you?"

Guerrera took a moment to respond. "My name is Guerrera. Jordan Guerrera."

The van went over a deep pothole, and the three men bounced in their seats, Zander's chains clinking and clanking.

"What do you want?" asked Zander.

"You."

"Why?"

Guerrera paused for a moment, rubbing his salt and pepper stubble with his metal fingers, pondering how to deliver a complex answer in the simplest way.

"Let's just say you have a hefty bounty on your head."

"What could anyone possibly want with me that they're willing to pay such a high price for?" probed Zander.

Guerrera narrowed his eyes. Were the boy's questions genuine? Did he know his own role in the prophecy and was just feigning ignorance to gain information? Or did he truly have no idea who he was and the potential power he wielded, and what would happen to him as a result of that power?

If Guerrera, right here, right now, gave him the answer to that question, would he then be arming the boy with the knowledge to carry out the very task that they were trying to prevent him from completing? If the boy was truly unaware, then wouldn't it be better to keep him in the dark? Or would he find out regardless, as that was his destiny? Were fates and destinies sealed? Was the future set? Or could it be changed? What if the oracle had prophesied that Guerrera would die next year? But then he brought his gun up to his own temple and blew his own brains out right here, right now in this moment? Wouldn't that mean he was changing his fate and dying before his time?

Or would the gun jam? Or would it fire, and he would somehow survive the injury and continue living on as a vegetable right up until next year when he was prophesied to die, thereby fulfilling the prophecy?

But then, if the future was set, what was the point of this task Guerrera was fulfilling?

Goddamn it.

Prophecies were a befuddling business. Headache-inducing. But Guerrera's thoughts were interrupted as Zander spoke again.

"It's for him, isn't it?"

"Him who?"

"You know who."

Guerrera felt a hint of an amused smirk creeping to his lips.

"What's funny?" asked Zander.

"Nothing. Just a book from the old world I read once. The villain of the story was always referred to as 'You Know Who' by those who feared him." He paused, collecting his thoughts. He continued, "So tell me, who is this 'him' you're referring to?"

Zander's gaze hardened at once. The look was very similar to the one he had earlier, in the moments before he had slaughtered Guerrera's men. Behind his cool, unperturbed exterior, Guerrera found himself recoiling a little from those brilliant green eyes.

"The Deceiver. The Impostor. The Great Liar. First claimed to be a prophet. Now claims to be God himself," replied Zander.

Guerrera said nothing.

"He performs miracles, right?" continued Zander. "Things no human could possibly do? Controls the weather. Brings the dead back to life?"

Guerrera remained silent.

It would have seemed to an onlooker that Jason, who was sitting next to Zander, seemed to have finally realised that Zander had awoken.

But Guererra knew better. The man was fighting an internal battle over something and had been since the moment they had set out. His concentration and performance had suffered because of it. Guerrera was keeping a close eye on him. Jason now sat there silently, watching the exchange between Guerrera and the boy, the introspective look of turmoil still plastered across his face.

"Have you ever actually seen him bring a dead man back to life?" asked Zander.

Guerrera nodded lazily.

"Before your very eyes?"

Guerrera took a moment before answering, "He brought back the long-dead parents of one of my men."

Zander smiled. "Those were not his parents. His parents are still dead. Those were Jinns. Demons who adopted the shape and appearance of your man's parents to deceive him and attribute the power of resurrection to this great deceiver."

A flicker of something flashed through Guerrera's mind.

Zander continued, "Think about it, Jordan—"

"Do not address me by my first name," spat Guerrera venomously without raising his voice, pointing a finger at Zander's face, his cool demeanour lapsing momentarily, an intense savagery replacing it. "I am not your friend."

Zander paused, seemingly unabashed, gave a benign smile, and continued, "Ok. I apologise. But think about this; has this deceiver ever killed anybody in front of you and brought that very same dead body back to life? On the spot?"

Guerrera was silent for a spell, then in a voice low and even, almost a monotone, said, "You have no idea what you're talking about, kid. You haven't seen what I've seen. You should sit there and conserve your energy, believe me, you're going to need it."

Zander merely blinked, leaned back, and gazed out the rear window, ignoring the hostile glare fixed on him from Jason.

Guerrera lit a cigarette, taking long, deep drags, filling the van's interior with smoke. He was a little irritated with himself for allowing this kid to control the conversation for so long, asking him questions, interrogating him, "educating" him. As if Guerrera were the prisoner and the kid the captor. But Guerrera had pushed back and established the boundaries again, so he had at least redeemed himself somewhat.

***

An hour had passed since Zander regained consciousness in the van. The sun had now completely dipped beneath the horizon. Guerrera continued to stare out of the window, and Jason had yet to utter a single word.

Guerrera, despite himself, lit another cigarette and spoke without turning to look at Zander. "Not far now, kid. Just approaching the Iraqi border." He was speaking more to himself than anybody else. But there was something about this kid. He was like a toothache. Impossible to ignore. Like a scab that just had to be picked. The kid was a lamb being led to the slaughter anyway, so what could it hurt to pick at him a little bit? Just to pass the time.

Guerrera could tell that the kid was the type of person who would speak in riddles. Deep, philosophical, and cryptic answers to simple questions. Like a philosophy or religious book in human form. He exuded an air of mystery and deep esoteric knowledge, and Guerrera, an avid reader and knowledge-seeker, simply could not pass up an opportunity to engage in dialogue with somebody like that. It was a once-in-a-lifetime opportunity, his instincts told him.

"You know," said Guerrera, pausing to take a pull on the cigarette, still facing away from Zander, "in all my years, I've never experienced time passing as quickly as it has over the last couple of years. Seriously. A year feels like a month; a month feels like a week. A day feels like a morning or an afternoon. What d'you make of that, kid?"

Jason's ears seemed to perk up. As if he had also experienced this phenomenon himself. He eyed Zander from the side, awaiting his response. When Zander did not reply, the man spoke for the first time, "Well?"

"Welcome, brother." Zander smiled pleasantly, turning to look at the man. "So glad you could finally join us."

Jason shot Zander a look of pure hatred and disdain. "He doesn't know shit, Guerrera. You're wasting your time. Chosen one, my ass. My cattle prod didn't seem to get that memo, did it?"

"Shut your mouth, Jason," said Guerrera in an ominously calm baritone.

Jason opened his mouth to say something, seemed to think better of it, and reverted to staring at the floor, the nervous, contemplative look back on his face.

"*Barakah*," said Zander.

Guerrera blinked. "What?"

"*Barakah*. It means 'Blessing.' Everything in this world runs on *barakah* or lack thereof. The human body, wealth, time, food, drink, actions, even the Earth itself. If one or any or all of these things involve transgressing the limits placed by the Creator, there will be no *barakah* in them. And anything that lacks *barakah* will never benefit.

"For example, let us look at an incredibly wealthy man. There is nothing inherently wrong with possessing, acquiring, or earning wealth. It is the manner by which it is acquired, earned, and spent that determines whether there is *barakah* in it or not. Let's use the currency of 'dollars' in the old world, for example's sake.

"Let's say this man is worth a billion dollars, earned through lying, cheating, stealing, and killing. Transgressing the limits set by the Creator. This money will have no *barakah*. Therefore, it will bring him no peace. No contentment. He will always want more, 'if the son of Adam had a valley full of gold, he would want to have two valleys. Nothing would fill his mouth but the dust of the grave' he will forever suffer sleepless nights and anxious days, constantly looking over his shoulder, constantly fearing that a person he hurt or cheated or stole from will return to destroy him and take his wealth. This lack of *barakah*, this poison, will affect even his physical body and his mind and seep into every other facet of his being.

"However, had he earned his billion dollars in a pure manner, without transgressing limits, he would not be plagued by these issues. A man who possesses a mere thousand dollars will live an easier, happier, and more contented life than this billionaire if he has *barakah* in those thousand dollars." Zander paused.

Guerrera waited silently.

"Let us look at the example of a man who lies with his neighbour's wife. There is nothing inherently wrong with the act of copulation. A man who lies with his own wife will find *barakah* in this action: pleasure, happiness, peace, love, warmth, comfort, and legitimate offspring.

"But a man who lies with his neighbour's wife is transgressing the limits. There is no *barakah* in this copulation. He may experience momentary, fleeting pleasure in the act, but it will be plagued by guilt, fear, anxiety, heartache, and conflict. And it will spread to the neighbour's wife, the neighbour himself, and any resulting offspring. Everybody will be touched by the stench in some way, shape, or form."

Zander paused. Guerrera still sat silently. Jason continued to stare at the floor, although Guerrera could tell he was listening closely.

Zander continued, "There is individual *barakah* and collective *barakah*. Over the last millennium or so, the collective *barakah* of humanity has progressively decreased directly in proportion to the progressive increase of corruption. Greed, war, lust, hedonism, godlessness, deception, consumerism. We are at the precipice. Never, in the history of humanity, has the collective *barakah* of the Earth been so low. Not even at the time of Noah and the great flood. Especially now with the appearance of this false God. Look at the land, the sea, the air, the animals. It hardly rains, and when it does, much of the time, it is acidic and of no benefit. The animals on the land are scarce, as are the fish in the seas, the fruits, the crops, the vegetables, trees, and plants. The deficiency of *barakah* has infected everything. And time itself is no exception.

"The *barakah* in time ensures that your experience of it is beneficial. When *barakah* is high, time seems to slow down, stretch out. You can achieve things in a month that most people couldn't in years. Even your lifespan seems to have expanded. If not the actual number of years, then at least your experience of those years. When *barakah* in time is low, your life passes by in a flash, even if you live the same number of years. Before you know it, you're old with one foot in the grave, wondering where your life and all that time went.

"So, in answer to your question, about this phenomenon of time passing very quickly. That's the answer. *Barakah*."

Guerrera was silent.

Jason, however, was much more vocal.

"Bull. Shit."

Zander turned his head to look at Jason as if to say, 'oh?'

"Never heard so much shit in my life. 'Berakka!' 'Berraka!'" He mocked, making exaggerated facial expressions and gestures with his hands. "Do you know why the Earth is in this state? Hmm, I wonder, maybe, just maybe it has something to do with the goddamn nuclear war?"

Zander nodded and smiled. "Oh, it does. But the Earth was steadily decaying long before the war. All the diseases were already present and growing. The war and the appearance of your filthy false God only accelerated the process."

Jason threw a vicious right hook which spun Zander's head as if it were on a swivel.

Zander turned back to Jason like nothing had happened, and a flash of reluctant admiration rushed through Guerrera.

Zander continued, "Besides, Jason, wouldn't you imagine that nuclear war qualifies as transgressing the Creator's limits? Thereby reducing *barakah*? By the way, that punch you just threw at me had no *barakah* in it." Zander smiled derisively, "That's why it's hurt you more than it hurt me."

Jason lunged forward again, but Guerrera slapped him in his face with his metal palm, bellowing, "ENOUGH!"

Jason looked livid, the area he'd been struck growing bright red. But he lowered his gaze and became quiet.

"See?" said Zander with a cocky smile on his face.

Jason raised his head again as though he'd suddenly been struck by an interesting thought. "Talk all the bullshit you want. The fact is, my God is real. He walks, talks, demonstrates his power and benefits us directly. I can see him, touch him and speak to him directly." He raised his hands, palms up, and looked up at the roof, shrugging. "Where's yours? Don't see him anywhere. Do you? Look at you. Sitting there like a trapped animal. You would think he would take better care of his chosen one, wouldn't you?"

Zander smiled but didn't reply.

Jason shook his head and sat back, satisfied he had won the exchange.

Guerrera stubbed out his cigarette on his metal hand and casually dropped the butt on the floor. He inhaled slowly, exhaled, looked at Zander, and said, "You're definitely no bore, kid. I'll give you that."

He leaned back and continued to gaze out of the window, watching the scenery blur past. His thoughts drifted, and his mind took him back to where he had been, this time last week.

Chapter 7: The Council of the Thirteen

Prophecies were such vague, sketchy things. Infuriating.

Why couldn't an oracle or a soothsayer or a fortune teller ever just say, "Next Tuesday at six o'clock, you will fall down the stairs, break your neck and spine, lose the use of your legs, resulting in depression and alcoholism for two years, after which you will die from liver failure." Or "Next week you will meet the love of your life, get married, her name will be Layla, you will have three children and live happily ever after."

No.

Instead, they would say, "Great trials and misfortune await you…" or "Happiness is on the horizon..."

Was it because they were all a bunch of crap? Deliberately vague, therefore difficult to disprove? Or was it because fate and destiny were complex and set things, set in a delicate balance that must be kept concealed from humans to prevent their intervention from interrupting this balance? Who knew?

These were the musings running through the mind of Jordan Guerrera and probably many of the other twelve men and women in the room.

These individuals were collectively referred to as 'The Council of the Thirteen' or often just 'The

Thirteen.' All handpicked, carefully selected by the 'Messiah' himself for their strength, courage, loyalty, wisdom, faith, and abilities. Each man and woman had proved themselves and passed tests with distinction. They sat at the long, oak table, six on each side with Guerrera at the head as the chairman of the council.

Guerrera watched silently as the twelve debated the best course of action.

"Look. It's simple," said Jason. "The Oracle said that 'The boy will strike a hefty blow and bring about His destruction.' So, if this boy is the instrument of His destruction, then we find him and kill him. Problem solved." He spoke in a patronising tone as if stating the obvious to a group of dimwits.

"It isn't, though, is it?" said a thin, pale, dark-haired woman who sat opposite and three seats down from Jason. She spoke in an oily voice with a strong French accent. "The prophecy is well known. The people are aware of it. If we somehow managed to locate and kill the boy, we would have no proof. The people wouldn't believe it had happened. They'd need to see it happen with their very own eyes. Until that happens, there will always be sceptics and doubters on our side and hope for our enemies."

"Well, then we bring back his head! Hell, bring back his whole body and string it up in the Square!" replied Jason aggressively.

"Goddamn it, Jason," interjected Esteban. "Don't you get it? It's not about them seeing the body or even the killing. It's about them being absolutely certain that the boy is indeed the boy from the prophecies."

"I agree. But how would we achieve this?" asked the oily-voiced woman.

"We capture him and bring him in alive so he can stand trial before Him. Before the people," said Esteban. "If the boy is as great as the prophecies say, then there will be no doubt as to whether it is the boy from the prophecies or not. Once this has been established, the boy can be executed publicly."

This is a waste of time, Guerrera thought. The decision had already been made after many a private discussion between Guerrera and Him. This council was just theatre. A performance to give the participants the illusion of progressive discourse, make them feel important and as if their plans and opinions mattered to Him.

They didn't.

But Guerrera needed the discussion to continue and play out for a little while in order to maintain the facade.

One of the men opposite Esteban mumbled in the ear of the man next to him. The mumbling man was Russian and the only council member who could not speak or understand English. The man next to him doubled as his translator.

The translator spoke in a thick Russian accent, enunciating each word slowly and carefully as if reading a passage out loud in an English language class. "Artyom asks, thet by bring ging boy here to KHim, are we not, err, how you say, pro po gating? Boy to fulfil his mission? What if this is how boy kill KHim?"

"Thank you!" said Jason raising his hands, then lowering them dramatically as if relieved that somebody was finally talking some sense.

"There's no way the boy can stand against His power. Alone, chained, and under heavy guard." Came a deep voice, sitting at the end of the table, the closest to Guerrera. Huge, black, and bald, this was Kofi. Kofi always seemed to jump in late and inject strength and confidence into the discussion.

The twelve-way discussion continued, "So how do we find him? We have a description and a rough area, but there really isn't much to go on. The prophecy says, 'He will appear between Turkey and Syria.' What the hell does that mean? 'Appear' what is he going to be born there? Travel there to make his first appearance to us? Fall out of the sky?"

"And when will this happen? Right now? Tomorrow? Next year? Next decade?"

"We'll just have to post guards across the entirety of the Turkey-Syria border twenty-four-seven."

"What? Are you insane?"

"You have a better idea?"

"We don't have the manpower for that, not to mention, we still don't know what 'Appear' means. What if it means that he was born twenty years ago? And has already raised an army and will 'appear' with them at the border? That's our whole plan up in smoke—"

"That's irrelevant!"

"How is that irre—"

"Enough!" The single word from Guerrera, delivered in an only slightly raised voice, but accompanied by his metal fist crashing down on the table like a judge's gavel, brought order and silence to the table.

Guerrera paused for a moment, then said, "We shall find the boy and bring him in alive to stand before Him. I have spoken to Him. He has dreams. Premonitions and visions pertaining to the boy. He is confident that in a very short time, he will see where the boy is. Rest assured; we will find him."

Chapter 8: The Hit

The van bounced and jerked over rugged terrain. Zander had lost all sense of time and had no idea how long they'd been travelling. As far as he was aware, they'd only stopped once to refuel at the southwest border when they crossed into Iraq. There was a solitary compound guarded by armed men who most probably worked for Him. That was over an hour ago.

"Can we pull over for a second?" asked Zander.

"Why?" said Guerrera.

"Toilet break."

"I knew I shouldn't have offered you water the second time."

"No good deed goes unpunished." Zander smiled.

Guerrera sighed, slid up the bench, and with his metal hand, banged on the partition, which separated them from the driver and the man in the front passenger seat. The partition slid open, and Guerrera shouted something in fluent Arabic to the driver. The driver nodded and closed the partition.

The van slowed, carried on for a minute or two, made a left, and stopped.

Guerrera opened the rear doors and jumped out with the grace of a ballerina half his age. He gestured to Jason, who stood, stepped over to Zander, and gripped his upper arm.

"Come on, move it."

It was a brilliant night lit by a salubrious full moon. They were somewhere in the northwest of Iraq.

They had stopped in what seemed to have been a hospital car park. Half the building remained, like a box of Kleenex with its top half aggressively torn off. Charred and blackened, almost invisible in this light. The remains of the hospital looked like a hoarder's apartment, with the remains of old-world electronic equipment, bones, beds, gurneys, and more, heaped everywhere.

A handful of burnt-out vehicles were scattered around the former car park, which no longer bore any resemblance to its previous purpose.

There was a sudden rustling sound and then a blood-curdling screeching coming from the ruins of the hospital. The shrill screech ripped through the quiet night, and the three men turned their heads in its direction. The driver and the man in the front passenger seat of the van jumped out, weapons drawn.

Three red, tiny, glowing circles floated in the ruins.

"It's a mutant rat," said Zander casually, as if describing the weather. "Kill it before it kills us."

As if it had understood Zander's words, the rat let out another terror-inducing screech and rushed forward into the moonlight. Despite being roughly the size of a German Shepherd, it was just as fast as a regular rat.

Guerrera and his men opened fire simultaneously. The gunfire rattled, spoiling the serene night atmosphere, bright muzzle-flashes lighting up the world around them, smoke and the smell of cordite assaulting the men. It lasted only a few seconds as riddled and torn apart by a couple of dozen bullets from four different weapons, the monster dropped just a metre away from Zander, flailing its legs and snapping its jaws helplessly, the three red eyes looking around frantically before it finally stopped moving.

Jason kicked it with his boot. "Christ, I've never seen one this big. Think there're more?"

"No," said Zander matter-of-factly. "They would have revealed themselves after all that noise."

Jason shot him a look of disdain. "Do it there," he said, giving Zander a little shove and gesturing towards one of the burnt-out cars nearby. The nervous look he had worn for most of the journey now back on his face.

Still in his hands and feet restraints, Zander shuffled forward awkwardly, a couple of inches at a time.

After he was done, Guerrera and Jason escorted him back to the van until Zander suddenly stopped.

"Guerrera. I have a favour to ask."

Guerrera looked at him.

"Would you kindly allow me to pray one last time? I've missed the afternoon prayer, and it's time for the evening one."

"No," said Guerrera.

"Come on, boss, he's getting his ticket punched soon anyway, let him have his silly little prayer," said Jason.

Both Guerrera and Zander looked at Jason in surprise.

Jason shrugged. "We don't let him pray? I've got a feeling we wouldn't hear the end of it for the remainder of the journey. And I've just about had enough of listening to his shit."

"Ay, Boss!" Came the driver's voice suddenly. Both he and the front passenger had returned to their positions in the van.

"Watch him," said Guerrera to Jason as he walked over the van, which was idling ten yards away.

Zander glanced at Jason, who was now looking his worst yet. Pale and sweating, his eyes carefully tracked Guerrera as he made the last few steps to the van, approaching it from the driver's side.

"This won't work," said Zander, looking at Jason.

Jason's eyes widened in fear as a yell and three gunshots, all in quick succession, sounded from the van. At the same time, Jason had drawn his pistol. He grabbed Zander frantically and placed him, facing forward, in front of his own body, the barrel of the pistol, kissing Zander's temple.

Guerrera approached. The right side of his face, stained with blood, his real hand pointing his gun at Jason and Zander, the metal one, open by his side. His eyes were dark with barely contained rage.

"What's this then, you stupid bastard? A mutiny?" he growled.

"STOP RIGHT THERE, GUERRERA! I'll blow his goddamn brains out! I'll do it. Don't test me!"

"Wasn't man enough to kill me yourself, ey? Had to get those dumbass Arabs to do it? Well, I'm here now. And I'm gonna rip your damn spine out. So, shoot me."

That was the longest speech Zander had heard the man construct up until now. It almost seemed like being forced to speak this much at once was partially the reason for his rage. As if he felt he was being garrulous.

Jason, shaking with the fear of a coward but driven by the determination of a zealot, moved the gun from Zander's head and pointed it at Guerrera.

"I said, stop! I don't want to kill you, but this needs to be done, and I won't let you stop me! The kid needs to die!"

"Listen to me, you idiot," said Guerrera, inching forward slowly, gun still raised. "What do you think this will achieve? You do this, and he will peel your skin from your body, and you'll wish you'd killed yourself instead of this kid."

"You can't kill me," interjected Zander with a level of somnolence that had no place in this situation. "It's not the way it's written."

"YOU SHUT YOUR FILTHY MOUTH!" screamed Jason desperately.

"Kid, shut up," said Guerrera. "You're not helping."

"I'm doing it for Him," said Jason, shaking uncontrollably now, almost sobbing. "Even if he kills me for it, it needs to be done! Taking his prophesied killer right to Him, it's insanity! He will thank me one day."

Zander, with blinding speed, suddenly lunged forward and wrapped the six-inch chain, which attached the two manacles on his wrists, around Jason's gun and ripped it from his grip. The gun clattered to the ground, and Jason dived after it. Guerrera also rushed forward, moving almost as fast as Zander.

A three-way scuffle ensued, with Guerrera violently shoving Zander out of the way. Zander shuffled over to the rear of the van in his chains and watched the two men battle.

Except battle was not the right word. It was over before it started.

Jason never stood a chance against the battle-hardened Guerrera as the grizzled, metal-fisted commander brought his iron fist down over and over again like a piston into Jason's face. Guerrera did not even attempt to reach for the gun he had stuffed in his belt or Jason's, which was lying just a metre away. He only continued to pound away until Jason's head resembled a dropped lasagne and, even then, continued until the relentless strikes hit nothing but the ground beneath it. The heavy clinks sounded like a particularly enthusiastic quarry worker breaking rocks with a sledgehammer.

Guerrera got up, at last, his breathing surprisingly steady, bloodstains on his face, hands, and clothes. He removed his brown leather duster, walked to the rear of the van, ignoring Zander, opened the doors, and threw the coat inside. He then took out one of the canteens and began washing the blood and gore off his hands and face. He must have suddenly noticed the pistol Jason had dropped as he walked over to it and stuffed it into his belt.

He looked at Zander. "Why didn't you try to escape?"

Zander smiled, raised his eyebrows, and gestured to his chains. "How far would I have gone in these?"

Guerrera studied Zander for a moment, face unreadable, then took out a carton of cigarettes, lit one, and began clearing the front of the van of the two dead Arabs.

Zander watched him as he cleared the front seats and imagined what must be going through the man's mind. He had begun this mission with a dozen vehicles and thirty men. And now, due to nothing more than two kids, one an insane giant, the other, probably in his mind, a religious nutjob, he was the sole survivor. The last man standing, driving the package home by his lonesome, in a banged-up Ford Transit. Zander saw him shake his head and laugh dryly to himself as he dumped the second body on the ground.

Chapter 9: The Sword of God

Zander finished tying the last of the supplies to Kaz's back.

He checked the straps holding the mountain bike on his own back. It was treacherous terrain. The climate, the mutant animals, the scarcity of clean water, the bandits and robbers. Kaz probably wouldn't see the end of the journey. The bike was cumbersome but necessary.

Uncle Mourad grasped Zander's shoulders, staring him dead in the eyes.

"Who are you?" he said.

"Zander."

"Who was your father?"

"A warrior. A lion. A *Mujjaddid*. The last bastion of light in a world filled with darkness."

"Who is your mother?"

"A sword of justice. A protector. A teacher. A legend."

"Can the offspring of such a union produce anything but a warrior?"

"No."

"Then who are you?"

"Zander."

"With whom do you walk?"

"I am the Wolf that walks alone."

"With whom do you walk?"

"Alone!"

"With whom do you walk?"

"Alone with my Lord."

"And when the Lord is with you, who can harm you?"

"Nobody."

"What are you?"

"I am the Sword."

"What are you?"

"I am the Sword of Peace!"

"What are you?"

"I am the Sword of Justice!"

"What are you?"

"I am the Sword of God!"

"Who are you?"

"Zander."

"Who are you?"

"Zander."

"WHO ARE YOU?"

"ZANDER AL MALIK!"

Uncle Mourad slapped Zander's shoulders and pressed his forehead against his. This litany had been drilled into Zander from the day he could string a sentence together. They had been his first words. This would very likely be the last time he would recite it to his uncle.

"You've got this, God willing," said Uncle Mourad, holding the sides of Zander's head, foreheads still pressed together. Zander felt tears fighting for passage to his eyes, but he held them back. He could cry all he wanted later.

But not now.

He saw his mother standing like a rock in the doorway to the great, underground silo in which they lived. A few escaped wisps of grey hair blowing in the breeze underneath her headscarf. Her one good eye fixed on him with a mixture of pride, sadness, and worry. They had already said their goodbyes. No tears were shed.

All around her stood Zander's people. Around fifty of them, men, women, and children, watching him with awe, admiration, and melancholy.

As he mounted Kaz and prepared to kick the horse into motion, a shrill, high voice stopped him.

"Zan, wait!"

Zander turned his head to the sound of tiny, hasty footsteps making their way towards him.

Fatia, his baby sister and only remaining sibling. She was six years old but already spoke three languages fluently; her skill with weapons and martial arts was almost on par with Zander's when he had been her age. But for all that, she was still a little girl seeing off her older brother with a heavy heart. Tears poured down her smooth rosy cheeks as she forced a brave grin across her face, which only managed to look like a grimace.

If Zander had thought it had been difficult to hold back his tears when saying his goodbyes to his mother and uncle, it was nothing compared to this.

Fatia looked up at Zander atop his mount, her eyes shining with tears, the forced grin still plastered across her face, "You forgot the date cakes I made you." she said, holding out a crumpled paper bag with both hands.

Zander took the bag and smiled pensively, "Thanks so much, Fatty."

Fatia began to sob. Her breath became shallow and panicky, the forced grin disappeared, "W... will... I... ev... ever... s... see you a... a... again?"

Zander bent down without dismounting, scooped Fatia up, and placed her on his lap. He wiped away her tears, held her face in his hands, and said, "Remember, it doesn't matter where we see each other again, but we will. In this life or the next. Be good. Keep reading your books, say your prayers and keep training. Take care of Mum and Uncle Mourad."

She nodded, eyes still flooding with tears as Zander kissed her on the cheek, gently placed her back on the ground, and kicked Kaz into action, hand raised, bidding farewell to his people.

Now facing away from them all, Zander allowed the tears to begin escaping from his eyes.

As Kaz took him steadily further and further from his home, the chants of his people rang in his ears.

"GOD IS GREAT!"

"GOD IS GREAT!"

"GOD IS GREAT!"

Kaz picked up the pace, and Zander inhaled the cold morning air. He began to focus his mind on the mammoth task awaiting him.

I am the Sword of Peace.

I am the Sword of Justice.

I am the Sword of God.

I am the Wolf that walks alone.

Chapter 10: Captive

They sat in front.

Both captor and captive. But for the chains, an onlooker might have taken them for a father and son returning from an expedition.

Zander, still in chains, yawned in the passenger seat.

Guerrera took one hand off the wheel and rubbed his eyes, also yawning. With only thirty miles to go, he was finally beginning to show signs of fatigue.

Zander marvelled at the way Guerrera changed gears with his metal hand. The fingers splayed in open mode, Guerrera pushed the gear stick around dexterously with the palm, steering the wheel with his normal hand.

"You have an interesting aura," said Zander.

"Jesus Christ, kid, do you ever shut up?" said Guerrera with an exasperated sigh.

"It's dark. Very dark."

Guerrera kept his eyes on the road. He didn't reply.

"But there is a light there. Very small, but very powerful. There is good in you, Guerrera."

"I saved you only to deliver you to a worse fate," replied Guerrera matter-of-factly.

"That's not what I'm talking about. There is a very powerful light in you, buried under layer upon layer of darkness. You need to act fast before it is snuffed out permanently."

"Whatever you say, kid."

"You wear your aggression, your callousness, your brutality, as a badge of honour. You revel in it. Take pride in it. Don't you?"

A muscle in Guerrera's grizzled jaw flexed, but he still stayed silent.

"These qualities have served you well in this world we live in now. But at what cost? Your eternal soul, for temporary pleasure and dominance in a temporary world. Is that what you want?"

"You got me all wrong, kid. There's no good in me. And you'll see that when I take you to Him. When you see the fate, I've delivered you to."

Zander looked at Guerrera, feeling something like pity. "Yes, that's what you tell yourself. That there's no good in you. In order to bury that gnawing feeling, that small voice that tells you that the things you do are wrong. You've been telling yourself this since you were eight years old... since the day you killed your father to protect your mother and your sister."

The van screeched to a halt, forcing both men forward, straining against their seatbelts. Guerrera swore and grabbed Zander by the throat with his flesh and bone hand, a mixture of violence and confusion in his eyes. The violence was more dominant, overshadowing and surpassing the confusion, which was simply a little salt and pepper on the main meal, but not the meal itself. Violence and enmity were this man's bread and butter: his default state, his first and last point of call.

Zander could feel the blood rushing to his face, his nose and face quickly beginning to feel like they would burst.

But he did nothing. He did not attempt to fight or protest but merely stared at Guerrera, whose rage-contorted face was now beginning to blur.

Guerrera finally released his hold, and Zander gasped for air, coughing and sputtering. He waited for Guerrera to ask him how he knew these things. He even had an answer ready, *"I serve the Lord, and in return, he lifts the veils from my eyes and unlocks for me the mysteries of the universe."* He at least expected the man to threaten him and warn him not to ever mention it again.

But he did neither.

Guerrera took a few inconspicuous, deep breaths, composing himself. He seemed almost ashamed that he had momentarily lost control. He shifted the gear stick into first and pulled forward again, the Ford Transit shuddering stationary for a second as the rear wheels spun in place before finding traction.

Zander, his breathing returning to normal, massaged his throat and craned his neck to look at

Guerrera. The man had returned to his cool, composed demeanour as if nothing had happened. His grey, steely eyes firmly fixed on the road ahead.

"It's easier this way," said Zander.

Guerrera turned his head and fixed Zander with a look of naked incredulity as if dumbfounded that Zander still thought talking was a good idea. This was the most complete expression Zander had yet seen on Guerrera's face. He savoured the moment, as he had a feeling it was a phenomenon that didn't, and wouldn't, happen very often.

"To just give in to the darkness and tell yourself that this what you are and that there's no changing it, so you might as well submit to it. But this is not true. This is the *Shaytaan* deceiving you. *Shaytaan*, the hopeless, the doomed, wants you to feel just as hopeless as him. And he is succeeding. Because change takes faith and effort. Facing your demons takes courage and pain." Zander paused, watching Guerrera's expressionless face.

"After the defeat of your false God, there will be so much *barakah* on the Earth that a child will play with a snake. A lion will graze with a gazelle, and a single pomegranate will feed an entire family for days. Peace and prosperity, the likes of which the world has never seen."

Guerrera kept his eyes on the road.

"I want you to be there when this happens, Guerrera. I want you to witness this blessed era. There is good in you, I swear by the Lord of the worlds. All you need to do is confess your sins, not to me, nor to any man. But to the Lord himself, and to Him alone. Come clean, confess your sins and make genuine repentance, and he will heal your scarred heart and clean your stained soul."

Guerrera sighed again and lit a cigarette.

***

"What is the matter Guerrera? You appear troubled."

Guerrera looked his master in the eye. A simple act he took great pride in as he seemed to be the only one capable of it. No other man, woman, or child seemed able to achieve this feat of courage, discipline, and endurance. When speaking to Him, they would study their shoes, or the ground, or something in the distance. The milquetoasts among them would even shut their eyes yet still lose control of their bladders. The braver or prouder ones would look above him or past him, sometimes up at the sky.

But never at his eyes. They seemed to suck the strength and will right out of you.

Though accomplishing eye contact, Guerrera struggled to find his words.

"Speak."

"I… I am concerned."

"Go on."

"The boy. He seemed to abandon all resistance as soon as he realised who we were and where we were taking him. He even had a chance to take a weapon and attempt to escape. But he didn't even try. And now, in his cell, knowing what awaits him tomorrow, he sleeps soundly after singing recitations from his scriptures. He seems content; I would say smug even. He wants to be here. The prophecy—"

"Do not speak to me about the prophecy Guerrera. Your knowledge is merely a drop in the ocean. I have told you as much as you need to know to complete your duty. Nothing more."

"Of course, my Lord. Forgive me," said Guerrera, although he didn't lower his gaze.

"The boy is a zealot, Guerrera. A religious fanatic. Do you worry when a captive, intoxicated with opiates or drink, or the like, smiles contentedly, sleeps peacefully, or laughs joyfully?"

"No."

"This is no different. As a wise man once said, 'Religion is the opiate of the masses.'"

"And opiate is the religion of the masses," said Guerrera with a faint smile.

"Indeed."

There was silence for a few moments, but tension was in the air. The tension of words still waiting to be released.

"Was there something else?"

Guerrera inhaled. "I do not know what you have planned, my Lord, and of course, you do as you please. But… I advise… implore you not to make this a gladiatorial contest against our men, as you have done with some of the others."

"Why?"

"I understand the importance of satiating the crowd's desire for entertainment and blood, and I know the odds stacked against the captive are always insurmountable. But I have never, in all my years and battles, seen a man fight like him. He fights like a hundred demons. He would best twenty of our best men singlehandedly in a single battle. I have no doubt of this. Were a captive to achieve this in front of the crowd? Especially this captive, it would do nothing but increase his mystique and his legend and lower morale on our side. Perhaps this was what the oracle spoke of when she said, 'He will strike a hefty blow.'" Guerrera broke off and hesitated for a second, realising he had mentioned the prophecy again, against the warning moments ago. He waited to be rebuked.

Uneasy silence descended for a few moments, then, not a rebuke, but a question. "What do you suggest?"

"A secure execution. But slow, painful, and humiliating. Spectacular. Bring him back to life. Kill him again. And again, and again. This will break even the likes of him, eventually. It will also tantalise the crowd and increase their faith in you, my Lord."

Both men were silent for a spell, but Guerrera could tell his advice was being chewed over. His master broke the silence.

"If this is true, then I suppose bribery with women, status, and riches will also be of no avail? I find turning someone to our cause raises morale to a greater degree than merely eliminating them."

"You suppose right, my Lord, a man like this cannot be turned or corrupted. Only broken or eliminated."

"Thank you for your counsel, Guerrera. You are dismissed."

Guerrera gave a deep nod, bordering on a bow, turned, and walked towards the door. Just as he opened it and was about to walk through, he heard, "Guerrera!"

He turned. "Yes, my Lord?"

"You have done well. I was right in entrusting this task to you. No other could have completed it. It was a perilous and difficult mission, and we have suffered great casualties. But you have delivered, as you promised, and as I knew you would. You have my gratitude."

Guerrera said nothing but nodded again. After he left the room, walking back to his quarters, he realised that his master's parting words had not had the effect he would have imagined they would. He felt no pride or relief. Just a gnawing uneasy feeling in the pit of his stomach. Something he had not felt in such a long time that it took him a few minutes to identify it.

Shame.

Guilt.

***

Zander awoke with a start.

He had been dreaming of Bossman. He had been riding Bossman's motorcycle when the dead man suddenly appeared, sitting on the handlebars facing him. Zander had asked him to move as he was blocking his view ahead. But Bossman's blood-stained face, a bullet hole in the centre of his forehead, had frowned angrily at him, eyes burning with rage. He had then pulled a shotgun out of nowhere, pointed it at Zander's face, and yelled, "YOU SNEAKY COWARD SUMBEETCH, ZEE. WE WAS SPOSED TO BE A TEAM! FIRST, YOU KILLS ME, AN' NOW YOU TAKES MY BIKE TOO?"

He had then cocked the shotgun and pointed it in Zander's face. "EAT LEAD, DOUCHEBAG!" and then pulled the trigger.

That was when Zander had awoken in a cold sweat.

He was lying on the floor in a bare, grimy cell, barely large enough to take three full strides in any direction. The door was made of steel with a sturdy flap at the bottom, and about eight feet above him, in the wall opposite, was a small window. No glass, but iron bars going along it. The moon was bright and shone right through into the cell, lighting it up.

Zander noticed a steel bowl of water glinting in the moonlight near the flap and a tray with what looked like bread and dried meat.

Famished, he walked over to the tray, knelt, and wolfed down the bread, leaving the meat. The bread felt and tasted like cardboard in his mouth, but he was grateful for it. The meat was tempting, but he did not know its origin. Nor did he want to.

He shoved the last piece of bread into his mouth, chewed it with effort, and forced it down his throat. He then picked up the bowl of water and drained half. He would leave the other half for ablutions.

As Zander set down the bowl, he caught movement out of the corner of his eye, in the rear corner of the cell, to his right. At first, he had dismissed it as his own shadow, but then he swivelled around and almost jumped out of his skin as his eyes began to focus on what they were looking at.

A man.

He was squatting on the floor, back resting against the wall.

"Don't be alarmed," said the man coolly, holding up his hands, palms facing Zander. He gave Zander a grin that was probably intended to be friendly but only managed to look horrendously mischievous.

Zander gathered himself for a moment, then said, "How did you get in here?"

The man's face broke out into another grin. He had the kind of face that was handsome but rang every alarm bell in one's brain. Like a beautifully patterned snake. Captivating and enchanting but frightening and anxiety-inducing all the same.

"How did I get in here? Who am I? What do I want? These are the most natural questions but also the most irrelevant and least important. Especially with your limited time."

Zander didn't reply.

"I am here to save you a great deal of pain and suffering." He paused as if waiting for Zander's reaction.

Zander merely raised his eyebrows.

"What he has in store for you, you cannot bear. Nobody can. You may think you can, but you can't. Believe me."

"Go on."

"So, you need to listen to me. Listen to me carefully and follow my instruction." The grin was gone, and the expression that replaced it was deadly serious.

Serious. This mere word was too abstract, perhaps too human even, to articulate the intense look on this man's face. Zander found himself wishing that the mischievous grin would return in its place.

"Tomorrow, at dusk, when they take you in your chains to meet him, you will pledge fealty to him in front of the crowd, fall to your knees and beg his forgiveness. He will spare you to show his followers how merciful he is. The crowd will be in awe. The boy from the prophecies? The chosen one? Even he can't resist this man's power? He must be the Messiah. He must be divine.

"The crowd's awe will, in turn, inflate his self-awe. He will spare you as a living reminder to all of his power and his mercy. He will imprison you for a while. But not long after, you will gain his trust, become one of his soldiers. Once you have cemented yourself in this position, with your skills, it will not take long; you can be the inside man. Inform your people of all his plans, tactics, and secrets. Destroy him from within.

"This is the wise way. The long game. Your way? It is nothing but the way of a mindless fanatic. Pain, suffering, and self-destruction, of no benefit to anyone."

Zander smiled.

The man seemed a little surprised by this response. He waited for Zander to speak, a reptilian quality to him, like a lizard watching its prey.

"I know who you are," said Zander. "I know what you're trying to do."

"Do you?"

"Yes. After all your years of experience and practice, I would have thought you could do better than this. You know who I am. I'm no amateur, yet you come at me with these juvenile tactics. You must be getting senile."

Something flickered in the man's face. For a split second, Zander could have sworn he saw the man's tongue flick out like a snake.

"You are the ultimate deceiver," continued Zander. "The master of manipulation. Even more so than this false messiah. Yet this is all you could come up with? You corrupt people in stages. Work on them slowly, over time.

"You're not just going to approach an ordinary man and whisper in his ear to encourage him to go out and murder somebody. That wouldn't work. So, you plant seeds. Small actions which seem innocent, even virtuous, on the surface but corrupt a person over time. Until eventually, murder is no longer out of the question. Like the story of Barsissa the monk, long ago. You remember what you did to him, don't you?"

Zander did not imagine that the man's face could darken any further. But it did.

Zander continued, "Poor old Barsissa. He was a very pious and dedicated servant of God. Lived his life praying in his church and engaging in good works. One day, three brothers who lived locally, therefore knowing of Barsissa's pure reputation, came to him, asking him to look after their poorly younger sister, as they were leaving on an expedition for at least a few months.

Barsissa, the God-conscious monk, right off the bat, refused. Said that this was from the devil's plans. But the brothers pleaded and pleaded, told him that there was nobody else they could entrust this task to. Barsissa finally relented. Looking after a vulnerable young girl while her brothers were away? This was God's work, after all. Better he, a good man, look after her instead of some corrupt individual with evil intentions.

"So, the brothers left. Barsissa allowed the girl to stay in the house opposite his church. For the first few days, Barsissa would go and leave food outside the front door of the house. He would leave food three times a day, knock on the door and hurry away in order to avoid seeing the girl and falling into any kind of evil temptations.

"Then you came to him. Told him that the girl was lonely. Afraid. Leaving her food and scurrying away was not sufficient. She needed company, protection. He should at least go inside and check she was ok. Talk to her, keep her company a few hours a day until her brothers returned. You convinced him. It was still from a good place, after all. Taking care of a young, vulnerable girl. Still God's work.

"So, Barsissa now began to take the food into the house. But still, the pious servant of God that he was, he would only talk to her through a partition, a curtain. So, then you convinced him that she needed face-to-face contact. She was all alone; she needed to see a human face now and then. So, the partition came down, and before long, Barsissa and the girl began interacting for hours every day. Soon enough, they fell in love, and Barsissa fell into the sin of fornication.

"Soon after this, the girl became pregnant, and nine months later gave birth to their baby. Barsissa was horrified. What would happen when her brothers returned? They would crucify him! What would happen when the whole town learned that he, Barsissa, the pious servant of God, had taken advantage of a vulnerable girl and was now fathering a bastard? His reputation would be destroyed.

"So, you came to him once again. Convinced him that his fears were not for himself. That would be selfish and cowardly. No. His fears were for the greater good. People would lose faith in the pious servants of God and even in God himself. They would become cynical and faithless after learning that a man such as he could become so easily corrupted. Something needed to be done. Not for Barsissa himself, but for the greater good. Nobody could be allowed to find out about this."

Zander took a breath and swept some strands of hair from his face. He continued, "So, Barsissa murdered both the baby and the girl. For the collective good. The greater good. He buried them in secret, in a location known only to him. He then created a fake gravesite out behind the church.

"A few weeks passed. The brothers returned. Barsissa gave them the sad news that their sister had died from her illness and showed them the fake grave, telling them this is where she was buried. The brothers, also being men of God and trusting Barsissa, grieved briefly, visiting the fake grave to say some prayers, but accepted God's decree and went home without any suspicion.

"That night, you visited all three brothers in their dreams. You informed them exactly what had transpired and showed the brothers where their sister and her baby were really buried. In the morning, the brothers conferred and were shocked to learn that they had all experienced the same dream. So, they went to the church and dug up the fake grave and saw it was empty. They then went to the location you showed them in their dreams and discovered the bodies of their sister and her baby. Furious, they went to Barsissa and snatched him from the church, escorting him to the authorities so he could be tried and executed.

"Along the way, you came to him for the last time. Told him that he was surely about to die. Told him that only you could save him now… if he would only bow to you in worship. Desperate and afraid for his life, he did. But of course, you could not, and did not, save him. You made it so that the once-pure, strong servant of God, now a fornicator and a murderer, left this world with his last act being one of worship to the greatest enemy of God. You stole his soul.

"So, no, you filthy deceiver. I will not take your advice or listen to you. You had better crawl back under that rock in hell you came from." Zander spat on the ground, looking at the man with as much disdain and hostility as he could project.

The man had not moved a muscle throughout Zander's entire speech. He now fixed Zander with a curious gaze.

"You fool," he said with a cruel smile, shaking his head. "You self-righteous, fanatical fool. I shall enjoy watching you tomorrow. I truly shall. You will beg for death before the end."

"You're boring me now. Get out. I need to make my ablutions and pray." With that, Zander picked up the metal food tray and hurled it at the man as hard as he could. The tray hit the wall where the man had been with a heavy clunk.

But the man was nowhere to be seen.

Chapter 11: Martyr

They grabbed him roughly, bound in his chains, from the jeep. A burly escort on each side, holding him under his armpits. An entourage of grim-looking hard men carrying assault rifles surrounded him. It looked like they were in the remains of what had been, in the old world, a car park.

The gravel was worn and full of potholes. The long-ago, painted lines to mark the parking bays were all but gone, a few remaining partial marks here and there. There were dozens of other vehicles parked around them: cars, jeeps, vans, motorcycles, car-tank hybrids, bike-car hybrids, and monster trucks. It looked like a convention of the lovechildren of a mad scientist and a petrol head.

A few yards ahead of them were the walls of the colosseum. The limestone, concrete, and tuff, constructed millenniums ago, battered, eroded, and barely standing. Large chunks were missing in random places, but the walls still stood, as if in defiance to father time himself.

As soon as he exited the jeep, Zander heard the roars of a thousand exhilarated people. Music, drumming, cheering, and laughing. He could feel the atmosphere already from this distance. They were giddy with the anticipation of blood, humiliation, and pain.

His blood.

His humiliation.

His pain.

Zander found himself grateful for the two stone-faced gorillas holding him on either side. Without them, he felt his legs would give out. They felt weak and rubbery. Decades of progressive muscle development, all gone in an instant.

They reached the entrance to the colosseum, and Zander's stomach dropped even further as he saw the full view of what awaited him.

Zander had never felt so terrified and alone.

He had been subjected to trials and training since the day he was born. Trials and training, which would have ensured he didn't see his fifth birthday had he been an ordinary human.

Two of his older siblings had died at birth. A younger one was born with a defective eye and every limb of a different length. He died at the age of three.

Yet Zander, like his baby sister, not only survived but thrived in the hostile new world.

He was born with full health and function. The sinewy muscles in his arms, legs, and torso already becoming visible on his tender, infant body a few months into life.

He had learned to walk at three months. Spoke fluently at twelve months. Learned three additional languages by the age of three and led raids, hunts, and expeditions at the age of seven. By the age of nine, Zander had begun to best his uncle, a master of combat, in their sparring sessions.

But no amount of training could have prepared him for this.

It was a shocking scene. Zander had seen some sights in his time. He was far from sheltered. He had seen much of the grim scenes this new world had to offer.

This was something else entirely.

There were at least two thousand people, most of them populating the stone pews sporadically, which went around the whole circular perimeter of the colosseum. The pews were situated in a dozen rows, broken in places, parts missing, each level below the other, descending and jutting outwards.

The top level must have been around fifty feet high, the bottom probably around ten feet off the ground. At its inception long ago, the colosseum could have held at least twenty thousand, so the lowest levels were sufficient to hold the crowd. That was where most of them sat, with a few more scattered around sporadically on the upper tiers.

The crowd's combined hubbub and excited murmuring, punctuated by the drummers and the flute players, was deafening.

There were also scores of people scattered around on ground level. Ugly, deformed, radiation-damaged, battle-scarred men and a few women. Some with extra limbs or missing limbs. Others, with extra eyes, one eye, or no eyes. Prosthetic body parts galore. Some crudely fashioned and attached, probably slapped on hastily and painfully for a few copper coins, or miscellaneous goods, in alleyways of shady businesses by two-bit surgeons or mechanics. Others, more sophisticated and well-crafted, attached with diligence and precision.

The aggression, hostility, and hate emanating from them were palpable. It was all-consuming, a type of nuclear radiation in itself.

There were huge mutant rats, eyes red, jaws snapping, held back by these men and women, on chain leashes, straining against them, hungry for flesh. Also on leashes were cat-sized scorpions with multiple pincers, rabid dogs, and even some chimpanzees, patchy-furred with sharpened teeth. They screeched spastically, swiping aggressively with their paws in Zander's direction. A grotesque spectacle.

But none of these were the worst.

The worst were the undamaged, primped, and preened women.

Dressed to entice and well put together, they were aesthetically beautiful. But they were banshees under the surface. They all had a demonic glint in their eyes and petrifying auras. They laughed at Zander. Leering. Mocking. Singing eerie songs in some strange, bone-chilling language, dancing, swaying, and moving seductively like possessed hippies, or exotic dancers, with a horrible kind of grace. They danced to the other-worldly music coming from the flutes and the drums, the combined effect of which penetrated deep into Zander's soul. It made him want to weep out of terror and anxiety, cry for his mother, and wish that the ground would swallow him whole.

As the crowd parted around Zander and his entourage, he saw a large platform raised around four feet above the ground in the distance. It was made of stone, stone steps leading up to it, with a twenty-foot pole bolted to the centre. The stage was situated in the centre of the colosseum. This is where it will all happen, thought Zander, as his stomach dropped yet further.

He found himself wishing that Bossman had killed him earlier. Or perhaps during one of the skirmishes or by one of Guerrera's men. The regret and hopelessness became unbearable. It seeped into the very marrow of his being. He wished that he had died at birth like so many of his siblings. The providential, comforting arm around his shoulders had disappeared when he needed it most.

Why had he, Zander, survived? Why him? Why did he have to carry out this impossible task? He simply could not do it. He could barely stand, and he felt like vomiting. And this was all before the main event had even begun.

Uncle Mourad's voice interrupted his thoughts.

"What the hell is wrong with you, you little maggot? Look at you; you're pathetic. Is this what I trained you for, for twenty-four years of my life? They haven't even lain a finger on you yet, and you're folding already. You best man-up quick, or there'll be hell to pay. Who are you? Who is your mother? Who was your father? With whom do you walk? Who is your Lord?"

His mother's voice cut in. *"You're a diamond sculpture Zander, the toughest and most valuable material on Earth. God gives his strongest soldiers the hardest battles."*

Now Zander's own voice rang through his head. *I am the sword of peace. I am the sword of justice. I am the sword of God.*

I am the Wolf that walks alone.

He breathed in deeply, held it for two seconds, then exhaled. He muttered a supplication under his breath.

Some of the strength had returned to his legs. He neared the stage, now only a stone's throw away, and as the sun began dipping behind the western wall, orange and gold, he held his head high despite himself and glared insolently, making sure to make direct eye contact with as many of them as he could.

The grotesque men and women shouted and leered, throwing missiles and spitting at him from a distance. Zander put on his best smug smirk and muttered, "Come on then, you dirty, Godless, motherless sons of whores. Let's do this."

Zander climbed the steps and stood in the middle of the stage, a few feet in front of the pole, still bound in his chains, his two escorts flanking him.

The sun peaked over the western wall, casting a dim, orange light and long shadows across the colosseum.

The hubbub died down in an instant as if a switch had been flipped. The men stopped roaring. The music stopped. The women ceased their dancing. Even the hellish animals seemed to have quietened down. The crowd bowed their heads as if in vigil.

There was movement in one of the archways next to a section of the seating pews ahead of him. The dozens of people gathered around it split like the Red Sea to allow the entourage to walk through.

Guerrera was in front, flanked by a huge, black, bald man on one side and a pale man with a blank expression on the other. The threesome walked forward a few paces in tandem and then stopped, stepping aside and clearing the path.

Another man emerged from the archway, and Zander felt his heart begin to pace. It was Him. The liar. The impostor. The false Messiah.

The impostor continued at his leisurely pace, now no more than thirty yards from the stage, eyes poring over Zander.

Zander's mouth was dry, his throat burning. What he wouldn't give for a cup of fresh, cool, delicious water. He felt the tremors beginning in his feet and making their way up to his legs. He tapped his feet very slightly to an unknown rhythm in an effort to hide his intense terror, which, he feared, was coming close to petrification. He desperately struggled to maintain control of his lower orifices. Still, he stood straight in his chains. He didn't lower his gaze and kept his chin up. He supplicated under his breath, with as minimal an amount of lip movement as possible, like a ventriloquist.

"There is no power or might besides God. There is no power or might besides God. There is no power or might besides God."

The impostor continued to walk with a completely relaxed gait, taking no notice of the crowd around him. Zander felt the man's evil hit him like an arrow. The hate, the despair, the hypnotic terror emanating from him. It was all so palpable that Zander could almost see it. Certainly, he could feel it assaulting him even from this distance, weakening his resolve.

The providential, comforting, guiding arm was still absent. He questioned why he had ever even considered putting himself in this insane situation. This miserable place. What had he been thinking?

He inhaled deeply. Held it. Exhaled.

I am the Sword of Justice. I am the Sword of Peace. I am the Sword of God. I am the Wolf that walks alone.

The impostor had now reached the stone steps leading to the stage. He climbed them gracefully, stepped onto the stage, and stopped an arm's length away from Zander, who raised his chin a centimetre. The crowd waited; breaths abated.

He looked young, in his early thirties at most. Zander was almost disappointed by his unremarkable appearance. His average height. His average clothes, his average physique, and a face bordering on handsome and unassuming. No scars, no marks. No red eyes or horns.

He studied Zander with no signs of urgency. He took his time looking him up and down like a child deciding which wing to pull off a butterfly first. It made Zander feel insignificant. Powerless.

After what seemed like an hour to Zander, the impostor finally spoke.

"I thought you would be bigger," he said with a playful and surprisingly disarming smile. His voice was much deeper than his physical stature would have led Zander to believe but silky at the same time. Seductive, even.

Zander didn't reply.

"You are, Zander Al Malik. Yes?" he continued.

Zander said nothing.

"Do you know who I am?"

Zander fixed him with what he hoped was an icy, defiant glare and shouted, "The false Messiah!"

He hoped he had been loud enough for his response to be heard by at least most of the crowd and steady enough not to betray his nerves. It had come out a little reedier than he'd planned though not embarrassingly so. But it had the desired effect as gasps and exclamations of shock and anger rippled through the crowd.

The impostor continued to ignore the crowd and appeared unabashed by Zander's inflammatory remark.

He continued to hold Zander's gaze.

Zander struggled to maintain eye contact and prayed it didn't show. The man's eyes exuded an otherworldly smoulder; it was almost like looking directly at the sun.

"My name is Naberius," he said. "And I am your Lord. I know your intended task. You have failed. But I am a merciful Lord. Submit to me right now, and you will be rewarded with a clean and swift death. Or perhaps even life. Who knows? We shall leave it up to the crowd." He acknowledged the crowd for the first time, half-turning to them, raising his arm in an exaggerated upward arc, gesturing towards them.

"Deny, and you will taste pain and suffering, the likes of which you have never known or imagined." He paused, gazing at Zander with a mild, relaxed expression on his face.

The colosseum was utterly silent. Over two thousand people, watching intently, holding their breath. Even the animals and beasts seemed temporarily pacified.

Zander glanced over Naberius's shoulder, and saw Guerrera in the distance, leaning against the wall of the first row of pews by the archway, arms folded, stone-faced as always. He met Zander's gaze, but his face gave nothing away.

His eyes moved back to Naberius, who raised his eyebrows as if to say well?

The tremors started in Zander's legs again. His heart hammered at a hundred miles per hour, mouth and throat dryer than ever.

Would it be so bad to take this offer? It would be with the best intentions, after all. Of course, he wasn't going to take the advice of his visitor last night, but he could still make that decision for himself, couldn't he? His faith was strong enough to feign loyalty to this impostor, just to get close to him and destroy him from the inside.

But doing it this way? He didn't even know if he could handle it. The other way would be wiser. It would save a lot of pain and suffering. The Lord could see his heart, his intentions. He would know that Zander was only feigning this fealty to deceive the deceiver. Play the long game.

No.

He couldn't let his mind be poisoned now or his courage crumble. He had come too far. This was his mission. His task. He had been chosen. It was the only way.

But where was the strength? The courage? The twenty-four years of physical, mental, and spiritual conditioning? The providential, protective arm? Why had he been forsaken in his darkest hour? Jason's words ran through his head, Where's yours? Don't see him anywhere. Do you? Look at you. Sitting there like a trapped animal. You would think he would take better care of his chosen one, wouldn't you?

He felt his heart bursting with fear, regret, sadness, and anxiety, and, with the sheer force of will from the depths of his soul, he glared straight into Naberius's eyes.

"SPEAK!" Naberius yelled, showing anger for the first time.

"I reject your offer, you filthy liar. You are not my Lord. You are a deceiver and an impostor who will be destroyed very soon. Do whatever you need to do to me. This is the truth, and it will not change." He, once again, raised his voice enough that he might be heard by at least those closest to them.

187

The crowd erupted again. Much louder this time. The animals, excited by the noise, screeched, barked, and yelped.

"DIRTY INFIDEL!"

"SCUM!"

"KILL HIM!"

"CRUCIFY HIM!"

"SILENCE!" boomed Naberius.

The colosseum became silent once again.

Zander could see the cogs turning in Naberius's head. As petrified as Zander was, he knew that this man was also in a precarious situation. He was in the spotlight in front of many of his devotees and supporters. Every utterance, reaction, and action he displayed needed to be measured very carefully. He could not afford to show any cracks in the façade of his divinity.

Naberius looked at Zander now, face electric with supernatural energy and excitement. Calmly, he said, "I understand you are young, Zander. You are vibrant, full of the energy and zeal of youth. Faith and commitment. You also, unfortunately, have been victim to an extreme, lifelong programme of grooming and brainwashing. This, coupled with the fact that I am a merciful Lord, means that I will forgive you for that little disrespectful outburst just now."

Zander felt disarmed. He had no response. He had been expecting a sadistic, raging monster. Not this ordinary-looking, calm, rational, and understanding human being.

Snap out of it, Zander rebuked himself. This man is the ultimate deceiver. He will act however he has to in order to manipulate the situation.

Naberius cleared his throat as if to make an announcement and, with all the charisma of a snake oil salesman, said loudly, "I would like to draw your attention to our three newest recruits!" He gestured grandiosely towards the archway he himself had emerged from earlier.

The sun had now completely dipped behind the western wall and, following Naberius's announcement, tall floodlights Zander hadn't noticed before, all around the colosseum thudded on and lit up the entire place.

Three people emerged from the archway and walked towards the stage.

Zander felt his heart leap to his throat.

He recognised them, even from this distance. But no, it couldn't be. Could it? No. No. Please, no.

Uncle Mourad, Sara, and Fatia had now reached the foot of the steps to the stage. They looked content. Happy. At peace.

His mother's face turned to concern. "Zander, my son. You've done so well. You've been so brave. But you can stop this now. I'm sorry, so so sorry for all we've put you through. We were wrong, so totally wrong." She began weeping into her palms.

Uncle Mourad placed his hand on her shoulder sympathetically and looked up at Zander, brow furrowed with genuine concern. "Zander, she's right. We're so sorry, buddy. Please, it's not too late. Just accept Naberius, beg his forgiveness, and he will forgive all your sins and disobedience. We can all be together again."

Fatia spoke, her high-pitched voice pulling every string in Zander's heart. "He's soo kind, Zan! He's amazing! Did you eat the date cookies? I've made more. Come on, hurry up and do what he wants so you can come and eat them."

Zander began to tremble. This was not his family. He knew Naberius could enlist the help of the Jinn. Make them adopt the shape of long-dead family members to fool people into believing he had the power to resurrect.

But his family were not dead…

Were they? Had the Silo been discovered and attacked by Naberius's forces at some point during Zander's journey? Naberius harnessed the Jinn to shapeshift into dead people. Surely that meant he could do the same with people who were still alive. Didn't it? Or were they real? Had they really been caught and corrupted by his power? That was a real possibility, wasn't it?

Zander clenched his jaw, closed his eyes, and shook his head. His first visible show of weakness.

It didn't matter who or what they were. All that mattered was his mission. His task.

When he opened his eyes, Naberius was watching him with a faint smirk. "Well?"

Zander closed his eyes again, opened them, and took a deep breath.

"Go to hell."

Naberius gestured to a group of armed men standing near the stage. Three of them approached Uncle Mourad, Sara, and Fatia and pointed their rifles, point-blank range, at their heads.

"My mercy has its limits," said Naberius. "Last chance."

"ZANNN!" screamed Fatia, sobbing, eyes full of terror. "Pleeease, you're killing us!"

"Don't do this, my son," said Sara morosely.

"This is crazy. Don't be stupid," said Uncle Mourad.

Zander fought to keep his composure, looked at Naberius, and said, "I said, go to hell."

Naberius sighed and nodded at his men.

The three shots rang out simultaneously.

His family's heads exploded, dead before their bodies thudded against the ground.

The crowd roared and cheered, exhilarated. They had come for blood and had gotten their first taster, whetting their appetite for more.

Zander turned away, his heart tearing in half. He breathed rapidly, supplicating under his breath, but did not allow himself to make a sound.

"That was unfortunate," said Naberius. "But you left me no choice; you understand that don't you? Your insolence, arrogance, and disobedience is destructive. It has cost your family their lives. You can still save yours. And, who knows, one day, if you impress me, maybe I'll even bring them back."

Zander spat at Naberius's feet.

The crowd erupted again.

A stone flew from somewhere and struck Zander above his right eyebrow, drawing blood. He did not flinch but felt the sharp, throbbing pain and then niggling pains in various other parts of his body. Almost as if the rock had struck a switch on his body, turning on his pain receptors so all the knocks, wear, and tear he had suffered over the last week came rushing back all at once.

The crowd laughed and jeered.

"SILENCE!" roared Naberius.

The colosseum became silent once again.

Naberius gazed at Zander. "As ugly as that was, it's about to get much uglier."

He turned and walked down the steps off the stage.

Zander suddenly noticed that his two escorts, who had been standing on either side of him, each a metre away, were now holding chains.

They grabbed Zander roughly and pushed him back against the pole. Hands and feet already shackled, the two men wrapped one chain around Zander's neck, securing him to the pole, and the other, securing his thighs.

When finished, the escorts followed their master off the stage, leaving Zander completely alone.

A wave of terror hit Zander as the realisation of what was about to happen hit him.

The stone that had hit his head earlier was not a random occurrence. He scanned the crowd around the stage, on the ground level, and saw that every one of them, around a hundred, held at least a couple of stones in their hands. Some of them, their pockets bulging with what must have been more stones, and others were carrying small sacks and reaching into them, drawing out yet more stones.

There was no dramatic speech.

No introduction or preamble. One second, they were all standing there, holding the stones, with maniacal, elated looks on their faces. The next, Zander was assaulted by an assortment of rocks, stones, and pebbles of different sizes, raining down on him from every side, even from behind him. Some missed. Others grazed him. Many struck him all over his body. Some hit him straight on like bullets. Others flew in a high downward arc before landing on him.

After what felt like an eternity, the deadly barrage seemed to have ceased.

Zander slumped forward against his chains, head almost hanging by his waist. Blood seeped into every inch and crevice of his body. The excruciating pain from where the first stone had struck him, he could still feel. Even after the hundreds of others that had followed. As if the first stone had claimed a right over his body for drawing first blood.

He could barely see. Could barely think. His vision was nothing but a blurry sea of red, with vague shapes moving in the distance. He tried to say something, but all that escaped his lips was a weak, hoarse whisper. He heard laughs and jeers.

"The scumbag's still moving!"

"Haha, he's trying to say something!"

"Aww, what's wrong little boy, between a rock and a hard place?"

"All hail the chosen one!"

"Hahaha, looks a bit *stoned* to me. Don't do drugs, kid!"

Zander opened his mouth in an attempt to retort, but no words escaped his lips. Instead, his mouth opened and closed silently, gulping like a fish. He realised it was becoming difficult to breathe. He felt the life seeping out of him rapidly.

And he submitted to the darkness.

Chapter 12: The Prophecy

"The Grand Shaykh's dreams have never been wrong. This is the truth. And the truth is always good. No matter how frightful. No matter how painful," said Sara in a fatalistic tone, her face both pensive and full of strength and belief.

Zander stared at his mother, horrified.

"How... how can I... it can't be... this... it's too much. I won't do it. I can't do it."

Uncle Mourad clasped Zander's shoulders firmly, gazing directly into his eyes. "You can. And you will. Who are you?"

Zander swatted his uncle's hands off his shoulders aggressively. "Screw that! This is messed up. I can't do it!"

"Yes, you can," said Sara. "You are my son. You are your father's son. You will, and you can, God willing."

Zander tried to calm his breathing, just as his uncle had taught him. He breathed in deeply, held it, breathed out. Then he said in an accusatory tone, "Why have you waited nineteen years of my life to tell me this?"

"Because it isn't something we could tell you until we believed you were ready. It is a very heavy burden," said Uncle Mourad.

Zander gave an incredulous scoff. "Yeah, no shit!"

Sara scowled at him.

"Sorry," said Zander, rolling his eyes.

All three were silent for a moment. Then Zander spoke. "Tell me the last bit again. From the first execution. Something's not making sense."

"He will be granted the power to kill and resurrect you three times. This is not his power. It is very important you remember that. It is not his power. This power will be granted to him by God for a short time. And after the second time, this power will be taken away. He cannot do this a third time," said Sara.

"But which power will be taken away after the second time? The power to kill me? Or the power to resurrect me?"

An uncomfortable silence permeated the room. Uncle Mourad bowed his head slightly and suddenly became interested in the floor.

Sara gazed at her son. "This is the part which hasn't been revealed."

Zander stared at his mother in disbelief. "You're joking, right? That's a pretty important detail, don't you think?"

"Maybe," she said. "But it doesn't matter. Your faith and your destiny are all that matter. This is your duty. This is the truth. And the truth is always good. No matter how frightening. No matter how painful.

What happens after the second time is in the hands of your maker. Whatever happens, it is good."

Chapter 13: Resurrection

Zander awoke with a start.

The pain was gone. The blood was gone. His vision was clear as he squinted in the bright floodlights, and his heart beat stronger than ever. He felt revitalised and recharged as if he had just woken up from a deep sleep.

But the fear and despair were still there, and his soul was still exhausted.

The deep sense of foreboding and anxiety suffocating him from within as the realisation of where he was and what he was doing slapped him hard across his face.

There were gasps and murmurs from the crowd. This must have been the first time they had seen Naberius bring a dead body back to life with their own eyes. After their initial shock had worn off, they resumed their cheering and jeering.

Naberius, a cocky smile plastered across his face, nonchalantly kicked stones and rocks out of his path as he made his way back to the stage. He stopped two feet from Zander, who was still chained to the pole, no longer sagging but standing straight, chin high.

The crowd quietened.

"That was unpleasant and could have been avoided," said Naberius. "What comes next will be worse. But this too can be avoided if you would but abandon your hubris and repent."

Zander was spent. Though all the signs of the hell he had endured moments ago had gone from his body, he could remember every second of it: the terror, the pain, the desperation, and the isolation. He could not take much more of this. He couldn't.

Naberius continued, "You need but to kneel and repent, and all your transgressions shall be forgiven."

Zander breathed hard. Conflicted. Tormented. There had to be an easier way.

He met Naberius's gaze with tired eyes and gave him a reluctant nod.

Naberius beamed. It was surprisingly charming. He gestured to the two escorts.

The crowd roared, clapped, and cheered.

The two escorts stepped onto the stage and unfastened the chains binding Zander to the pole. They held him up as if fearing he would collapse, hands and feet still shackled by the manacles.

Naberius nodded at the escorts, and they released their grip.

Zander swallowed. His throat was on fire, and his tongue and lips felt like sandpaper. What he wouldn't give for a drink of water.

The entire colosseum again became silent.

Zander slowly shuffled towards Naberius until he was less than an arm's length away from the man.

Gingerly, awkwardly, heart racing with the anticipatory dread of what he was about to do, he dropped to his knees. He bowed his head and raised his hands, slightly apart, palms facing towards himself.

"Oh, Lord. The most beneficent. The most merciful. Deliver me from the evil of this false idol. Grant me the strength and the patience to bear his trials. Destroy him as you destroyed Pharoah before him. There is no power or might besides you."

The shock and disbelief on Naberius's face brought Zander a brief rush of satisfaction. But this look of shock quickly turned to an expression of malicious rage as the crowd booed and hissed.

"You fool," he spat. "You, self-righteous, sanctimonious fool. Remember this mercy you have rejected. Remember this opportunity you have squandered when you experience what comes next."

The escorts manhandled Zander and dragged him back to the pole, the insane roaring of the crowd filling his ears as his legs shook, and he struggled desperately to control his bladder.

***

This can't go on much longer, Zander thought as he looked at his severed limbs littered around him.

One of his arms lay a metre in front of him to his right. His left leg, a few feet beside it, and his right, further down. The other arm had been tossed into the crowd like the scraps of a meal thrown to a pack of dogs. The crowd had gone wild, fighting over it, passing and throwing it up and down the stands, like a grim game of pass the parcel.

Zander looked down desperately at the cauterised stumps that were, a few moments ago, his arms and his legs. He had passed out many times during the ordeal. Only to be woken by the searing pain of the continuous cutting and sawing or the cauterisation of one of his limbs.

The butcher stood in front of him. A fat man with yellow teeth and bad body odour. No glee or pleasure on his face. But no disgust or conflict either. Just a cold, clinical countenance. A man engaged in his craft. Zander was nothing more to him than a pig's carcass on a meat hook.

Zander looked up to the sky, his vision blurry, the muscles in his neck barely able to move his head, which now felt more like a boulder.

"My Lord where are you?" he murmured weakly. "Where?"

A tear rolled down his cheek. His breathing became uneven and ragged. Where was the help? Where was the providential, protective arm he had felt guiding and protecting him for so long? Why had he been abandoned in his hour of greatest need? He couldn't go through this again.

This time he was certain of it.

He would die again soon. And be brought back again. But this time, he would take Naberius's offer. It wouldn't be genuine allegiance but merely self-preservation. Live to fight another day. He would still fulfil his mission in time if he could. God would understand.

The distant memory of a passage in the scripture came to the foggy forefront of his mind. God does not burden a soul beyond that it can bear.

Well, he couldn't bear this. He couldn't. He couldn't.

Memories flashed before his eyes. His mother stroking his hair tenderly with her rough hands. Fatia, drawing pictures, baking cookies, running down the stairs to show him, her big brother, her latest pet project, eagerly watching his face to see his reaction. A sweet smile lighting up her face, penetrating Zander's heart.

Uncle Mourad, groaning and clicking his back after a hard sparring session, looking at Zander with thinly veiled pride and admiration.

He had failed them.

Whether they were alive or dead, he had failed them all.

Tears flooded down his face as he lowered his head again, just in time to see the butcher's blade driven into his chest.

For the second time that evening, Zander died.

***

Zander woke up in the colosseum.

But something was wrong.

The crowd was gone. Naberius was gone. The beasts, the creatures, the blood, the stones, his chains, and shackles had all disappeared. His limbs were whole and attached to his body, and he moved them to make sure they worked.

He tried to figure out what time of day it was. There was no sun. No moon. The floodlights were off, but everything seemed to be lit by a strange purple light. Like a strange kind of twilight, he had never seen.

Dumbfounded, Zander turned all around him, scanning the colosseum. He stopped as his gaze fell on a shape in the distance.

Zander could make out the vague shape of a person. A man sitting in one of the spectator seats at the top level in the otherwise deserted stands.

"HEY!" Zander yelled. "Who are you? What's going on here?"

There was no reply or movement.

Zander walked off the stage and made his way towards him.

As he drew closer, climbing the stairs, nearing the top level, Zander saw that it was indeed a man, sitting straight-backed, facing forwards towards the stage. He was wearing what looked like a dark-green cowl, hood up, face hidden from the angle Zander approached from.

Zander, reaching the top level, now made his way down the aisle of seats. "Hey! I'm talking to you!"

The man still did not respond, as if transfixed on an invisible show, down on the stage.

Zander had now reached him, placing his hand on the man's shoulder.

The man stood up slowly, taller than Zander, turned to him, and pulled down his hood.

Zander was astounded. This was the most beautiful human being he had ever laid eyes upon. Inhuman in its beauty. His face was a chiselled tapestry of elegant but masculine perfection. A thick, neat, jet-black beard adorned his features and brilliant green eyes, full of mercy, compassion, and wisdom.

"Who are you?" Zander asked.

"You have done well, Zander Al Malik," said the man, as if he had not heard Zander.

Zander said nothing for a moment. Then, "What is this? Where am I? Am I dead? Is this a dream? A hallucination?"

"All of these. And none of these."

Zander stared.

"You have done so well, Zander," the man repeated. "You have come so far. Why do you resign now?"

"I…I can't take anymore! He has abandoned me. Why? I've done my best! I can't do anymore. I can do it another way!"

"There is no other way."

"Then where is he!"

"He is near. He is always with you. He never left you. But you must keep going. You must finish the task. Fulfil your destiny. You are close. So close. Paradise awaits you, both in this world and the next. You cannot give in now."

Zander shut his eyes, bowed, and shook his head. "No, no, the next one will be even worse. I can't. I can't."

The man placed his hands on Zander's shoulders, bringing his face close, those captivating eyes spilling warmth and comfort into him. "Listen to me, Zander. Listen to me carefully. The Oracle who informs him. She has told him things. Informed him of the prophecy. But the oracles are servants of the devil. They interact with the Jinn and only know what the Jinn tell them. And, as you know, the Jinn mix the truth with incomplete truths, half-truths, and lies. She has told him you are the chosen one. She has told him that you will bring about his destruction. She has told him that he will be given powers of resurrection only for you.

"What she doesn't know and hasn't told him is that these powers are only temporary. What she also hasn't told him is that you will not kill him. You are only to strike a hefty blow and turn the tide. Bring about his eventual destruction by another from your line. Your mission is but the second-to-last rung on the ladder. By attempting to kill you, he is, unwittingly, fulfilling the prophecy and paving the way to his own demise, 'They plot and they plan, and God too plans, and he is the best of planners.' Had he merely left you alone or had his men kill you instead of bringing you in alive, you would not have been presented with the opportunity you have now been presented with. He would have been safe."

Zander was deep in thought. This was making his head spin. He asked the question. The one question he needed the answer to. "What happens on the third time? Does he fail to kill me again? Or to resurrect me again?"

"This knowledge is not with me."

"I thought as much," said Zander, exasperated. He added, "So how is it I 'Turn the tide?' How do I 'Strike a hefty blow?' I can't do that if I'm dead, right? Right?

"You like to read, don't you?" the man asked.

Zander was taken aback by this sudden change in subject by such a random and trivial question.

"Yes."

The man gestured past Zander.

Zander turned and saw a book sitting on one of the seats, one level down from theirs. He turned back to the man, frowning curiously.

The man gave him a look that said, "Go ahead."

Zander turned reluctantly and climbed over the seats to the next level down. He walked to the book and picked it up. It was *The Screwtape Letters* by C.S Lewis. He had read this book many moons ago. He could not remember much of it except that it was a good book and was about conversations in the form of letters. Advice and counsel from a senior demon to a junior demon on corrupting his subject.

"What would you like me to do? Read the whole thing or—" Zander broke off as he looked up and saw that the man had disappeared.

He whirled around, scanning the whole colosseum, but the man was nowhere to be seen. Perturbed, and without knowing why, he looked up at the sky.

Zander could have sworn he saw a pair of shining wings, bright as the moon, beating in the far distance. He blinked, and they were gone.

He looked back down at the book, thumbed the pages, and opened it to a random page. His eyes pored over the words.

Merely to override a human will (as His felt presence in any but the faintest and most mitigated degree would certainly do) would be for Him useless.

He cannot ravish. He can only woo. For His ignoble idea is to eat the cake and have it; the creatures are to be one with Him, but yet themselves; merely to cancel them, or assimilate them, will not serve. He is prepared to do a little overriding at the beginning. He will set them off with communications of His presence which, though faint, seem great to them, with emotional sweetness and easy conquest over temptation. But He never allows this state of affairs to last long. Sooner or later, He withdraws, if not in fact, at least from their conscious experience, all those supports and incentives. He leaves the creature to stand up on its own legs—to carry out from the will alone duties which have lost all relish. It is during such trough periods, much more than during the peak periods that it is growing into the sort of creature He wants it to be. Hence the prayers offered in the state of dryness are those which please Him best…. He cannot "tempt" to virtue as we do to vice. He wants them to learn to walk and must therefore take away His hand, and if only the will to walk is really there, He is pleased even with their stumbles. Do not be deceived, Wormwood. Our cause is never more in danger than when a human, no longer desiring but still intending to do our Enemy's will, looks round upon a universe from which every trace of Him seems to have vanished and asks why he has been forsaken and still obeys.

Zander put down the book and closed his eyes, tears leaking out of them.

Then the world began to spin. Faster and faster until he could no longer see where he was. The sky, the colosseum, and everything in it blurred into a mishmash of shapes and colours. Zander felt like he was about to throw up.

And he was gone.

Chapter 14: The Wolf That Walks Alone

Zander opened his eyes.

He was back in the colosseum.

The real one.

The roaring crowd was back, elated at seeing their master resurrect their enemy to face yet more torture. His chains, his shackles, the pole, his limbs (now reattached to his body), the creatures, the blood, the stones, and Naberius had all reappeared.

But this time was different.

Zander could feel it in his very bones. It was an indescribable sensation. It was as if his definitions had faded. His identity, his name, his very self. They no longer existed. He was no longer Zander. He was no longer bound by these chains and shackles and labels constructed by humans. Much less the literal chains and shackles constructed with physical, material elements that thought they were binding him. It was as if a veil had been lifted, and he could see the reality beneath the reality. He was everywhere and nowhere, beyond this physical plane they called "The world." He was in the world beyond the world. Was this God?

No.

Even this word was too small. Too simple to capture the essence of a reality too deep and complex to ever be articulated by a word or words.

What he felt now was beyond happiness or joy or contentment. He had been consumed, annihilated by love. Beyond words or ideas or comprehension. The peace and serenity came upon him in waves. Wave after blissful wave, as if he was standing on the shore of a sea of tranquility and peace.

It was as if he was connected to every single atom. Every human, plant, and animal. Every creation there ever was, is, and would be, from the beginning to the end of time.

His heart felt like it would burst from the ecstasy. If this feeling could be bottled, put in a pill or a syringe, humanity would beg, borrow or steal it from him. Even kill.

It was all so suddenly clear. It was as if he had lived his entire life up until now in a beautiful palace. Only with the lights off and the windows shut. And now, the lights had come on, and the windows had opened, and he could see and appreciate the palace in all its glory.

Zander looked up at Naberius, who stood at the edge of the stage in front of him, and gave him the broadest, most genuine grin he had given anybody in a long time. He felt no fear. No anxiety. He could not even feel hate for this man, his tormentor.

Naberius stiffened. There was a sense of unease in the crowd; they knew something was not right. Even the animals were becoming restless.

Naberius composed himself. "Aah! The prodigal son returns! I hope you had a restful slumber." The words, spoken loudly and jovially and intended to inject confidence back into the crowd, fell flat. There were no whoops or cheers or jeers. They merely observed uneasily, waiting...

Naberius's face darkened, and he continued, business-like this time. "This has gone far enough. This is your final chance. Repent or die."

Zander, ignoring Naberius's final ultimatum, spoke loudly. "SONS AND DAUGHTERS OF ADAM! A new age has begun! An age of peace. An age of freedom. An age of hope. Leave this place. Leave this place now and head west. The armies are rising. This impostor is at the precipice of his destruction. His days are numbered. Remain by his side, and you shall also be destroyed. Leave! Leave now for your own sakes and for the sake of your children!"

The crowd did not make a sound. They seemed frozen in place, looks of terror, anxiety, and confusion on their faces.

Naberius's face contorted with rage. "Enough!" He gestured to the spectators on the ground level, holding weapons and the mutant animals on leashes. "Finish this."

The spectators let go of their leashes, and dozens of feral and mutated dogs, rats, and chimpanzees leaped towards Zander, rushing to tear him apart.

But they didn't.

Most of them stopped, turned, and pounced on their owners, tearing apart their limbs, sinking their teeth into their flesh, shrieking, barking, and screeching. Screams of pain, panic, and gunfire tore through the colosseum as the confused owners fought for their lives against their own pets.

A few of the animals ran over to Zander. Two muscular, mutant chimpanzees, a huge mutant rat, and a feral dog. The chimps began to tug at the chains and shackles binding Zander, the rat nuzzled his legs like a cat, and the dog stood in front of him, facing Naberius and the crowd, growling, teeth bared.

It was complete and utter pandemonium. There was a stampede as the crowd rushed to leave the stands. Bodies fell from the upper levels, tumbling down the stairs and falling off the edges. Spectators scrambled over the seats in a mad panic to head towards the exits.

Naberius roared at a dozen of his die-hard followers on the ground level, still standing fast, not knowing where to aim their guns. "What are you doing, you fools? Kill him!"

They raised their weapons, aimed at Zander, and opened fire.

Six of the guns backfired with loud bangs, and three of them jammed.

Only three fired.

The bullets whizzed past Zander and indiscriminately hit other unintended targets behind him.

The chimps had broken the chains and shackles, and Zander was now free. He walked calmly off the stage, the animals walking with him, the dog in front, the rat at his heels, and the two chimps on either side of him, like some strange protective detail recruited from a carnival.

He walked past Naberius, who was still surrounded by a few of his hardcore followers. The man looked ready to faint. He stood, gaping at Zander, his complexion pallid, mouth open, and eyes gaping.

Zander smiled at him and continued to walk towards the exit. He penetrated through the sea of chaos like Moses through the Red Sea. Around him, there were still hundreds of people. Some continued to fight desperately against the savage animals trying to rip them apart. Others lay dead on the ground. Hundreds continued to trample over each other, desperately trying to leave the colosseum.

Only a couple of dozen yards from the exit now, Zander saw a figure standing just by it, holding Zander's sword in his hand.

The other calm eye of the storm.

It was Guerrera.

Although he seemed to have aged a decade since Zander had last seen him up close, the look on Guerrera's face was unplaceable. It was possibly sadness and regret. Even now, the man couldn't express any shock or fear.

Zander stopped a few feet in front of Guerrera. The dog turned to Zander briefly, then stood in front of him, within arm's reach of Guerrera. The chimps and the rat stood in place.

The two men and the animals seemed to be in a bubble of their own, a separate world, unaffected by the madness and chaos still taking place all around them. It was a surreal scene.

Zander nodded. "Guerrera."

Guerrera gripped Zander's sword. The dog growled, and the chimps tensed, sinewy muscles rippling under their skin.

He extended his arm and held the sword to Zander, gripping it by the hilt, blade facing down. "This is yours."

Zander took it. The beautifully crafted, dark-green leather hilt felt soothing in his hands. He had not anticipated holding it again. He looked at Guerrera and could not feel any hate or bitterness towards the man for the part he had played in Zander's suffering. He would gladly suffer through it all again if it meant he could experience the current state he was in.

Then, Guerrera did something Zander never thought he would see him do, even if he lived with him for a hundred years.

He collapsed to his knees and began weeping profusely.

Zander watched him cry, curiously. Even his tears seemed hard. Even now, on his knees, tears pouring down his face, there was a toughness to him. He barely made a sound. He shuddered and jerked quietly, face reddening, the veins in his neck protruding and throbbing, hands clenched into fists on his knees. He breathed and growled as he wiped the tears from his face, not with open palms but with clenched fists.

This continued for about a minute until Guerrera wiped the last of the tears from his eyes with his sleeves and, still on his knees, looked up at Zander and said, "Kill me. I deserve it."

His voice was steady, controlled. Nobody could have guessed that this man had been crying his heart out just seconds ago.

Zander smiled down at him, and the dog moved out of the way so that Zander could step closer. He placed his palm gently on Guerrera's grizzled head.

"I forgive you, Guerrera. By God, I forgive you. Stay strong, stay on the straight path and be true to yourself. Leave this place and head west. Do not delay. We will meet again."

Guerrera bowed his head and began to weep again as if death would have been preferable to forgiveness.

***

The chaos had died down a little.

There were still scores of people escaping the colosseum. Some dashing frantically on foot, others scrambling into their vehicles, engines rumbling to life, wheels screeching and spinning madly before shooting off.

Zander walked through the car park, his heart floating, his step light, his little entourage still walking with him.

The sun was beginning to rise, hinting at the beautiful day to come. As he reached the edge of the car park, leading onto a straight road, stretching as far ahead as his eyes could see, he saw something a hundred yards ahead and grinned broadly.

He walked towards it; it was parked by the side of the road.

It was a beautiful Indian Chief Dark Horse motorcycle. Black and gleaming in the rising rays of sunlight. The key was in the ignition.

The dog barked at him as if saying goodbye. The two chimpanzees shrieked and patted him on the back. The rat whipped his leg with its tail, and they all trotted off together, back in the direction of the colosseum.

Zander climbed on the bike and was about to turn the key when he heard footsteps behind him.

He turned his head and saw the unsettling grin. The terrible but handsome face. The mysterious visitor in his cell the night before.

"You have done well. I commend you. Sincerely. Well done," he said, clapping slowly.

"Well?" said Zander.

"Well, what?" asked the man, attempting to look curious and innocent but failing miserably.

"You haven't come here just to congratulate me. So, what is it?"

The man smiled. "Just an idea. A suggestion. The impostor has been struck. Very hard. His support will surely wane after the show you've just put on. Thousands of his devotees have witnessed your power. Why leave now? Why not go back and start your own following? You are good. Kind. Just. You can lead them away from him and to you. Save people from him and have them revere and serve you instead. You can't just leave them at his mercy; this is wrong."

Zander let out a harsh, dry laugh and shook his head, turning back around and twisting the key in the ignition. He pushed the start button, and the engine roared majestically to life. The low rumbling, music to his ears. He wondered whether his family was still alive or if they really lay dead back in the colosseum.

No.

They were alive. They had to be. He could feel it.

He looked behind him again and saw that the man had disappeared. A meow came from in front of him, and Zander whipped his head forward and saw a brown tabby cat had jumped on the bike's handlebars. It looked clean and healthy, unravaged by the new world. It jumped onto the bike's tank, between Zander's thighs, looking up at him with round marble-like eyes.

Zander smiled and stroked its head gently. It purred and nuzzled his hand.

Fatia had always wanted a cat. He could imagine her face lighting up and her squeals of delight when she saw it.

He scooped up the cat, which offered no resistance and placed it under his shirt like a baby kangaroo, its head poking out of the collar.

"I'm naming you Pilgrim," he said. "Don't look at me like that. It's a cool name, and don't you dare let my sister change it."

The sun had now risen and cast a brilliant golden glow over the road ahead. Zander breathed in the air, feeling it was much fresher and cleaner than it had been just the previous day. The Earth seemed to have started healing itself already.

"In the name of God and all praise is for God. How perfect He is, the One Who has placed this (transport) at our service, and we ourselves would not have been capable of that, and to our Lord is our final destiny."

He kicked the bike into gear and twisted the throttle. It shot forward like a missile, rushing along the open road. The sun beat on his back and the wind whipped through his hair. The engine vibrated underneath him, and Pilgrim purred beneath his shirt, head exposed, watching the scenery, unperturbed by the noise and speed of the bike. Zander smiled contentedly. He could do this forever.

I am the Sword of Peace.
I am the Sword of Justice
I am the Sword of God.
I am the Wolf that walks alone.

Sleepers

Had they offered peace, we would
have sent them a diplomat
Had they offered ignorance, we
would have sent them a teacher
Had they offered knowledge, we
would have sent them a scholar
Had they offered trade, we would
have sent them a merchant
But they offered war, so we sent a
soldier

—Unknown

The man's hands were bleeding from the knuckles. It was a sticky, humid night in the middle of summer, worsened by his already bad insomnia. It was three in the morning, but his brain was wired and awake as if it were eight in the evening, and he was watching a live sporting event in a busy bar.

His eyes were tired and burning, begging him to close them, his body exhausted, but he simply could not switch off his mind.

Five minutes earlier, he had somehow managed to begin powering it down. He could feel himself drifting off, eyes closed, body floating away into the abyss of a well-deserved slumber... but then it had slipped away. Abruptly. As if to say, "Ha! Fooled you! You think you deserve this gift? No. Not you, my friend!"

This happened repeatedly for the last three hours.

And so, he had given up.

He jumped out of bed, switched on the bedside lamp, roared out of frustration, and punched his wooden wardrobe half a dozen times as hard as he could, cracking it, splinters sticking out of his bleeding knuckles.

He sat on the edge of his bed, knuckles dripping crimson, naked from the waist up, head in his hands, tugging at his hair.

He could feel the wraith.

The heavy, black thing.

The unwanted companion, holding him from behind in a piggyback wherever he went, weighing him down constantly, whispering in his ear and intruding on his thoughts. The metaphysical manifestation of all that was negative in this world. Hate, despair, fear, sadness, grief, anxiety, and rage. It would follow him no matter where he went and what he did. It was exhausting to fight it every moment of every day, and even when he did have the energy to fight it, he would rarely defeat it.

In the few instances, he managed to strike it a hefty blow, it would go down for the count, and the man would have a few moments of peace and tranquility.

Absolute bliss.

It would be as if he had been on fire for days and had finally jumped into a swimming pool. He was amazed that a normal person always felt like this yet still complained about life.

But, like a durable boxer, the wraith would be down but not out, and it would get back up before long, before the ten-count, and jump on the man's back again, heavier and more garrulous than ever——

PTSD, depression, insomnia, and a load of other things they probably didn't even have names for yet. Or maybe they did, and he could learn what they were if he bothered to visit a doctor or a therapist again.

He only had four moods. Two sets of opposites. Ecstatic or depressed. Emotionless or extremely angry. There was no happy medium.

He never took drugs nor alcohol; his reasonably religious upbringing didn't allow it, although he had smoked tobacco on and off over the years. The depression he had suffered for as long as he could remember. But the PTSD and insomnia crept up on him later in life.

Now nearing thirty years of age, the man had had a promising military career, then the police, and finally the secret services. But all three of these had been cut short, one after the other, by these mental health disorders. The PTSD had been the final nail in his coffin.

He had always thought he was immune to PTSD. All the things he had seen and done over the years in the military, then the police, had never bothered him. But then he joined the secret services and realized just how wrong he had been.

He was charged with infiltrating a terrorist group overseas. Behind enemy lines, deep undercover, he was instructed by his new "comrades" to execute a prisoner by slowly sawing off his head with a hunting knife. He, of course, thought about refusing. But it had been a test. It would surely have blown his cover if he failed to follow the order, and he would subsequently have been tortured and killed, failing the mission.

It was for the greater good.

He would kill one person to save thousands.

And so, he had done it. He had slowly sawn off a man's head as if it were nothing more than a piece of lumber, devoid of any sentience. The squelching of the hunting knife as it sawed through flesh and gristle, the warm blood squirting onto his face like a gruesome fountain, and the horrific screams, begging, and protests of pain and terror from the victim, etched into his memory for all eternity. And now he had PTSD and deep self-loathing to add to his resume of mental illnesses.

After being diagnosed and discharged from the service, knowing he was damaged goods and an unemployable liability to any government agency, the man transitioned to the private sector and utilized his unique skillset there instead: private security, bodyguarding-close protection, and other similar roles, all over the globe.

But as damaged, broken, and flawed as he was, he still managed to grasp on to his deeply embedded morals, and so he refrained from any mercenary or assassination type of work, just guarding and protecting. Strictly defensive and passive, but in high-risk and hostile environments. He had no qualms about killing, but it had to be exclusively in self-defense or defense of another.

After an eventful couple of years abroad, the man returned home briefly. He stayed at his parents' house for almost a year before leaving again. This time Libya for a few months, before returning and settling for work domestically, in London, a lot closer to home. He found private security work with a company that paid for his accommodation here.

He thought about going home, maybe finding a nice girl to marry and settle down with, along with his tight-knit family with a 'normal' sensible job.

But during the job in Libya, he met a girl whom, at the time, he imagined himself marrying and bringing home to his parents.

Zahra.

She was pretty, shapely, wholesome, and intelligent. A Libyan native, she spoke English fluently with only a hint of an accent which only made her all the more endearing.

But, as with most other things in his life, it had ended abruptly and violently when the man she had been promised to, learned of their relationship and informed the family.

It ended with the man shooting dead, the husband-to-be, in self-defense, subsequently losing his job with the company, and escaping the country by the skin of his teeth.

The entire situation was utterly insane and physically and psychologically exhausting. But the worst part of it all was that Zahra stopped speaking to him.

After returning to the UK, he sent her messages via WhatsApp, seeing that she was online and reading them, but would receive no replies. Not even a "Piss off and leave me alone."

But she didn't block him on the app either. Just silence. That, somehow, was even worse and more anxiety-inducing than being blocked.

He didn't have the opportunity to say goodbye or even speak to her about the whole debacle (let alone talk about seeing each other again), which made him very antsy and restless.

As a force of habit, over the following few weeks, he opened his WhatsApp every few hours to see if she was online, and eventually ended up sending her a few more messages.

Zahra finally replied. Only to tell him she never wanted to speak to him again, and then she finally blocked him.

Back in Libya, she had told him she loved him. And he had ended up killing a man because of her. Or was it for her? Maybe both. It didn't matter.

After everything they had been through together, all the plans they had made for their future, she didn't even think he was worth a text message. Not even to talk about the whole mess and let him know how she felt about it all. Or to check how he was doing. Or even just to say goodbye.

To hell with her.

As his friend Mitch would say, "That girl is for the streets."

That's what happens when you get sappy, emotional, and let your guard down for some silly girl, he thought.

That was six months ago. He still missed her. It hurt and constantly replayed memories of her in his head. Every little thing reminded him of her. But there was no point in wasting energy thinking about something that no longer existed. Nothing lasted forever.

He also missed his mother and his father. His siblings. His friends.

So why didn't he go home?

He couldn't.

He needed this type of work. The adrenaline and the danger. It was the only substitute for the alcohol and drugs he couldn't consume. It was the only way he could grasp onto some semblance of control and sanity. And by God, was he good at it.

It also distracted him. It kept him busy and his demons at bay and slightly blunted his existential angst. Many times, on his jobs overseas, he found himself half-hoping for a bullet to catch him in his head or a bomb to blow him to bits so he could escape this miserable existence.

He knew what his late grandfather would say if he were here. He would quote the scriptures and tell him, "Have *Sabr* my son, have *Sabr*."

Sabr meant patience, and the man found himself reciting a few verses of the scriptures pertaining to this. "And We will surely test you with something of fear and hunger and a loss of wealth and lives and fruits but give good tidings to the patient."

It brought him calm and serenity for a few moments. He was hoping against hope that the effects would be more lasting over time.

***

His bleeding hands throbbed with pain, but he enjoyed it. It gave him a sense of temporary relief from the inner turmoil and restlessness. The external, physical pain redirected the focus from his constant inner pain. A bit of peace for a few moments. He sat there, chest heaving, trying to calm himself.

He got off his bed, walked to the battered wardrobe, and opened the door. On the inside of the door, still undamaged, was a full-length mirror. The man studied his reflection for a few moments.

He saw a man, whose next birthday would be his thirtieth, who, although felt twenty years older, looked his age—a face that managed to be both femininely delicate and ruggedly masculine. He saw a man unusually tall for the area of the world from which his genetic heritage originated. A man who was still lean and aggressively muscular with a slender waist, huge shoulders, and chest, and arms like tree trunks, even though he had not engaged in any strenuous physical activity or practiced any sort of diligence towards his nutrition for the past month or so.

He witnessed a man whose physical appearance did not match the myriad of mental disorders he suffered or the chaotic lifestyle he lived. This was the result of a lifetime of fanatical physical training, exceptional genetics, muscle memory, and abstinence from alcohol and drugs, both of which he could have been forgiven for falling into, considering the state of his mental health.

Throughout his entire adolescent and adult life, physical exercise had been a form of constructive self-harm. Blood, sweat, tears, and pain to award him the benefits and the satisfaction of a self-harmer with none of the negatives. A type of self-harm and pain which, ironically, made him stronger, and that meant the result was not really "harm" but improvement.

At times, he trained for hours on end to utter exhaustion, depleting his energy to such an extent that he would have none left to fret or think about anything. Or to do anything other than collapse into bed and fall asleep.

It was a form of alchemy. Transforming the hate, rage, trauma, and self-loathing into a constructive activity. The perfect antidote to the dark, tormented maze which was his mind... If only the results were more absolute... more permanent. But it did help. It got him through to the next day, which was definitely something.

The mobile phone on his pillow suddenly lit up and vibrated on silent mode. He wondered who it could be at that hour. Even during sensible times, his phone barely rang. He had been completely unsocial, isolating himself for the past two months, and most people had taken the hint.

He thought it might be Zahra for a split second, and his heart skipped a beat.

He returned to his bed, dragging his feet unenthusiastically, and looked down at his vibrating phone at the caller I.D.

Not Zahra, of course, but it was a recognized number in his contact list, and the name flashed across the screen.

The man debated whether to answer the call. He was in no mood for conversation, especially with this caller.

It vibrated four times. He still wasn't sure. Five times. Six. Then he picked it up and answered the call.

And his life changed forever.

Day One: Thursday

Farah and Nasir Khan couldn't help but blame themselves. It was the harsh, illogical, overly self-critical self-reflection of a mother and father—the curse of being a parent.

Why hadn't they seen it coming? Why hadn't they recognized all the signs? Why hadn't they done something sooner? If only they had been more vigilant, more aware, more assertive, their twenty-one-year-old son would still be here.

But they hadn't. They had dismissed Kamran's aloofness as a phase.

It was a late teenage angst, they thought. His temper was just hormones. His secrecy and suspicious behavior were merely the concealment of the typical questionable activity that young men and women went to great lengths to keep hidden from their parents.

And now he was gone. And there was a good chance they would never see him again.

One week had passed since his disappearance. The Khan couple, shocked and distraught, had contacted the police as soon as they realized no friends or family had seen him for two days. He would never just disappear. He was a good boy. Intelligent, thoughtful, and though, like any young man, he would often come home later than curfew, he would never stay out for an entire night or more. Especially not without making some contact. Something had to be wrong.

Then they received the letter.

It was on the third day when an unknown person dropped a small, white envelope through the Khan family's letterbox. The envelope had no stamp or address, just a scrawl in black ink in what appeared to be their son's handwriting, *To my family*.

Anxious and shocked, they frantically tore open the envelope to find a single plain white piece of paper filled with writing on one side. It read:

To my family

I appreciate that this will come as a shock. But please try to understand.

Over the last couple of years, I have grown weary of this life. This existence, this world. The chaos. The filth, the corruption, the disease. It is everywhere. It smells. It stinks like faeces and I cannot get rid of the smell. The lies, the hypocrisy. It seeps into everything. It is inescapable. Everywhere I turn there is ugliness. Dishonesty. Lies upon lies. Evil upon evil. Even amongst my own so-called "respectable" family.

I have a father who cheats on his benefits and taxes. A mother who supports him. Two older brothers who are nothing but self-serving materialists, caged and controlled by their own desires. And a younger brother who will most likely grow up to be the same.

I do not say these things to hurt or insult you. I do not hate nor harbor any ill-will against any of you. On the contrary, I am doing this because I love you and want to save you all.

This world is collapsing. Global-warming, climate change, financial collapse, nuclear war.

Agenda 21 is no myth. It is happening as we speak and has been for decades. The endgame is on its way. But there is no need for it because the world is nearing its sixth extinction event. And this time the extinction will be us. Humans. There isn't much time. We need to change our ways and repent before it is too late.

I have been in contact with a secret society who understands all of this. They have set up their own community and follow a Messiah who provides for us, protects us and has created for us a paradise on Earth. Away from all the filth. All the corruption and all the evil. And when the world does finally come to an end, we will die together in our paradise, and enter a new, everlasting one.

My being here, whether you join me or not, ensures your salvation in the hereafter. Of course, I would prefer you to join me in this world too, but if not, at least you will be safe in the next, where we shall all meet again in our final and eternal abode.

Yours lovingly

Kamran

The receipt of this letter resulted in the police calling off the search for Kamran. It was clear that he willingly left home and joined some sort of cult, but a twenty-one-year-old was legally an adult. And an adult who had left home and chosen to live somewhere else had every right to do so and had not broken any laws, regardless of how brainwashed or deluded he might be.

So now, one week after his departure, every adult member of the extended Khan family sat in the dining room at the large table for twelve, discussing their limited options.

"Have you thought about hiring a private investigator?" Nasir's younger brother, Hamid, suggested.

"Yes, but where would he start?" Nasir replied. "We have no idea where Kam is or what this ridiculous group he's joined is. He could be anywhere in the country or even abroad. He has taken his passport with him."

"Well, that's the investigator's job, brother. To find out these things," Hamid said.

"No," Farah interjected, sullen and tearful. She had lost her bubbly personality ever since her son had left. "We don't know anything about that kind of thing. We don't have that kind of money either. Besides, we wouldn't know where to go, who to hire, who's honest and reliable, and who's not."

"Well, that's what the internet is for. You can easily find out things like that these days," Hamid's wife suggested.

"No, I have a friend who hired one of those people from a company once," Farah's sister, a paralegal, said. "He charged a fortune and never even finished the job. These are private companies and private operators. They're not even vetted. By law, they don't have to be. Any idiot can pick up a magnifying glass and charge you money to 'investigate.' It's just luck of the draw whether you end up with Sherlock Holmes or Walter Mitty."

"But we have to do something, don't we? We can't just sit here and hope he changes his mind and comes home, can we?" said Hamid.

"We can pray!" exclaimed Hamid's wife.

"Of course, we can, and we will! But prayer isn't a substitute for action. You pray and act!" replied Hamid.

"You're right. I'm not just going to sit here and leave my son in God-knows-where. These cults are dangerous. They abuse people, mess with their heads, carry out sacrifices, and even mass suicide. Remember that documentary on BBC we watched that time? Who knows what they'll do to him! or make him do!" said Nasir.

"But what are we going to do?" said Hamid. "We have no leads. Nothing to go on. If we at least had a rough location or could speak to someone who knows something, we could try to do something. But we have absolutely nothing. Just this letter. This is driving me mad! Goddammnit!"

"Mind your language!" warned Hamid's wife.

"Well then, that settles it," said Nasir. "I guess we have no choice but to contact Suleiman…"

The chatter died instantly as if somebody had flipped a switch.

The tension was palpable, and it seeped through the air like a thick fog.

The dozen or so members of the extended Khan family held their breath, exchanging furtive glances around the room. Each man and woman, waiting for another to break the unbearable silence.

Finally, Hamid spoke.

"Suleiman? Are you crazy? He's insane. A head-case!"

"Watch your mouth, Hamid. That's my son you're talking about!" said Nasir

"I know who he is, bro. He broke my jaw."

"You deserved it." Someone muttered.

The twelve-way discussion continued.

"Do you even know where he is? When's the last time you spoke to him?"

"Last I heard, he was halfway across the world, on ships, shooting up Somali pirates with a machine gun!"

"I thought he was in prison in South Africa?"

"He's more likely to end up joining that cult himself than to bring back Kam!"

"Come on, don't exaggerate. He's not that bad."

"Ha! Compared to what?"

"QUIET!" Nasir's voice boomed through the dining room like a judge's gavel, and the room became utterly silent for a second time.

Even though he was pushing sixty, Nasir still struck an imposing figure and presence. Though average in height for a south Asian man, he was stocky and solidly built in his youth. His advancing years and decreased physical activity had resulted in a little fat gain, but this only added to his overall bulk and the impression of raw physical power as he had lost none of the brawn underneath.

"Look, you can say what you want about my son, but the fact is, he's the toughest and most intelligent human being I have ever known, and, regardless of his mental state, he still cares very deeply about his family. More importantly, he's the only one who has the experience, skills, and connections to stand even the slightest chance of finding Kamran and bringing him home."

Nasir Khan had spoken. His tone had a finality, like a closing statement, which indicated that the conversation was over. The rest of the family knew better than to argue. Besides, what better ideas did they have?

Day Two: Friday

It was early evening. Suleiman Khan sat at his parents' dining table.

His mother sat next to him, his father opposite. He studied both his parents.

His mother had changed in the six months since he had last seen her. Already rather petite, she had lost more weight and collected more grey hairs than he remembered. She had gone from slim and healthy to fragile and ill-looking. She was usually bubbly, warm-spirited, and enthusiastic but she now looked drained. Plain. Grey. Like a picture in a child's coloring book which had yet to be colored. She had always been a tough and resilient woman underneath all the brightness and warmth. But this latest challenge seemed to have put her down for the count. Temporarily anyway, Suleiman hoped.

His father hadn't changed a bit, aside from the slight signs of stress due to the current situation. Still big and broad. Short, iron-grey beard, grey hair. His default tough-looking, stern face, punctuated by wise, piercing dark eyes, curiously gazing at the troubled, enigmatic fruit of his loins sitting opposite him.

Suleiman had always admired his father. His physical and mental fortitude. His bravery. He exuded authority, maturity, and wisdom. Growing up, the main recurring characteristic he noticed about his father was that when he spoke, people listened.

Whilst in his prime, he had looked like a fit heavyweight boxer, he now instead resembled a retired overweight strongman competitor, the type that pulled trucks and airplanes with ropes and ate five times as much as the average man.

The old man was hard as nails. He had killed two invading soldiers in his home village during the civil war with a butcher's knife when he was barely a teenager. He immigrated to the UK as a young man, working hard physical jobs and fighting mobs of marauding racist skinheads throughout most of his youth before finally getting married, starting a family, and building his own removals business from the ground up.

Suleiman held the sort of respect and reverence for his father, which made it difficult to make prolonged eye contact with him. Not due to a fear of the man himself or a lack of confidence, but for fear his own eyes might betray the ugliness, defiance, and hostility there was within them. Almost like refraining from shining a flashlight directly into somebody's eyes or shaking somebody's hand when his hand was dirty.

He inhaled deeply. Exhaled.

***

Nasir Khan studied his firstborn, sitting across from him. The boy managed to look both unhealthy and vigorous at the same time. Both capable and vulnerable. Suleiman had half a dozen plasters over his right hand, around the fingers and knuckles, dark circles under his bloodshot eyes, and he avoided eye contact, looking past Nasir instead of directly at him.

But Nasir knew it wasn't fear or timidity. It was something else.

Suleiman's hair was the longest he had seen it, half-groomed, a few strands falling over his face. Nasir's eyes fell on what used to be his son's right ear but was now a misshapen tiny lump of skin the size of a cherry—the result of a particularly nasty street brawl involving knives two years ago in South Africa. An incident that had resulted in his son spending three months in a South African prison.

The trio sat there for a short while, Nasir and his wife asking the usual parental questions.

"How have you been?"

"How are you feeling?"

"Have you eaten anything?"

"Are you still having nightmares?"

"Are you taking your medication?"

Then they updated Suleiman, about the situation with his younger brother in detail.

Suleiman had listened intently throughout, his expression unreadable. Face immobile. But there was clearly a lot going on behind the poker face. He inhaled and leaned back in his chair.

"Ok...ok," he said. Slowly nodding as if he already had the situation under control. He continued, "First things first, does anyone recognize this guy?"

He took his mobile phone out and held the screen up to his parents.

Nasir and his wife studied the picture.

It seemed to be either a still or paused video footage. Nasir recognized the scenery immediately as their front garden. Less clear was the man in the picture, dressed in dark clothes and wearing a cap whose peak was pulled tightly downwards towards his face, casting a shadow over it.

"How did you get this?" Farah asked.

"I'll explain in a bit," said Suleiman. "First, I need to know if you recognize this guy. It's very important."

"I need my glasses," Nasir muttered. "Can't bloody see anything."

Farah squinted, studying the picture intently for a few seconds.

"That… that looks like…Tarik!" she exclaimed.

Nasir took the phone from Suleiman and held it at arm's length. He studied the screen for a few more seconds before his face lit up in agreement with his wife. "You're right. That is him."

Farah nodded. "Look at the nose. The cheeks. Yes, that's definitely him."

"Who's Tarik?" Suleiman inquired.

"Kamran's friend from school and now uni," Farah replied.

"Tell me everything you know about him."

"Well…he studies journalism at uni, a couple of years older than Kamran, I think. But his closest friend. They've been inseparable since secondary school. I've met his parents a few times, really nice people. They visited just the other day after they'd found out Kamran disappeared. Tarik was with them. He didn't say much, just seemed really upset and withdrawn," Farah said.

"What else?" Suleiman asked.

"Let's see… oh… if I remember correctly, he works part-time at the Co-Op across from the uni, I remember Kamran saying. It was only a month or two ago, so chances are he still works there."

"I take it he still lives at home with his parents?"

"Yes, I think so."

Suleiman nodded slowly. Contemplating. Nasir could see a plan already formulating behind his son's eyes.

As much as Nasir's proud, dominant, alpha-male personality hated to admit it, he knew that if it ever came to physical violence, his son would come out on top. No question about it. Even the thirty-year-old version of himself wouldn't stand much of a chance. As tough and capable as Nasir knew himself to be, the boy was something else entirely.

One in a million. He could see it in his eyes. Training, physical fitness, age, and all else being equal, it would be the boy's spirit and determination that would win it in the end. He was the type of individual who would still try to beat you with his teeth if you cut off his limbs. He simply had no quit in him—just pure determination and aggression.

But Nasir knew that underneath the toughness and the ferocity, his son had a good heart and a fierce love. When he contacted him earlier that day, a few hours after midnight, knowing he would be awake at that hour, informing him of the situation with Kamran, Suleiman had not hesitated. His car in the garage for repairs, he had instantly booked the first available coach and travelled the four-hour journey to meet them.

"So, how did you get that picture then anyway?" Nasir asked.

"It's not a picture," said Suleiman. "It's paused CCTV footage. I had a former colleague of mine from MI6, years ago, install it all around the outside of the house without any of you knowing. The footage streams and saves directly to a special app on my phone, which I can access whenever and wherever I want. With all the unsavory individuals I've tangled with over the years, I wasn't going to leave this place unmonitored. Especially with all the time, I spend away.

"And after you told me on the phone about the letter that was posted through our letterbox, I put in the rough time and date, and before long, found our friend Tarik in the footage, posting the note through our door and quickly scurrying off. So, if anyone knows where Kam is, it's him."

***

Suleiman's mother and father exchanged subtle glances of pride. He could see a sudden change in their demeanor. They seemed a little hopeful for the first time. Their spirits lifted ever so slightly.

The dining room door flew open, and Suleiman's youngest brother burst in with purpose. He froze in his tracks, and his eyes widened with surprise when he saw Suleiman sitting at the table.

"Mosh," said Suleiman, smiling and nodding at his brother.

Mosh stood by the doorway as if he had forgotten why he had come in. His deep-set eyes appeared much older than his mere sixteen years. The innocence of youth that had always been in them had disappeared.

"Hey," he replied unenthusiastically and hastily broke eye contact.

"You ok?" Suleiman asked.

Mosh quickly scurried past the dining table with his head down and picked up a rucksack off the floor. "Yeah, just going out."

"Where're you going?"

"Gym."

"Nice, I was just going to say you're looking a bit bigger."

Mosh gave a weak smile and nodded. There was an awkward silence for a moment.

"Anyway," said Suleiman. "We'll catch up when you get back, yeah?"

"Yeah. Cool," said Mosh flatly and hurried out of the room.

Silence, again, permeated the room for a few seconds until Suleiman said, "He blames me, doesn't he?"

His parents shifted uncomfortably. Then his mother spoke. "He's young, sweetheart. This is all very overwhelming for him. He's always looked up to you, almost like a superhero. Wanted to be like you. So did Kamran. I think he's got it in his mind that if you had been home, this would never have happened. That, somehow, something like this could never happen on your watch."

It was Suleiman's turn to shift in his seat.

"What are you going to do, son?" His father asked, hastily changing the subject.

Suleiman paused, then said, "It's best you don't know."

"I don't care what he does," said his mother, eyes glistening with tears. "You do whatever it takes."

As his parents rose from the dining table and left the room, Suleiman picked up his phone, swiped the screen a few times, and held it to his ear. He heard the dial tone ring three times before a rough, deep voice answered.

"Hello, my friend. Back from the dead, I see! Finally, had enough of sitting in your PJs, crying, eating ice cream, and watching chick flicks like a little bitch?"

"Mitch?"

"No. It's Mary bloody Poppins."

"I'm calling in a favour, brother."

"About time. What do you need?"

"You. You and your toys…"

The man on the other end of the line let out a dry but satisfied laugh. "Let's play, Sul… let's play."

Day 3: Saturday

Darren Mitchell, or "Mitch," was Suleiman's closest friend. A few years older than Suleiman, they had been colleagues in the military, then MI6. They had gotten each other out of countless sticky situations and saved each other's lives on various occasions.

Suleiman wasn't sure whether Mitch currently owed him or if he owed Mitch. It didn't matter. They were brothers in arms. Thick as thieves. Each man was always available at a moment's notice for the other.

Mitch had been dismissed from MI6 for gross misconduct soon after Suleiman had and had narrowly avoided prison.

He had always been a loose cannon, a free spirit, and he wouldn't change for anybody. Not even Her Majesty's Secret Services. And so, he now earned a living as a professional problem solver. A "Fixer." A kind of private investigator/security specialist/enforcer/mercenary hybrid. He would sell the vast number of skills he had acquired over a decade in the military and espionage field as a service to anybody willing to pay for it.

It hadn't taken long for Suleiman to gain enough knowledge about Tarik to organize a kidnapping. It amazed him how freely people today surrendered their personal information for the whole world to see. There was an era during which a person would write personal thoughts, feelings, and events in a personal diary and become enraged if another person read it without permission. Now, people would publicize their entire life on social media and become upset if others didn't read it.

Though Suleiman had an active Facebook account, he had very little personal information displayed on it, had rigorous security settings, and only kept his account active for situations such as this.

After the phone call to Mitch the previous evening, Suleiman logged on to Facebook, and after a quick skim of his own bland, rarely updated profile page, he typed in Tarik's full name in the search bar.

There were numerous search results, but Suleiman's target was the first on the list. He recognized the profile picture as his man immediately. After a fifteen-minute study and analysis of Tarik's profile, including his past statuses, posts, pictures, comments, and location check-ins, Suleiman deduced that Tarik would start work at the CO-OP at 5 PM on Saturday and finish at 10 PM. Also, he commuted to and from work on his moped. Suleiman had then decided that he would intercept him as he was leaving after the end of his shift, as opposed to his arrival at the start. This would afford them the cover of darkness and less interference or potential witnesses from busy streets full of vehicles and passers-by.

Suleiman then contacted Mitch and, this time asked him to prepare one of his unmarked, untraceable vans, balaclavas, two Glock 9mm handguns with live ammunition, and some tools.

***

It was ten minutes to ten. Suleiman sat in the front passenger seat, next to Mitch, in his van.

They had parked in the CO-OP car park. It was almost deserted, with only a handful of vehicles littered around sporadically, most of which probably belonged to the remaining staff members on shift. The plan was for Suleiman to exit the van and intercept Tarik whilst he concentrated on starting the moped. Driving right up to him and jumping out wouldn't work like it did in the movies. The car park was too quiet. Too desolate. Seeing a strange van approaching would be too conspicuous. Tarik might be alerted and make a run for it.

After grabbing Tarik, Suleiman would carry — or drag— him to the van. Mitch would be behind the wheel, as he currently was, with the engine running. As soon as Suleiman grabbed Tarik, Mitch would drive towards them to close the distance. Suleiman would then bundle him into the vehicle, and they would drive to a desolate location and have as much time as they needed to extract information from Tarik.

He was only a uni kid, barely out of school. Not a hardened criminal or agent. Therefore, it was very likely that the shock and trauma of the situation alone, along with a few threats added for good measure, would be sufficient to loosen his tongue. The guns and tools were mainly just for show and partly a precaution for unplanned incidents. An intimidation tactic. They wouldn't need to resort to physical violence. Hopefully.

Mitch had parked parallel, one row behind, and six bays along from the parking bay where Tarik's Moped was and directly facing the exit of the car park and the front entrance of the shop, twenty yards away.

Had they parked any further, the interception risked becoming sloppy with more distance to cover, meaning more chance for something to go wrong and longer exposure. Any closer, they risked spooking Tarik before he even reached his vehicle, especially at this time of night with so few vehicles in the car park.

Suleiman had briefly surveilled the shop earlier in the day to confirm Tarik would be there. There was always the chance he would call in sick or not come in due to other unforeseen circumstances. He might have even booked the night off or recently decided to resign.

But, sure enough, Tarik arrived five minutes before the start of his shift, and, satisfied, Suleiman returned home and prepared for the night ahead.

It was now five minutes to ten, and the two men sat in the van, facing the shop's front entrance. The van's headlights were switched off, but the engine was running, making a smooth, quiet purring vibration. The soft sound of the engine was deliberately chosen for its inconspicuousness.

The CO-OP was all but empty, and Suleiman could see staff members through the glass doors and windows, every minute or so, appearing then disappearing from his line of sight, mopping, cleaning, stacking items, and frantically trying to finish their remaining tasks for the night so they could leave on time. He even spotted Tarik a few times, breathing a sigh of relief, thankful his target hadn't left early for some reason.

This had to be done tonight. Time was of the essence. The longer his little brother was with that cult, the higher the likelihood of him refusing to return, whether in body or mind or both.

Three minutes to ten.

The frantic movement in the CO-OP had now stopped, and the automatic metal window shutters began to descend, inch by inch. The front entrance shutter was still open, so the staff members could exit. The lights were still on but wouldn't be for long.

"Get ready," said Suleiman, pulling on his balaclava.

Mitch nodded, pulling his balaclava on over his head. "Let's do it."

Dressed in black from head to toe, Suleiman jumped out of the van and hurried around to the back, crouching, out of sight to anybody in front of the van, only his left eye visible through the left eyehole of the balaclava as it peered out, watching, waiting for the moment. His heart rate barely rose. The stakes weren't high enough with all he had experienced and seen over the last decade. A defenseless uni kid outside of a quiet CO-OP in a quiet car park? And on the other side, two armed, extremely capable, and seasoned operatives? His adrenaline receptors were fried. Burnt out. Desensitized. It took a lot for Suleiman's adrenaline to begin pumping. He couldn't remember the last time his hands and legs had shaken.

But no matter. It was an advantage. Although adrenaline took blood away from the vital organs, blunted pain, slowed down the perception of time, and primed you to fight or flee, it also tended to affect performance and degrade hand-eye coordination and clarity of thought, among other faculties. A lack of it would make things run smoother.

Two minutes to ten.

All the CO-OP lights had now been switched off, and the staff members began leaving the building. There were four of them in total. One girl looked to be around her late teens, an older lady who appeared to be in her fifties or sixties, a middle-aged man... and Tarik.

Tarik waved his colleagues goodbye and walked towards his moped. He glanced briefly at the van parked a few bays across from it, but with its headlights off and its tinted windows and the indiscernible sound of the running engine, it must have looked unoccupied to him, and he probably thought nothing of it.

The other three staff members had stopped just outside the front entrance of the CO-OP for a quick chat, forming a semi-circle with the middle-aged man in the middle. His demeanor, body language, presence, and the way the other two responded and interacted with him told Suleiman he was probably a manager. There was definitely something about him. He looked fit. Whippy. Serious and intelligent eyes emitting strong "Don't mess with me" vibes. He could potentially be a problem.

But they were not moving. The manager seemed to be giving the other two instructions before they went their separate ways, perhaps plans for the following day or discussion about the day's events just passed.

Good, Suleiman thought. No immediate interference from that distance. The girl and the older woman would not intervene. That only left the manager as a possible obstacle who, if he chose to intervene, would have to first recover from the initial shock of what was happening. This would take a second or two. Then another five or six seconds to cover the twenty yards to the space between the moped and the van.

The kid looked light. Probably around ten stone. By the time the manager arrived at the scene, Suleiman and his target would be more than halfway to the van.

Tarik reached his vehicle. He secured his rucksack and began to unstrap his crash helmet, ready to wear.

Suleiman made his move.

He leaped out from behind the van like an Olympic sprinter and swiftly, but quietly, like a cat, covered the ten yards between the van and Tarik. Tarik had his back to Suleiman, so he didn't notice the black-clad figure racing towards him like a silent, sinister bat out of hell until it was too late.

Just as Tarik turned to the sound of rapid footsteps, Suleiman grabbed him from behind, with his right arm around Tarik's throat in a rear-naked chokehold, and his left arm scooped under Tarik's left leg, lifting him off the ground and carrying him, almost horizontally, like a roll of carpet.

"What the—!" Tarik yelped in shock, dropping his helmet, fighting, kicking, and squirming, but to no avail against his attacker's python-like grip.

The teenage girl screamed and pointed.

The older woman froze.

The manager did not hesitate.

The one or two seconds of frozen shock Suleiman had predicted did not actuate.

"OI!" he bellowed. Bolting towards them like a greyhound. "LET HIM GO!"

Suleiman sighed. He had hoped for this to be quick and clean. No blood. No broken bones. But this now seemed highly unlikely.

Skipping the shock and freeze phase, the manager reached Suleiman and Tarik before they had even covered half the distance to the van. He immediately grabbed Suleiman in a headlock with one arm and repeatedly punched him in the head with the other, shouting and cursing, demanding Suleiman release his captive.

Hands occupied, refusing to release his grip on Tarik, Suleiman began kicking and shoving at the manager. The three men became a tangle of limbs, almost like a Loony Toons cartoon... until a deep, rough voice shouted, "STOP!"

Mitch.

He stood between the skirmish and the van, three or four yards away, black-clad, with a ball hammer in his hand. The duo had agreed that they would not use or even brandish the Glocks before arriving at the planned location unless it was absolutely necessary. A couple of thugs with hammers and balaclavas kidnapping somebody in the south of the UK? Already a fairly big deal for the police. But add in guns with live ammunition in a country as gun-free as this, and the whole department would be after them: helicopters, dogs, and armed response units. It would enter a whole new level, and they didn't need or have time for that level of heat.

Suleiman, Tarik, and the manager stopped struggling and froze in their positions, breathing hard, gathering their bearings. Suleiman still had Tarik around the neck and under one leg, the other leg barely touching the ground. The manager still had Suleiman in a headlock.

"OI! Hero!" shouted Mitch. "This ain't gonna end well for you, mate. Let him go, or you're gonna get hurt!"

The manager was defiant. He didn't move. "I'm ex-forces, mate! I didn't fight for this country, so that scum like you could run riot in the streets! Walk away now, or you'll be the ones who get hurt!"

Wrong answer.

Suleiman could feel Mitch grinning behind the balaclava. He was enjoying this. Sure enough, he let out a loud, dry laugh, mocking the former soldier. "Ha! This ain't Baghdad, bud. Where's your rifle? Where's your medevac? Air support? Eh? You think a few hours of hand-to-hand combat drills makes you a proper scrapper? You're in way over your head, fella! Last chance. Let him go and step away." He spoke the last sentence ominously. Like a countdown had ended.

The situation had already lasted longer than anticipated and was quickly spiraling out of control. The two female staff members hadn't moved from the shop entrance. The older woman was frantically speaking on her mobile phone to what was surely the police, and the younger woman had her phone held out in front of her, horizontally, recording the action.

Had it not been for fear of Tarik escaping, Suleiman would have released him for a second or two and made short work of the former soldier. But Tarik was too important at this juncture. Too valuable. If he managed to get away, it would be nearly impossible to chase, relocate and abduct him with the police, who were probably already on their way, trawling the streets.

They had to leave.

Now.

Suleiman acted fast. Like a cat on speed, he released his hold on Tarik, grabbed him, and threw him at Mitch with all the strength he could muster. Mitch caught Tarik and held him in another rear naked choke hold with his free arm, the ball hammer still in the other. Wasting no time, Suleiman, still restrained in the headlock, bent down and violently lifted the ex-soldier's legs from underneath him, and they both thudded down backwards onto the tarmac with Suleiman on top, head now free of the hold. The ex-soldier lay there, dazed from the impact of Suleiman's entire one hundred kilos of bone and muscle, slamming him into the ground. Suleiman then struck his jaw with a savage elbow for good measure.

Mitch threw Tarik back to Suleiman. "Get in the van. I'll be right behind you."

"What the hell are you doing, man?" exclaimed Suleiman, holding on to Tarik. "Let's go!"

Mitch ignored Suleiman and hurried over to the ex-soldier, who was groaning, bravely trying to get up to continue to fight the good fight, but in vain. Mitch

S. I. ALMANZA

raised the ball hammer and brought it down viciously on the man's left kneecap.

"Mitch! DON'T!" Suleiman yelled.

Mitch raised the hammer again and brought it down on the other kneecap.

The ex-soldier roared in pain, and there were high-pitched screams and protests of shock and horror from the staff members at the shop entrance. The older woman shouted, "LEAVE HIM ALONE! The police are on their way right now!"

Mitch lifted the hammer for the third and final time.

Suleiman swore and screamed at the top of his lungs, voice full of fury and venom, "MITCH! GET IN THE GODDAMNED VAN NOW! DON'T DO IT!"

The hammer came crashing down again, this time on the ex-soldier's forehead. It cracked open and dark liquid poured out, quickly forming a pool on the tarmac. He lay there, no longer screaming. Motionless.

"Not such a big man now, are you? Soldier boy." Mitch gloated at his handiwork, gave a mock salute, and rushed back to the van, passing Suleiman and Tarik, shrugging. "In case he tried to follow us."

***

It was a little after 11 PM. Tarik sat on an old, battered chair with his hands zip-tied behind his back. He was a small kid with a distinctive face: hollow cheeks and an

261

aquiline nose. He was visibly shaken, dazed and confused.

Suleiman stood in front of him, face still covered by the balaclava. Mitch was outside, keeping watch.

They were in a decrepit, abandoned warehouse on the outskirts of the city. The operation hadn't gone as smoothly as planned, but at least they had achieved their objective. They had also managed to avoid police and, to their knowledge, had left no evidence at the scene.

But there was, of course, the minor fact that Suleiman had committed a silly schoolboy error and shouted Mitch's name on a couple of occasions. But that wouldn't be much of a problem. "Mitch" was, of course, an abbreviation. That much would be obvious to an investigator or anyone with common sense. But it was an abbreviation of his surname. Most people were called by an abbreviation of their first name, not their last.

Add to that the fact that it was a common name and that Mitch lived in another city. An investigator would probably assume that any names used verbally or otherwise in such an operation would be codenames designed to hide the perpetrators' real identity anyway. And in the unlikely event, it was traced back to Mitch, who had only managed to operate freely up until now by always covering his tracks with the utmost diligence. There would be no solid proof or evidence against him.

What had disturbed Suleiman more was Mitch's behavior with the manager. The former soldier was only doing what he had thought was right. His actions had been downright heroic. He hadn't deserved what had happened to him.

Mitch had always been a loose cannon, but Suleiman had never seen him do something of this sort. He had possibly killed a man who had no longer been a threat. After Suleiman had incapacitated the man, he would have been in no position to recover quickly enough to get into his vehicle, assuming he had one to follow them, as Mitch had remarked.

Even if he had been, the first hammer to the kneecap would have been sufficient in neutralizing that threat. Certainly, the second kneecap. But the final blow to the head had been an act of utter, premeditated savagery for which there was no need. The man could quite possibly be dead for simply selflessly attempting to assist his fellow man.

Of course, they hadn't had a chance to speak about this during the journey, as Mitch had been driving and Suleiman sat in the back, guarding Tarik. But they would have to, at some point.

"Wh... who are you people? What do you want from me? I haven't done anything!" Tarik cried. Trembling. Visibly terrified.

Suleiman wasted no time with preambles or theatrics. He cut straight to the point.

"Tarik. Listen," he said. "Listen very, very carefully to what I'm saying. I know who you are. I know you're intimately familiar with the individual I've been tasked with finding and bringing home. He's a close friend and classmate of yours. Kamran Khan."

A look of recognition flashed across Tarik's face. But he said nothing.

Suleiman continued, "Good. I haven't got time for pathetic attempts at denial and pretend ignorance, so you're doing well so far. Now, I don't want to hurt you. But believe me, I will if you lie to me or refuse to tell me what I want to know. Now, as I know you're aware, Kamran has joined some kind of a cult."

Tarik nodded. Smart enough not to feign ignorance.

"We have you, on video, delivering the note Kamran left for his family, explaining why he left. All I want to know is where this group is based, who they are and what they're about."

Tarik hesitated.

Suleiman held his breath. He was nervous. He prayed Tarik possessed some useful information. The whole operation had been a long shot from the start. It was a hail-Mary. A lead he was following simply because it happened to be the only lead he had.

There was always the possibility that Tarik knew nothing. Kam may have simply handed his closest friend and most trusted confidant a sealed envelope with instructions to post it through his door on a specific date, instructing him not to open or read the letter himself. He might not even have informed Tarik of what the whole situation was about and that he planned to leave home to join a cult.

But Tarik needn't know this. Suleiman had to project certainty and act as if he knew with full confidence that Tarik knew everything. Because if by some chance he did, he had to be given the impression that lying wouldn't get him anywhere and that the masked man in front of him knew without a doubt that he had the knowledge and would do whatever he had to to extract it from him.

"Look. I posted that note! I'm not going to deny that. But I swear that's it! I didn't even read it. He just gave it to me a few days before he left and told me to post it on the day I did!" Tarik pleaded.

Suleiman stared coldly. His gaze pierced right through Tarik, studying him, attempting to penetrate his mind and unsettle him psychologically. He could feel his energy exuding and pouring out onto Tarik. Barely contained rage.

"OK," Suleiman said. "I don't care about what you've done or not done. Just tell me where he is. And who these people are."

"I don't know!"

Suleiman narrowed his eyes. The kid was lying. He was no trained agent, that much was obvious, probably not a sleeper cell for the cult, but he was still hiding something.

"Fine," said Suleiman matter-of-factly. "I guess we're going to have to go to that nasty place I said I didn't want to go to." He reached into his pocket and pulled out a black Stanley Skeleton Liner lock knife.

"Please..." Tarik pleaded, eyes widening, fixed on the knife.

"I'll be generous," said Suleiman. "Three choices. Left eye, right eye... or the truth." He bent forward and displayed the knife in front of Tarik's face menacingly. But a sudden jolt of searing pain shot through his head.

The room was stuffy, starved of air. He could smell blood, stale sweat, and tobacco.

"Do it! He's a spy! A traitor! Worthless scum. Cut the dog's head off. Do it slowly."

The hunting knife in Suleiman's hand shook, he didn't want to do it, but he had to. A dozen armed men surrounded him. If he didn't proceed, his cover would be blown. What they were asking him to do to the prisoner would pale compared to what they would do to him. More importantly, the mission would fail, and the prisoner would die regardless.

He held the knife to the man's throat and looked in his eyes. Terror, hopelessness and sadness looked back at him.

Suleiman began to cut and saw, blood spurting onto his face, screams of unbearable pain filling his ears.

"The Excitatus."

The words brought Suleiman back to reality. He found himself leaning on a pillar with one hand and holding his head with the other. The knife lay on the floor near Tarik's feet. He gathered his bearings for a moment.

"What?"

"The Excitatus. Latin for 'The Awakened.' It's what they call themselves."

Suleiman walked to Tarik, who looked a little calmer now, picked up the knife, and slipped it back into his pocket, head still throbbing from the flashback.

"I'm listening."

"They're a cult. I don't know exactly when they were formed, but it wasn't that long ago. Their leader is a man who calls himself Nathaniel. A billionaire. On the outside, they're like a cross between the Amish and the Doomsday Preppers. They believe the world is ending soon, maybe by the end of the century. They believe that it is all corrupt and filthy and that we should spend what little time we have left living a pure life away from all the 'chaos and filth.' Apart from their inner circle, nobody uses modern technology, electricity, internet, and so on.

"It doesn't sound too bad on the surface, except they've been suspected of dozens of abductions up and down the country over the past couple of years. Men, women, and even children. Amongst various other crimes. But they're smart. Careful. There's never enough evidence to justify the authorities going in with a warrant. They've even let investigative journalists and police in voluntarily."

"So why have these journalists and cops not exposed them?"

"Why do you think? There's nothing to expose if you let them in voluntarily. Think about it. When you invite guests round to your house, you know exactly when they're going to show up. You tidy the place before they get there. Bring out the best silverware. Hide anything you don't want other people to see. Even your behavior. You don't swear, abuse your wife, beat your kids in front of the guests, and leave empty beer bottles and rubbish lying around, do you? Even if that's what you usually do when guests aren't there. And as guests, they're not going to go into any part of the house you don't allow them to go to. Living room, dining room, and restroom, maybe. But you're not going to let them snoop around your bedroom or your basement or anywhere else where you have private, or illegal or questionable things hidden. Same thing here but on a larger scale.

"There're three types of people in there. The elite, as in, the leader and those who work for him. The voluntary residents like Kam, who choose to be there and think they're doing the right thing. And the prisoners. As long as the prisoners are hidden when someone goes to investigate, along with anything else illegal, then there's no evidence of any wrongdoing."

Suleiman furrowed his brow. Brooding. He felt better than he had a few minutes ago. Like a weight had been lifted off his shoulders. Even excited. His worst fear had been that this would be a dead end. But the kid was a legitimate lead. He was definitely in the loop, and Suleiman would wring him dry for information.

"So why are they still active?" continued Suleiman.

"What?"

"I mean, if you know all this, then you've either been living there as one of those three categories of people, which I doubt, or someone told you. And if someone told you, then they could just as easily tell the authorities and get the whole place shut down, couldn't they?"

Tarik shook his head rapidly, frustrated. "It's not that simple. It's much bigger than that. You have no idea how powerful they are. How deep it goes. They have agents everywhere. Sleepers. Government, police, NHS, military, media. Even churches, mosques, schools, colleges, and universities. I mean, it wouldn't even surprise me if one of them works at the CO-OP with me or serves me coffee in the morning. It starts right from the very top and ends right at the bottom.

"I'm not saying that the poxy five to ten acres of land this cult leader owns and operates in is the base of all this power and that he's the head of the snake. No. What I'm saying is that he's one branch, one tentacle of a much larger monster with many tentacles just like him. And if you try and cut off or attack this one tentacle, then you will only anger the rest of the monster, and it will come and destroy you and everything you hold dear.

"A few have spoken out. Or at least tried to. Three disillusioned former members. And they're just the ones I know of."

"What happened to them?" asked Suleiman, already knowing the gist of the answer.

"One was found stabbed to death a hundred meters from the local police station. Probably on his way to it. Another 'jumped' off the roof of his flat, and the last one, the one who told me all this, mysteriously disappeared off the face of the Earth two weeks ago. Before he disappeared, I spoke with him a few times, only over the phone. And he would only call from pay phones.

"He would call me from a different pay phone every day. Extremely paranoid. I could feel his terror over the phone. Hear it in his voice. He sounded like he was losing it. Sometimes he would cry uncontrollably. I could almost see him tearing his hair out.

"He told me he was being followed constantly. Everywhere. From the moment he left his home every day to the moment he returned, there would be somebody in the shadows, lurking, watching. Even at home, he would sit there with the curtains closed, afraid to communicate using his mobile, landline, or even the internet, convinced they would be monitoring every word. Afraid to contact the authorities, knowing there would be at least a few of them planted in every department.

"That's how they operate. On the surface, they make it look like every member has the freedom to leave whenever they want. And they do. But as soon as someone does leave, they put them under constant surveillance and when they think the time is right, get rid of them."

"So, who was he? How did you know him? Why did he come to you and not someone else?"

"He was a good friend of mine. He trusted me and knew I study journalism. Journalism means I like a good story. I have a thirst for exposing the truth. More importantly, journalism means I know people. Have a lot of contacts and ways of getting the truth out there."

"So how did Kam… Kamran get involved in all this?" asked Suleiman, hoping Tarik hadn't noticed his stumble.

"A classmate at uni."

Suleiman raised his eyebrows underneath the mask.

"Like I said," continued Tarik. "They're everywhere. Kam started becoming more and more distant from me and our other uni mates. He, this classmate, and a few other kids began their own little clique.

"I knew something was wrong. Kam's smart. Very smart. And they say the smart ones are the easiest to brainwash. Something about them having a lack of narrow-mindedness. Open to new ideas in order to learn and expand that intellect. You give an idiot a new idea with a logical train of thought, he'll reject it because he thinks he's smart and already knows it all. That's what makes him an idiot. He knows what he knows. Any new thought strains his limited brain capacity. Whatever side of the fence he was born and raised on, that's where he'll stay. If he was born and raised in this cult, for example, he'll stay in that cult. If he was born and raised outside of it, he'll never go into it. He's stationary. Stubborn.

"But an intelligent person can be swayed and convinced to hop over to the other side of the fence. An intelligent person acknowledges how little he really knows and wants to know more. Therefore, opens himself up and becomes vulnerable to new, sometimes dangerous ideas, as long as these ideas are well constructed with evidence, a logical thought process, and conclusion."

"And as his closest friend, you didn't try to stop him?" asked Suleiman, a hint of accusation in his tone.

"I didn't know! People drift in and out of friendships all the time. They go through phases. That's life. I knew something was up, but I never dreamed he would do something like this!"

Suleiman scoffed. "Even when he gave you a mysterious envelope with instructions to post it through his door on a specific date?"

Tarik hesitated. "I… look…I told you. He's smart. I had a lot of respect for him. I still do. He spun me a convincing story about needing to go away for a few days to sort something out and made me promise to post the envelope and not open it myself. He assured me he would explain it all when he got back. I trusted him more than anyone and have never known him to lie, so I respected his privacy and didn't ask too many questions."

For the first time, Suleiman sensed that Tarik wasn't telling him the entire truth. But it didn't matter.

Judging Tarik was not the objective. All Suleiman needed to know now was the location of the cult's compound and any other details that might help him rescue his brother.

They spoke a little while longer. Tarik informed him of the compound's location, size, and the rough layout, among other details. His knowledge was limited as he could only re-iterate what he had been told by the former member he had spoken to over the phone. But it was enough. At least Suleiman now knew where he needed to go.

Suleiman took out his knife again, but this time he bent over Tarik and cut his restraints. "I think we're done here."

Tarik looked a little relieved but still apprehensive. He rubbed his wrists where the restraints had been. "So, what now?"

"Now? Well, I'm going to go and finish the job I was hired to do. I'm going to bring my..." another stupid slip, "your friend home and slaughter anybody who gets in my way."

"What about me?" Tarik asked hesitantly, afraid of the answer.

"You can go back to your life, working at the CO-OP, exposing the truth and posting mysterious letters through friends' doors without reading them, and posting what you had for dinner on Facebook and Instagram and whatever else you like doing."

Tarik said nothing.

"You'll have to walk home, I'm afraid. We'll give you your belongings back so you can use your phone and "google maps" the way home. It will take you a few hours, but I'm sure you can appreciate that we can't give you a lift back, especially after your colleague called the police and reported the whole thing, meaning we can't risk being pulled over by the cops and being seen with you or that van. Or feel free to call a Taxi once you get far enough away from here."

"Yeah, and especially after you beat my manager potentially to death with a hammer."

Suleiman felt a sudden pang of guilt and anger. "That wasn't my doing. My partner can get a little excited sometimes. That was very unprofessional of him, and it shouldn't have happened. I sincerely hope your manager is OK, and I will be having some severe words with my partner.

"But having said that, you even think of going to the police about any of this, you don't know who we are or what we look like, and we've covered our tracks well, so they'll never find us. But we know who you are, where you work, what you look like, where you study, and even where you live.

"So, believe me, when I tell you, I will find someone even worse than my partner, pay him a couple of hundred quid, to find you and make what happened to your manager look like a picnic. Or scratch that, I'll find somebody to do it for free just for the sheer pleasure of it. Are we clear?"

Tarik nodded. Convinced.

"Good. Come with me. We'll get you your things back, and you can go," said Suleiman.

As Tarik got up and walked towards the exit, he stopped for a moment. He turned and looked at Suleiman as if he wanted to say something but wasn't sure if he should.

"What is it?" asked Suleiman.

"Two things."

"Go on."

"Firstly, if you're one of them, if this whole thing is a setup and they've sent you to pose as a rescuer for Kam, in order to find out how much I know about them, please rest assured that everything I've told you is just pure hearsay.

"I've got no proof of anything, and I'm not planning on doing anything or saying anything to anyone. Not that anyone would believe it even if I did. I know what your organization is capable of, so even if I had the proof, I wouldn't dare do anything with it. I won't make any problems for you, I swear. I'm a nobody. You've seen for yourself I'm just a uni student who works part-time at a CO-OP.

"If they've sent you to vet Kam by interrogating his closest friend under the guise of finding him

S. I. ALMANZA

because they're suspicious of newcomers and want to find out everything about them. Then all I can say is that you've read the letter he made me post to his family. So, you can see how serious and dedicated he is to your cause. Please treat him well and don't hurt him."

Suleiman looked at Tarik for a few moments, then said, "Relax. If I were one of them and wanted to kill you, right here would have been the best time and place to do it. What was the second thing?"

"If you really are who you say you are, some kind of professional bounty hunter or something, then I don't care how much they're paying you. It won't be enough. All the money in the world wouldn't be enough because you won't live to see it.

"The fact that Kam wants to be there makes your job even harder. It won't be a rescue mission. More like another kidnapping. You should forget about this one job and move on. As much as I want Kam back home, it's not going to happen. They will kill you. And they'll do it slowly to make an example."

Suleiman smiled beneath the mask.

"I died a long time ago…. I just haven't been buried yet."

Day 4: Sunday

It had all gone wrong.

So utterly, horribly wrong.

How could he have been so stupid? So defenseless and unprepared? So oblivious to reality?

Suleiman stood, naked from the waist up, with his toes barely touching the ground. His arms were stretched above his head, chained by the wrists, attached to one of the thick wooden beams going horizontally from wall to wall above him. His hair was a bloody, matted, tangled mess and sat plastered all around his face. His nose was bleeding profusely, coupled with swelling around his left eye, and he felt like one of his ribs was broken.

The entire mission had failed before it had even begun, and Suleiman was in the dark, staring at a locked door, contemplating the gravity of his situation and the grim, inescapable depths of his failure.

Twenty-Four Hours Ago

After Suleiman had cut Tarik loose and torched the kidnap van, destroying all evidence of the preceding events of that night, he drove, with Mitch, to Mitch's home using the backup vehicle they had stored at the abandoned warehouse before the abduction. Once there, Suleiman ate, showered, rested, and discussed options and strategies with Mitch.

For a brief moment, Suleiman had thought of going in, Old Testament, all guns blazing. Contacting a few operatives and going in as a team, armed to the teeth, decimating anyone who got in their way, and bringing home Kam against his will if necessary. But he realized immediately that this was an extremely unwise strategy.

They would be going in completely blind. He didn't know whether the upper echelons of the cult were armed, their numbers, or the layout of the whole compound. Tarik had either not possessed or provided this information. It would be messy. Lives would be lost, some innocent, and the authorities would be called. Even if they managed to evade the authorities, rescue Kam and bring him home, which was extremely unlikely anyway, they would all become fugitives, wanted for firearms possession, usage, and murder, amongst various other crimes.

So, they concluded that infiltration would be the best strategy. Suleiman would go in alone and unarmed, posing as a new member. He would play the long game. Embed himself into their society. Talk face to face with Kam and perhaps, over time, deradicalize him and bring him home. They were, after all, free to leave any time. As for what came after, they would cross that bridge when they came to it.

The worst-case scenario would be that he would be unable to convince Kam to come home or to extract him alone. But at least he would have spent days or weeks gaining crucial, first-hand information about the place, so he could leave and formulate a new plan, armed with all the knowledge he needed to organize a forceful extraction.

And so, Mitch provided Suleiman with false documents, including a passport and birth certificate. Going in with his real name and address would arouse suspicion as this information would match his brother's. If both brothers had arrived at the same time, it would have been less suspect. But an older brother arriving at the gates a couple of weeks after his younger brother had? A diligent or paranoid sceptic would quite easily put two and two together. And this organization was anything but careless.

With the documents and a few other essentials packed in a large sports bag, and after discussing what Suleiman's cover story and fake persona would be, Mitch drove Suleiman five hours to the grassy hinterlands of the far north of England. They stopped a mile away from the compound and buried a mobile phone under a tree, marking the trunk, engraving it with a knife. The cult would not allow any electronic items to be brought in by members.

Once Suleiman had escaped with Kam, whether in a few days or weeks from now, the buried phone would be excavated and used by Suleiman to contact Mitch, who would collect him from that location.

Suleiman left his phone with Mitch after making a quick call to his mother. He was careful not to reveal too much, both for his family's safety and his own. The details of the mission had to be sealed, airtight. Only Mitch and he could know. So, he merely told his mother to be patient, not to worry, and that he would have Kam home in less than a month.

The two men stood by the tree. Suleiman handed the folding shovel to Mitch and wiped his hands on his trousers.

"What's up, bro?" said Mitch.

"What?"

"Look like something's on your mind. It ain't nerves about the mission, I know you. It's somethin' else."

Suleiman's eyes bored into Mitch's, but he said nothing.

"Well? Go on, spit it out, man, you've gotta get goin' soon. Whatever it is, unload it. You don't want it buggin' you when you're in there, gettin' Kam. You need focus, a clear mind. So, tell me now."

Suleiman still did not speak.

"It ain't that Zahra chick, is it?" said Mitch, grinning. "I know you're an ugly bastard, mate, but I'm sure there'll be others."

Suleiman did not return the grin but said, "Why did you have to go so OTT with that guy outside the CO-OP? He was down. Neutralized. He was in no shape to get up and cause any more problems."

Mitch laughed dismissively. "Come on, man, really?"

"I'm serious. The guy was just doing the right thing, and you messed him up bad. He could be dead."

"He ain't."

"How do you know?"

"Checked the news."

Suleiman paused for a moment. Then he said, "Even so, you could have killed him, bro. That was wrong."

Mitch sighed, then fixed Suleiman with a steely gaze. "Listen Sul, this ain't about me, or you, or that dumbass good Samaritan back there. This is about your brother. That's the mission. That's all that matters. That guy could easily have got back up after you hit him, jumped in a car, and followed us. He was that type of guy, I can tell. And so can you. I wasn't takin' no chances. I wasn't gonna let anythin' stop us from gettin' your brother back. You're family. That means Kam is too."

**

After bidding farewell to Mitch, Suleiman travelled the last mile to the compound on foot.

He contemplated the difficulty of the mission. He would be going in, unarmed and alone, to an unknown place: right into the lion's den, deep behind enemy lines. His extraction target was there of his own free will. He didn't want to be rescued. But perhaps seeing a familiar face would trigger something in him. Maybe seeing his own flesh and blood brother would open him up to seeing some sense. There was no time limit to this, after all. Suleiman had all the time he needed to infiltrate, then slowly, day by day, work on his brother. Deradicalize him. That would be the 'easy' way— the path of least resistance.

Failing that, he would have to take him, undetected, by force. Calling this the 'Hard' way would be an understatement.

Upon arrival at the front gates, just as the sun began to disappear behind the woods in the far distance behind the compound, he knew immediately that something was wrong.

The two guards at the gates were unarmed, but Suleiman had no doubts that they were professionals. The appearance, the presence, the body language.

But it was how they reacted as soon as they saw him that unsettled him.

They were expecting him.

They made a beeline for him as soon as he came within twenty yards of them, trying his best to look as unassuming as possible. Both moved at the same time, walking briskly and in tandem.

Suleiman stopped walking, raised his hands, and said, "Whoa, easy lads, my name's Reza. I'm here to join. I've got all my paperwork. You can search me. I'm unarmed."

But his words had no effect on the guards, and they continued to move forward like automatons and once they reached him, one of them swung a fist at Suleiman's ribs. Although Suleiman could easily have blocked the blow, he decided within a split second that he would not fight back. Incapacitating or resisting the guards would only make infiltration more difficult. Maybe there was nothing wrong. Maybe this was how they greeted all newcomers, to test them. He would allow them to rough him up so he could continue to act as if his intentions were innocent and play his role. Fighting back would be counterintuitive. And so, he allowed the blow to land squarely on his ribs. He doubled over, coughing and spluttering. Immediately after this, a knee struck him hard in the nose, followed by another fist, crashing into his left cheekbone, knocking him unconscious.

***

Suleiman awoke to two new guards, roughly attaching chains to his wrists, fastened to a wooden rafter above him. He must have been carried into the compound whilst unconscious. He was in a small building that looked like a barn that had been emptied of its animals, stables, and most of its hay but still smelled like a barn.

It was now night, and the barn was dimly lit by half a dozen wall-mounted flame torches scattered around it.

They had stripped him down to just his trousers, pockets emptied, and his sports bag was nowhere to be seen.

When they were satisfied that Suleiman was secured, the guards left the barn, leaving him alone.

A short while later, four men entered the barn.

And Suleiman's blood ran cold.

The first man must have been some kind of a right-hand man to the cult leader, Suleiman thought. Too much presence, too physically formidable and distinctive to have been an average or low-level goon. But too reserved, aloof, and unapproachable to be a charismatic, billionaire cult leader capable of convincing hundreds of men and women to give up their lives and join his cause.

The second man was almost certainly the leader—the big boss himself. Appearing to be in his late forties, with average height, average build, an all-round average, and unremarkable appearance, but exuding a powerful, dark aura, thinly veneered by a bright, charismatic countenance and energy, as if lit up by an invisible spotlight.

The third man caused Suleiman's stomach to jolt with excitement. Young, slim, and short. But dark and intelligent eyes, full of wisdom beyond their years.

It was Kam.

The fourth and final man who entered the room left Suleiman dazed and confused, shocking him to his very core.

The man stood a few inches shorter than Suleiman but was stocky. He was packed with hard, dense muscle. His upper back was particularly well-developed, so much so that it gave him the appearance of a hunch-back. His arms were long, almost like an ape's, slightly disproportionate but also heavily muscled. His face was rugged and angular with a thick, dark stubble, framing a self-satisfied smirk as he gazed at his helpless captive.

Mitch.

Suleiman stared. Shocked, defeated, and betrayed. Mitch. His closest and most trusted ally. It couldn't be. All those years together. All the sacrifices, all the good times. Telling Suleiman how he was family just hours ago.

Mitch's smirk grew. "Aw, don't look so surprised, Sul. Why the long face?"

Suleiman recovered fast. He was not going to give Mitch the satisfaction. He adopted a stoic, controlled front and uttered a single word, "Why?"

Mitch's smirk grew wider. "Why? Well, why not? After I was booted from MI6, there was bugger all I could do. Who would hire me after what I did? Who do you think kept me out of prison? And after all the things guys like you and me have seen and done, delivering pizzas or guarding a building site for the rest of my life just wasn't gonna cut it bro. So, these guys found me. They took me in. It's an amazing life really, Sul. We're the top of the food chain—"

"The food chain?" Suleiman interrupted viciously. "We'll see where you sit on the food chain after I rip your heart out of your chest and eat it in front of you, you dumb son of a—"

"Ah Sul, typical you, mate. Always have to play the hero. Always have to do the right thing. That's the main reason why I never approached you with any of this. We could have done amazing things together, but I knew you would never go for it. Because you always gotta to do the right thing. Family, morals, religion, and all that shit. And look where it's gotten you." He nodded towards Kam. "At least your little brother's got some sense, not some stupid, whiny pussy like you."

Suleiman stared at Kam. His brother had not reacted to the last comment. His face was a mask. No remorse, anger, or sadness. Just a blank canvas. Whoever this kid was in front of Suleiman, he was no longer his brother; that much was certain.

Then the leader spoke. "My name, as I'm sure you already know, Is Nathaniel."

"Couldn't give a shit, mate," replied Suleiman. "Met your sort before. Just another rich scumbag who would be nothing without his money." He was firing himself up. Making himself angrier to counteract the fear and despair he felt. He was breaking all the rules he had been taught and trained in about being held captive. Say little, remain calm, and don't aggravate your captors. But he didn't care. All he felt was anger and hate. He was going to kill these rats. He didn't know how yet. But he would.

Even if he died in the process.

Nathaniel laughed.

"Incredible."

His speech was cultured and refined—a stark contrast to Mitch's common, lowbrow deliverance.

"When my sleeper agent, Mr. Darren Mitchell here, informed me about you, who you were, your formidability, and your brazen plan, and especially after getting to know your impressive, younger sibling here, I must say I was very much eager to meet you. And now that I have, I can say I am not disappointed. You have an inextinguishable fire in you. A darkness, even, I daresay. Had you only channeled it into wiser ventures."

Suleiman said nothing.

Nathaniel continued, "Young Kamran is most impressive. Perhaps not a warrior like you, his elder counterpart, but most impressive indeed. What he lacks in terms of the gifts of physicality endowed to you, he more than negates with his other faculties.

"I knew, from the first moment I met him, that he was destined for far greater things than the other faceless peons in this community. So, almost immediately, I have given him greater privileges. Greater tasks. I trust him more than the rest. I am even considering hiring him as the PR manager of this community, creating and editing websites, writing articles, and speaking to the media, promotion, and the like. Perhaps even more than this in the near future.

"The very first moment your brother came to us, and I learned from Darren who he was, Darren knew you wouldn't be far behind. He told me all about you. Warned me, actually. Told me that you were the last person in the world whom we wanted pursuing us or looking for vengeance. He said you were a born killer and that you were the kind of man who, like the biblical Samson, would tear down the whole temple with himself still in it.

"And, looking at you now, I can see what he meant. But, young Suleiman, you should take solace in the fact that a man like you was always going to die in a manner such as this. Men like you don't grow old and gradually fade away. You are merely here one day, full of life and energy, then explode out of existence the next, whether in your twenties or seventies."

Nathaniel paused for a moment. He spoke like a man accustomed to delivering grand, lengthy speeches. He did not appear the least bit tired from talking so much.

"Are you finished?" asked Suleiman. "Thank God for that. I was starting to think that the plan was to bore me to death by talking shit."

Nathaniel resumed as if he had not heard Suleiman, "Your brother has one final task. A task which will leave no doubt in my mind about his complete and utter commitment to the cause. A task he has already agreed to complete. Tomorrow, at noon, you will be executed in the square in front of the entire community. Your brother will be the one to carry out the execution."

Suleiman stared at Kam, jaw clenched, keeping his lips in a straight line.

Kam met his gaze for the first time, and it was at that moment that Suleiman knew that his baby brother was ready and willing to carry out his execution. Kam's face was devoid of emotion, and his eyes were like two dark marbles.

He really was gone.

Day 4: Sunday

It had all gone wrong.

So utterly, horribly wrong.

How could he have been so stupid? So defenseless and unprepared? So oblivious to reality?

Suleiman stood, naked from the waist up, with his toes barely touching the ground. His arms were stretched above his head, chained by the wrists, attached to one of the thick wooden beams going horizontally from wall to wall above him. His hair was a bloody, matted, tangled mess and lay all around his face. His nose was bleeding profusely, coupled with swelling around his left eye, and he felt as if one or two of his ribs were broken.

The mission had failed before it had even begun, and Suleiman was in the dark, staring at a locked door, contemplating the gravity of his situation and the grim, inescapable depths of his failure.

Not only had he failed miserably in rescuing his brother, but he had also managed to get himself captured in the process, and his life would be coming to a violent and painful end in less than twenty-four hours. The hope he had instilled in his family, his mother, and his father, would come crashing down on their heads, quickly turning into anguish, pain, and despair when they realized that they had now lost two sons instead of being reunited with both. It would destroy them.

Perhaps it was for the best? His life was just a steaming pile of shit anyway, wasn't it? He was failure personified. He couldn't keep his careers, his women, his friends, or even his sanity. He had hoped for it to all end many times before, and now the end was here. So why fight it?

No.

This wasn't just about him. It was more than that now. This was about his brother, his family, and all the innocent men, women, and children whose lives these people had ruined. His slimy, traitorous, former best friend. They all needed to pay. Not just for what they had done. But for Suleiman's trainwreck of a life too. They had nothing to do with all the pain in his life. But they would pay for it regardless. Someone had to. And as long as it wasn't an innocent person, it didn't matter who footed the bill. Executing a rapist for the crime of murder instead of rape was no big deal. As long as the perpetrator was executed.

But how? He was bound and unarmed. In a place he knew nothing about and didn't even see, coming in. He was behind enemy lines, surrounded by hostiles, with no idea of their numbers, weapons, or positions.

His thoughts were interrupted by steady footsteps on the gravel outside.

Suleiman stared at the barn door.

The footsteps stopped just outside the door. Suleiman heard the clinking and clanking of the chains being unlocked and unwrapped. Then the doors opened with a creak and a groan, making the flames in the torches flicker.

Kam walked into the barn.

Suleiman glared at his brother and would-be executioner for a few seconds.

Kam closed the doors behind him, walked forward a few paces, and stopped an arm's length from Suleiman. He was wearing a large, single-strapped backpack. His face gave nothing away.

"You gonna kill me right now, bro?" said Suleiman venomously. "Thought it was supposed to be in public, at noon, tomorrow? Just couldn't wait, huh?"

Kam's face split into a grin. "You've lost weight, Sul. Do you even lift, bro?"

Suleiman frowned, confused. "You've lost the plot, Kam. Get the hell out of here before I beat the shit out of you. Who the hell do you think you are? Do you have any idea what the f—"

"Sul, shut up and listen for a second," said Kam. The grin had disappeared, and his face was deadly serious. "We don't have much time."

Suleiman's eyes bored into his brother's.

"I'm not one of them," said Kam. "I'm undercover."

Suleiman's eyes widened in shock. Kam seemed to wait for him to ask what he meant, but Suleiman said nothing, so Kam continued, "I first found out about them around a year ago. A close friend of mine at uni, Jay, just disappeared one day. Vanished into thin air. Called his phone, texted him, messaged him on Facebook, etcetera. Nothing.

"I called and messaged all his other friends, got in touch with his family on Facebook, put posts out on

Facebook, too to ask if anybody had seen him. Nothing. Three days after he'd disappeared, his parents messaged me, worried sick. They asked me to call the police and report him as a missing person. They thought it'd be best I did it, as I was the last person to see him and had been with him almost every day before he'd disappeared.

"So, of course, I did. Long story short, the police followed all the leads, but before long, the case went cold. Four months after he went missing, they approached me."

Suleiman, still tied to the rafter, arms above his head, stared at his brother. Kam. Heroic, social-justice-warrior Kam. He had always been a rescuer. He always had the insatiable need to fix all the world's problems. Suleiman and the rest of his family had joked that Kam would find the cure for cancer when he grew up. Or solve world hunger. Before he even said it, Suleiman knew exactly what would happen next in Kam's story.

"This guy I hadn't noticed before in my lectures approached me in the campus café. Looked ordinary enough, like a normal student. But he must've been one of their agents. A recruiter. He told me where Jay was. Told me about the Excitatus. Who they were, what they were about, what they did. It was no accident that Jay got recruited. And that they tried to recruit me. They headhunt.

"Sit in the lecture halls and observe the students. Which students have a passion for social issues, climate change, war, religion, politics, and morality? Which ones are outspoken? Which ones fit in or don't fit in? Which ones exhibit angst and a jaded kind of indignation and resignation about the current state of the world. What are they tweeting online, posting on Facebook, etcetera? Both Jay and I were very vocal about that kind of thing. Both online and offline.

"So, anyway, I played along with the guy. I didn't want to seem too eager. Told him to leave me alone at first, pretended I wasn't interested. Approached him a day later, acting like I was debating the idea and wanted to find out more. It worked. Before long, he introduced me to other recruits who were planning to join. These guys, and some girls, were so deeply brainwashed, it was surreal. Many of them were outcasts and incels. Sitting there with them in living rooms and cafes and online group chats, listening to them rant and rave about science, politics, religion, corruption, social ills, and climate change. Some of them seemed like they were one day away from getting a gun, walking into a school, and shooting it up."

"So why didn't you go to the police?" asked Suleiman.

"That was my initial plan. I'd recorded all the conversations, both the online chats and in person. But, as I dug deeper and learned more, I learned two things: one, I couldn't trust the police. That's how deep this organization went. And two, there was some horrific shit going on in this place. I'm talking some truly depraved, next-level shit. Rape, torture, child molestation, murder. That's when I knew that I had to do something. Something big, to bring the whole temple down." Kam paused as if listening for movement outside. He continued, speaking in a more hurried tone now, "So, I hatched a plan. I was to infiltrate the cult. Penetrate deep into the inner ranks. Where the illegal stuff happens. Record it with a secret camera" — he tapped a button on his shirt with his index finger— "and release it to the media. Online, major news networks, social media, YouTube, everywhere. Expose them to such an extent that the authorities would have no choice but to act."

"All by yourself?"

"It had to be airtight. They're too powerful. As I said, they're everywhere. Couldn't risk anyone ratting me out. These people don't mess around. Any loose lips, they'd kill me. So, I only told one other person."

"Tarik."

"Yeah," replied Kam, frowning curiously.

"Well, you picked the right guy."

"What do you mean?"

"He's how I found you. I kidnapped the guy and scared the shit out of him. Would have hurt him badly, too, if he hadn't told me where you were. But my point is, he never told me your real plan. I knew he was hiding something."

Both brothers froze and stopped talking as they heard footsteps outside.

The barn doors creaked open, and a man walked in, hand on the hilt of a sheathed sword at his waist. Dressed in black robes and medieval plate armor. Lean, with salt and pepper stubble on his face. He looked from Kam to Suleiman suspiciously.

Kam fixed him with a cold glare and raised eyebrows. "What?"

The man, like Suleiman, seemed a little taken aback by Kam's cold, indifferent confidence.

"I was on my patrol," he said. "Saw the chains were off the door. What are you doing here? Nobody is to have contact with the prisoner."

"Well, the prisoner may have useful information for us. Information I've been sent to extract."

The night guard did not look convinced.

Kam continued. "You got a problem with that? Go take it up with Nathaniel. I'm sure he'll be overjoyed at being woken up at one in the morning to have his orders questioned by the help."

The guard narrowed his eyes, suspicious and possibly offended by being referred to as "The help." But he wouldn't back down.

"What's in the bag?" he asked.

Kam, feigning exasperation, rolled his eyes. "Balloons and party poppers."

The guard was not impressed. "Show me," he said.

Kam exploded with rage, swore, and grabbed Suleiman roughly by the throat but did not take his eyes off the guard, glaring at him.

Through gritted teeth, he said, "Enough! Look, brother Daniel. This scumbag piece of shit"— he paused to throw a hard punch into Suleiman's gut— "used to be my brother. He came here to infiltrate and destroy our kingdom. He's no brother of mine anymore. Nathaniel has given me a small amount of time to have my way with him and get whatever info I can. You wanna keep up this hero Sherlock act? I'll go to Nathaniel myself and tell him you're interfering with his orders!"

The rage, the hate, and the violence emanating from Kam made Suleiman uncomfortable. It was so real, so convincing that for a moment, he forgot it was an act, and Kam was on his side.

The guard must have felt the same as he raised his hand and said, "Apologies. I was just doing my job." He hastily left the barn.

Suleiman stared at Kam. "Damn, little bro. I don't know what to say. Did you have to hit me that hard?"

Kam smiled and shrugged. "Had to look convincing. Let's hope he doesn't go and wake Nathaniel."

"What is in the bag anyway?"

Kam took the bag off his back and opened it. Inside was a handgun, ammunition, a hatchet, a ball-pein hammer, and an M16 assault rifle.

"Shit," said Suleiman.

"Listen," said Kam, now speaking with urgency. "We really are out of time. I've raided the secret armory. Disposed of most of most of the weapons and kept these for us. They still have a few weapons. But only their personal ones that some of them carry around with them.

"This is what we're gonna do. I'm going to free you. Then, I'm gonna go blow up the blacksmiths. It's the furthest building from here. It should be enough of a distraction for us to get to the front gates. There are only two guards at the front, and they're unarmed. So, it should be easy to get past them."

"Why don't I come with you to the blacksmiths?" asked Suleiman.

"No. I can get away with being seen out and about freely. You're supposed to be a prisoner. We don't want you seen until the fighting starts. Even after I've blown up the blacksmith's, I can blend into the chaos of dozens of people milling about and meet you back here."

Suleiman nodded. "Makes sense."

Kam unfastened the chains binding Suleiman's hands. Suleiman stretched and rubbed his wrists.

"You ok?" asked Kam. "Can you run? Fight?"

Suleiman nodded. "Did you bring me a shirt?"

"Damn. Didn't think about that. It's cool. You can look like Rambo, firing guns shirtless."

"Douchebag."

"Got you some water, though, and a banana," Kam said, taking out the items from the side pocket of the rucksack.

Suleiman snatched them greedily, wolfed down the banana, and drained the water bottle, coughing, and spluttering.

"Right. You good?" said Kam.

Suleiman nodded.

"Let's do this," said Kam.

***

Twenty minutes had passed since Kam left. Ten since Suleiman heard the explosion.

He stood behind a wooden pillar, facing the door with the M16 rifle stock buried in the area where the chest met the shoulder, the barrel facing the door, finger on the trigger, ready to fire.

Suleiman could hear the pandemonium and the panicked voices outside. Kam should have returned by now.

Then he heard footsteps approaching the barn.

They stopped, and he heard the chains clinking on the door.

Suleiman inhaled and braced himself.

The door opened.

Suleiman pulled the trigger.

11 Months Later

"It's starting! Hurry up, bring the plates!" said Nasir Khan.

"Dad, it's Sky Plus. Just pause it," replied Mosh. "Here." He stretched his hand out for his father to hand him the remote control.

"No need, here we are," said Farah Khan, her sister, and Kam, walking into the living room, each carrying a tray laden with plates of tandoori chicken pizza, fried chicken, and glasses of Pepsi.

Mosh waited until the clinking and clanking of plates and cutlery being passed around died down, and everybody had their plates in front of them, ready to eat. He pressed the play button on the remote, and the channel four intro music, befittingly rather sinister, began to play in tandem with the announcer's voice.

"Now, an undercover investigation into the most powerful and influential cult in British history, brought to you by a Dispatches two-hour special. This programme contains strong language and real footage of abuse and violence. Viewer discretion is advised."

The programme began with the usual previews and fast cuts of the action to come, but the voiceover of the narrator, this time, was familiar to everybody in the room.

"I infiltrated deep into the upper ranks of the most violent and powerful cult in Britain, armed with nothing, but a hidden camera, disguised as a button on my shirt. This is an independent investigation. I have no affiliation with Channel four or Dispatches. And only one other person knows of my task and my whereabouts. I witnessed online radicalization, brainwashing, murder, kidnapping, child and animal abuse, and torture. Culminating in the appearance of a familiar face, another infiltrator, here in an attempt to rescue me. My brother."

***

The extended Khan family sat in the living room, dinner plates now holding nothing but the scraps of their meal. A few half-eaten slices of pizza, crusts, and chicken bones littered their plates.

Of course, they all knew the story long before the programme aired. They had been told all about it, in detail, by Kam. They had seen the hundreds of hours of footage captured by Kam's hidden camera. Kam had immediately released all the footage in a preemptive blitzkrieg to every social media outlet, explaining exactly what it was and his story. It was of utmost importance that the exposure was extremely widespread in order to avoid any repercussions and to destroy any possibility of the whole thing being swept under the rug.

But to see it all edited and put together. Polished, background music added, narrated, dramatized.

That was something else.

They had seen Kam introduce himself, recording himself in the bathroom mirror, face digitally blurred. They had seen him attend the meetings and communicate in the online chat rooms. They had seen him travel to the cult's commune and embed himself within them. They had seen the murders, the abuse, the torture.

And, finally, they had seen Suleiman and Kam's final stand.

With only fifteen minutes remaining in the programme, the room was silent. Tears poured down Farah's face. Nasir was ashen-faced, and the entire Khan family watched the last act of the documentary with a melancholy tension.

"Can you talk us through what we've just seen?" said the interviewer, sitting across from Kam, whose face was still digitally blurred.

Off-screen, Kam was poker-faced. On-screen, Kam's chest rose and fell as he inhaled deeply, and began to speak. "So, as you've just seen, after I blew up the blacksmiths, there was, just, absolute chaos. All hell broke loose. The residents are running around all over the place. Security are rushing to the explosion site with their swords drawn. Everybody is running in the same direction. Except me.

"The plan was to cause a diversion with the explosion. Then I go and meet back up with my brother at the barn. We sneak out, with everyone half a mile away at the blacksmiths, then we take care of the guards at the gate and make our escape on foot through the woods.

"But, as you saw, it all went wrong. As I got to about a hundred yards from the barn, I saw one of the security guards, Daniel, you know, the one who walked in on my brother and me earlier? Approaching the barn door with his sword drawn. Whether he returned because he was suspicious from earlier or he was sent there, I don't know. But he had the keys to the chains on the door. As soon as he opened the doors, BANG! Headshot. My brother."

On-screen, Kam took a pause. Digitally-blurred face, seemingly gathering his thoughts. Off-screen, Kam seemed to have aged about ten years since he had left home to undertake his task. His skin and hair were the same, but it was the presence. The poise. Eyes that had seen things that would ensure he would never be the same again. He absently fingered the missing tip of his left earlobe.

The Kam on TV continued, "The two guys in the distance that shouted my name? After the security guard was shot dead? That was Nathaniel Jackson, the leader, and Darren Mitchell, one of his most trusted lieutenants, my brother's former best friend. The one who set him up and betrayed him. At this point, there was no point of any more pretense. So, I aimed my pistol at them and fired three times.

"I missed, of course, but it surprised them and gave me enough time to run to the barn. They recovered just as I reached the doors, and bullets whizzed past my head and into the door. I shouted out to my brother to identify myself so he wouldn't shoot me by mistake. He let me in, and we took positions.

"My brother looked through one of the bullet holes in the door and said that Nathaniel and Darren had been joined by another four armed men and were fast approaching us. He asked me if there was another building or area we could go to, which would be easier to defend, as the barn was flimsy, soft materials, not enough cover, and too many potential entry points. Also, wood, hay etcetera, easy to burn us out if they couldn't get in.

"I told him yes, the school, around two hundred yards from our position. Only two entry points— I mean, windows too, of course, but once you got up the stairs from the ground floor to the first floor, which was also the top floor, no more entry points. Also, many rooms, narrow corridors, and made of bricks and mortar. He said this was perfect, as their limited ammunition would run out soon, and they'd have to come in and fight with melee weapons. Small rooms and narrow corridors, stairs, etcetera, would have a funnel effect, and their numbers wouldn't count as much.

"Anyway, we had to leave sharpish before they surrounded us. Another four had joined them now, which made ten in total, eight of them armed with guns."

On-screen, Kam paused again and took a drink from the glass of water on the table in front of him. He continued, "My brother opened fire with the M16 through one of the bullet holes in the door. This was basically covering fire. It would force them to take cover and hesitate for a few seconds, by which time we could run out the back and get a head start to the school.

"Bang bang bang bang bang! I'd never heard a machine gun fire in real life before that point. It was deafening... and pretty exhilarating, to be honest. He emptied the whole magazine as I ran out the back to lead the way. He followed shortly. As we ran, I asked him if he thought he had hit any of them. He said he was pretty sure he'd got two. I asked if either of those was Nathaniel or Mitch. He said he didn't think so.

"We got to the school with them around a hundred and fifty yards behind us. Their numbers had gone up again, around fifteen now. They carried on running towards us, opening fire at the same time. I shot the lock on the school door and suddenly felt a burning pain in my left ear. One of the bullets had taken my left earlobe off. As more bullets whizzed and pinged all around us, my brother shoved me through the door, turned to them, now around ninety yards away, and opened fire. He didn't take cover, duck, or move. Just stood there straight, like something out of an action film, and emptied the last magazine of the M16.

"It was a miracle he wasn't hit at least once. He hit another three. Again, unfortunately, Nathaniel and Mitch not amongst those. So, we run up the hallway and up the first flight of stairs and take position round the bend, on the landing before the second and last flight of stairs. This was the best position as they could only come at us one way, up the stairs, the same way we had.

"So, weapons-wise, we're now both down to a handgun each, two magazines each, a hatchet, and a ball-pein hammer. The idiots outside start going crazy. Opening fire at the school, wasting ammo, hoping one of them might hit us.

"This goes on for a couple of minutes until two come through the front door with guns. We shoot them dead. Down to ten men now, as far as we're aware.

"So, they take position outside the front door, and we have a gun battle for a few more minutes. Us on the top of the stairs landing, round the bend. Them behind the front door. Firing at each other through the corridor. During these few minutes, I don't think we hit any of them. But I almost took another bullet, just grazed my right shoulder, and my brother had his pinky shot off, causing him to drop his gun down the stairs into no-man's land. It was probably empty by then, anyway. I'm out of ammo now too.

"But so are they. I hear Mitch's voice shouting at the both of us. Abusing us, calling me a rat, and telling us that he couldn't wait to shove a knife in both of us and rape our dead bodies. Telling us that we only had seconds to live. My brother shouts back. Calls him a cowardly, back-stabbing piece of shit and tells him to hurry up and come and try it.

"I remember looking at my brother and being amazed at how calm he looked. I was absolutely shitting myself. Almost literally. My arms and legs were shaking out of control. My brother clapped me on the back and told me it was just adrenaline. Told me to jump up and down a few times and clench my buttocks, my quads, and my fists. Direct the fear and energy towards the enemy. I did, and it worked.

"Four men burst in through the front door and run up the corridor and come running up the stairs. We stay on the landing, shoulder to shoulder. My brother kicks the first one in the face just as he reaches the third-to-top step. He goes tumbling down the stairs, knocking another one down with him. The other two reach us, and my brother buries his hatchet into the head of one of them, and I bring my hammer down on the top of the other's head. They go down. The two that fell down the stairs get back up, and another seven rush in through the front door, and I catch a glimpse of Mitch amongst them.

"They keep trying to come up the stairs, and we keep beating them back until I lose my balance and fall down the stairs and land right at the bottom. In no-man's land. I go into the fetal position as they start hammering me with metal poles, chains, fists, and legs. It only lasts about two seconds, though, as my brother yells my name, then Mitch's, and kind of, what's the word... kamikazes. Jumps from the sixth step, hatchet in his hand, and lands on top of the nine men battering me. Bodies, arms, and legs tangled and flailing everywhere. I open my eyes and see that they've forgotten all about me, and my brother is taking all nine of them on by himself.

"I jump back up and grab a pole off the floor and go to work, helping my brother. Whilst I'm struggling, fighting for my life with one or two of them, my brother is holding his own against seven or eight. I catch a glimpse of his face. His eyes look like a shark's, like he's not there anymore, and he's making kind of animal-like grunts as he hits and hacks with his hatchet, over and over and over, like a machine. Blood and body parts everywhere. Mitch keeps trying to get at him with his hunting knife, but in this enclosed area, with so many moving bodies, he's finding it hard to reach him.

"Five minutes later, and there's bloody and mutilated bodies all over the corridor floor. Only three people left, moving or alive, in the corridor.

"Me, of course, my brother and Mitch. My brother is sitting on the stairs, covered in blood, breathing hard, exhausted. I'm sat a couple of metres away from him, against a wall, pretty much in the same state as him. And Mitch is doubled over, a few yards from me, breathing hard but otherwise looking quite fresh. He straightens up. I remember looking at him, his face, his body, his aura, and thinking that this guy literally looks like a bull that's been taught to walk on its hind legs. Like if God created someone just for the sole purpose of violence, it would be this guy. I had a feeling he would give us more trouble than the previous ten or twenty guys combined. I was right.

"My brother asks him where Nathaniel is. Mitch tells him Nathaniel is long gone. Tells him not to worry about Nathaniel. To worry about him instead because he is going to kill us both. He raises his massive hunting knife, and I remember how casually he says it. I mean, you heard it on the video, didn't you?"

The interviewer nodded. Brow furrowed, engrossed by Kam's tale.

"He says, 'Come on boys, pick up your toys, let's play.' And he has this excited look on his face like he's a kid about to play the latest PlayStation game his parents bought him for his birthday. Anyway, my brother, one second, he's sat there, looking ready to collapse. Then, he suddenly picks up his hatchet and runs at Mitch. He brings the hatchet down on his head. Mitch grabs my brother's wrist with his free hand, stopping the blade about an inch from his skull. He stares at my brother, smiling, enjoying himself.

"I force myself on my feet and rush Mitch with a knife I picked up. Without even looking at me, he elbows me in the stomach before I can do anything with the knife, and I fall back against the wall, winded. He then thrusts his knife at my brother's stomach. My brother grabs Mitch's wrist in the same way Mitch is still holding my brother's. The knife blade inches away from his stomach. It looks like a wrestling match now, my brother with his hatchet an inch away from Mitch's head and Mitch with his knife inches away from my brother's stomach.

"Mitch is fresher, uninjured, and probably a bit stronger than my brother. The hatchet keeps moving back, away from his head, centimeter by centimeter. The knife keeps moving forward towards my brother's stomach. Mitch laughs and, like you just heard on the video, says something like, 'This is what you get for sitting around eating ice cream and watching chick flicks, feeling sorry for yourself over some girl. Pussy.'

"My brother headbutts him in the face and kicks him in the groin. This makes them both drop their weapons, and Mitch rugby-tackles my brother. They're scrapping, rolling around on the floor.

"I pick up the knife again, just as they both get to their feet, and Mitch throws my brother against the wall. He turns to me and picks up a hammer off the floor, batting the knife out of my hand and punching me in the face, knocking me off my feet.

"My brother gets up and rugby-tackles him. They wrestle for a bit, then Mitch has my brother against the wall, hands round his throat, trying to choke him to death.

"I try to get up to help but realize I can't. I feel weird. Light-headed. I suddenly feel sharp pain in the area between my hip in my stomach. I look down and see that my clothes are drenched with blood, mainly around that area. I lift my shirt and see a deep gash with blood pouring out. I realize I've been stabbed at some point without even noticing it. Probably earlier on when I fell to the bottom of the stairs.

"I look up. Mitch is still choking my brother. He's going purple. Still grabbing and punching Mitch, trying to break out of the hold."

Kam paused.

The interviewer looked at him sympathetically. "It's ok. Take your time."

"The last thing I saw before I passed out was the look in his eyes. It wasn't panic. Or fear. Just a calm kind of resignation. Like he knew this was coming. Like it was relief that it finally had. At the same time, he made eye contact with me, jerking his head as much as he could, jerking it towards the exit, signaling me to escape. Then I passed out."

On-screen, Kam's hand rose to his blurred face and moved across it, probably to wipe a tear.

Nasir's face was grave. Farah had a hand across her mouth. Eyes still spilling tears profusely. Mosh put an arm around her tenderly and handed her some tissues. The rest of the family watched in grim silence.

"So, what happened next?"

"I woke up in the same place just as the paramedics were putting me on a gurney. I panicked. Flailed my arms, screamed my brother's name, demanding to know where he was. I looked up and down, seeing bodies, police, paramedics, etcetera. But I couldn't see my brother, or Mitch, anywhere."

"Mitchell, Nathaniel. Your brother. Those are the only three that are unaccounted for. Their bodies not at the scene. No sightings of any of them since then. Do you think your brother is still alive?"

"I'm not sure. It doesn't make any sense."

"How so?" the interviewer asked.

"If he's dead, then where is his body? If he's alive, then where's Mitch's body? And why hasn't he made any contact with us in all this time?"

"If he is alive and is watching, is there anything you'd like to say to him?" asked the interviewer.

On-screen, Kam took a breath. His blurred face turned slightly to face the camera.

"Come home, bro. I know you're hurting. You've been hurting your whole life. I know you're in pain. I know you blame yourself for a lot of things. I know you've never forgiven yourself, and probably never will, for some of the things you've done in the past. But you need to. You have to. God forgives all sins. God loves you. Your family loves you. I love you. We never stopped, not even for a moment. All the bad you've done or think you've done. You've redeemed. You're my big brother. My hero. Always have been, always will be. Come back to us, brother. Come home."

The scene faded; the screen went dark.

Silence.

Then, writing appeared on the screen. A quote from Kam (uncredited, of course) that he had previously used in one of his articles about the whole saga.

Had they offered peace, we would have sent them a diplomat

Had they offered ignorance, we would have sent them a teacher

Had they offered knowledge, we would have sent them a scholar

Had they offered trade, we would have sent them a merchant

But they offered war, so we sent a soldier

—Unknown

The silence in the room was interrupted by a knock on the front door, followed by the sound of something being pushed through the letterbox, followed by rapid footsteps, as if somebody wanted to disappear in a hurry.

"Who's that at this time?" said Nasir, brow furrowed curiously.

Mosh went to the front door. He opened it, then closed it again. He returned to the living room and said, "Someone posted this and ran off."

He held up an envelope. Handwritten on the front was.

To the Khan family.

About the Author

S.I. Almanza was born and raised in Portsmouth, England. In school, English was his favourite subject, specifically creative writing. He would write stories for schoolwork and recreationally at home, often scoring top of the class for his writing.

Almanza is a former prison officer, bouncer, and security professional, working in chaotic roles and locations up and down the country. Many of these roles included managing a team of security professionals. He currently works for a company in partnership with the city council as a senior support worker in a high-risk, high-support homeless accommodation unit.

Almanza's passion for creative writing was reignited in 2018. Thus, in four years, in between the chaos at work (assaults, medical emergencies, deaths, murders, racial abuse, death threats), marriage, divorce, and other major life events, like a phoenix from the ashes, Almanza's debut book, Rusted Hearts was born. An anthology consisting of two short stories and a novella. Almanza used his extensive and intense professional experiences and his love for creative fiction to craft three gritty, fast-paced, and action-packed stories filled with twists and turns.

When not working or writing, S.I. Almanza can be found cycling, motorcycle riding, driving his sportscar, working out in the gym or in the park, boxing, playing basketball, reading books, and socialising with his family and friends.

Printed in Great Britain
by Amazon